Daring and Decorum

A Highwayman Novel

Lawrence Hogue

Supposed Crimes LLC • Matthews, North Carolina

Published in the United States.

ISBN: 978-1-944591-42-7

Special thanks to Karen Hopper Usher and Mari Christie for photography and graphic design.

www.supposedcrimes.com

This book is typeset in Goudy Old Style.

For all the L, G, B, and T people in my life,
who have taught me so much.
I've always been a little bit Q,
and you showed me that's okay.

And still of a winter's night, they say, when the wind is in the trees,
When the moon is a ghostly galleon tossed upon cloudy seas,
When the road is a ribbon of moonlight over the purple moor,
A highwayman comes riding –
Riding – riding –
A highwayman comes riding, up to the old inn-door.

- Alfred Noyes, "The Highwayman"

CHAPTER ONE

THE FIRST time I encountered the highwayman, his hand was upon my breast and his tongue was in my mouth. The rogue and his accomplices had stopped our carriage in a dusk-darkened wood, no doubt attracted by the lavish nature of the coach-and-four, with its elaborate gold trim and yet more elaborately bedecked footmen.

"Have no fear, ladies," said Anthony Cranford, Lord Burnside, the son of our neighboring Earl, as he reached for the door. "I'm sure these louts want only my purse." Anthony – I call him by his Christian name, for we were old childhood friends – had kindly offered to convey me, along with my companion, Mrs. Simmons, to Exeter on a shopping excursion. We were late in returning, as he had been detained longer than expected by his own business in town.

Before Anthony could open the door, however, it was thrown open from without, and there stood the masked villain, holding a pistol aimed upwards at Anthony's chest. He wore the dress of a gentleman: a finely-cut coat of claret velvet, buckskin breeches, and high leather boots, a large cocked hat topping it all. With a black crêpe cloth covering most of his face, only his eyes were visible, eyes that seemed calm, almost merry, as they surveyed the interior of the carriage.

"Yes, ladies, have no fear, for I never harm those whom I rob, as long as they cooperate. If you'll just return to your seat, my lord." As Anthony resumed his place across from us, the highwayman's gaze swept over Mrs. Simmons and then myself, at which point he brought up short.

"Oh, my, what a pretty – bauble." His eyes swept from my face to my throat, and lower, then back again. "Your necklace, I mean," he said, giving me half a wink. I caught my breath at the frankly appraising manner with which he had surveyed my person and at the knowing look he now gave me, for I was unaccustomed to being treated with such lewd impertinence.

He held his free hand out to me. "Now, if you'll just hand that necklace over, I'll proceed to his lordship."

My hand went to my throat, almost of its own accord. "This is my last memento of my departed mother. I will not part with it."

The highwayman only laughed, then spoke in a voice that attempted gruffness more than achieving it, like a boy straining for the tones of manhood. "Then I'll have it, with interest." His boot leather creaked as he stepped up onto the runner of the carriage and leaned in through the doorway. I felt my color rising as he placed a gloved hand on my cheek, his eyes gazing into my own with that merry, knowing glint, as if he knew just what feelings his bold manner was provoking.

Mrs. Simmons, seated next to me, took me by the arm and tried to pull me from the rogue's clutches, to no avail. Nor could Anthony restrain himself. He rapped on the floor with his walking stick. "Look here! Take our valuables if you must, but leave the young lady in peace."

The highwayman levelled his pistol at Anthony. "Oh, I will have your jewels and your coin, Lord Burnside, but I'll hazard the young lady is the most valuable treasure in this carriage. Now if you'll just toss that stick out the window – we must avoid violence where we can."

Anthony hesitated a moment, then did as commanded, leaving the highwayman free to return his attentions to me.

I don't know how he managed it, what with leaning through the carriage door and keeping the pistol aimed at Anthony. With his free hand, he lifted his crêpe mask and placed his lips on my own, just as I gave a gasp of surprise. His tongue entered my open mouth and began exploring within in a most lascivious manner. I couldn't help noticing he was remarkably clean-shaven, with none of that scratchy, three-days' growth of beard one associates with a ruffian. Too, he must have been fastidious in his toilette, as I caught a scent of rosewater. While his tongue was busy in its explorations, his free hand was having its pleasure at my breast. At first I felt only shock at such astonishing behavior, but then such a feeling came over me as I can hardly describe: a warmth flooding through my limbs as my heart beat faster – if that were possible – and my breath coming rapidly.

Leaving off with his kissing and groping, his hand went to the back of my neck and deftly undid the clasp of the necklace. While he performed this operation, his eyes remained fixed on my own; even in the dim light, they were alive with a merry glint, as though robbing carriages and molesting their occupants were the most exalting occupation in the world. And something more: those eyes saw deep into me, as if they knew with a certainty the feelings those lips and that roving hand had caused.

For my part, where I should rightly have felt fear, I felt something else entirely. Before I could check myself, I slapped him hard across the face, the blow softened by the cloth of his mask.

"Lizzie!" exclaimed Mrs. Simmons. "Do not provoke him!"

Yet the highwayman seemed to smile all the more, judging by the deeper crinkles around his laughing eyes. "What a remarkable young woman!" he said as he pocketed the necklace. "It's been a pleasure doing business with you, my lady."

He dipped his head to me, then turned his attention to Mrs. Simmons. "And you must be the young lady's governess, if I'm not mistaken."

Mrs. Simmons, trembling slightly, replied, "Yes, or a lady's companion, if you will, as Miss Elizabeth is done with her tutoring."

I placed a hand on her arm to calm her, as her fright had evidently made her chatty, but she kept her hands clutched tight together in her lap.

"Very well," the highwayman said with an air of gallantry, "then I'll have nothing from you, and that wedding band you're so assiduously hiding may stay in its place. Now, Viscount Burnside, what baubles do you have about you today? Ah, yes, you must have a valuable watch in your pocket, judging by the gold chain adorning your waistcoat. It will do nicely, I'm sure, and please spare us the stories of its importance as a family heirloom."

Anthony looked over at me as he reached for the watch. "Elizabeth, I promise I will do whatever I can to apprehend this rogue. I won't rest until I have gained satisfaction for this insult to your honor."

"An insult!" the highwayman exclaimed in mock umbrage. "I believe she rather enjoyed it, my lord. It seems she's never been properly kissed ere now – surprising, considering the two of you appear to be on a first-name basis." As he looked at me, I felt my cheeks flush an even deeper red. He turned back to Anthony. "You don't mean to tell me you haven't sampled the wares before completing the purchase?"

Anthony had the watch out and was ready to hand it over, but now he clenched it in his fist, ready to strike out at the rogue. "You will not speak of Miss Collington in such a – "

"We are old friends, nothing more," I interrupted, hoping to calm the situation as much as to correct the highwayman's mistake. For, contrary to the style the highwayman had given me, I was not of the nobility. My father was Vicar of Leighton Parish, of which Anthony's father, Earl Highdown, was the patron. As I was neither wealthy nor of ancient, noble lineage, there could be no question of our marrying, Anthony's increasing affections and Father's and Mrs. Simmons' hopes notwithstanding.

My statement had rather the opposite effect to what I had intended, spurring Anthony to yet more gallantry. "If you are any kind of gentleman, you will settle this now, with pistols at twenty paces." That such a challenge to an inferior violated the gentleman's code of honor – and that Anthony seemed to have forgotten it – could only be explained by his anger on my behalf.

The highwayman regarded Anthony wryly for a moment, then gave a snort. "Of all the countless noblemen I have robbed, you are the first to challenge me to a duel. I suppose I should feel honored that you would treat me as your equal." Here he ironically tipped his hat. "But who will be your second? And where are your pistols?" When Anthony merely shrugged, he laughed out loud. "And do you propose that I loan you the weapon with which you would send me to the undertaker?"

Anthony raised his chin, managing to look superior to the rogue. "Very well then, name the time and place and I will meet you to have satisfaction. You have my word not to warn the Constable of our meeting."

"Anthony, let him take your watch and be gone," I said.

"Miss Collington is right. We highwaymen leave the dueling to our betters. Now, the watch, if you please."

"I should have known a rogue would have no honor."

"Honor, is it?" For the first time, the humor went out of the highwayman's gaze and his voice took on an edge as hard as the single diamond he wore in his cravat. "And do you lords call it honor when you enclose the commons and horde your grain, driving the price of bread beyond the reach of the common laborer? No, that is theft, as surely as this. Now hand over that watch before I forget that I never harm my marks."

"Anthony – " I wanted to reach out to him, but the highwayman was between us. The moment stretched on as Anthony glared at the rogue.

"Very well," he said at last, handing the watch over.

"That's right, my lord. And now your purse. I imagine it's considerably lighter after your excursion to Exeter."

Anthony brought the purse forward. "I'll see you hanged for this!"

The highwayman gave an exaggerated sigh, his humor returning. "A sentiment one hears all too often in this trade, I'm afraid. Fortunately for me, it has yet to be acted upon with any effect. Now, ma'am, those packages beneath your seat."

Tossing the items to his waiting associates – yards of good muslin and a new set of silver spoons, for Father and Mrs. Simmons hoped to entertain Lord Highdown and his son in grander fashion than we had done in the past – the rogue made his farewell. "Ladies, gentleman, we thank you for your kind patronage, and may you have a safe journey home." A moment later, the thunder of hooves carried the outlaws away.

Instantly Mrs. Simmons turned to me, clutching my arm. "Miss Elizabeth, are you well? Did he harm you in any way?"

"It was quite a shock," I said, my hand to my breast, as if to calm my fear, "but no, I cannot say that he harmed me."

The coachman returned Anthony's walking stick and checked to see if we were well. "To the vicarage, Shaw," Anthony ordered. "We should get Miss Collington home as quick as may be so she can rest."

I accepted Anthony's and Mrs. Simmons' unnecessary attentions as gracefully as I could. When their talk turned to the state of the roads and the advisability of better arms for the footmen, I let my thoughts wander over the strange events, not at all sure that rest was what I most needed at the moment.

CHAPTER TWO

THAT SUNDAY week, Father discovered a pair of new parishioners in the receiving line after church, a handsome young gentleman and lady. "Ah, newcomers!" he said warmly. "We are always most gratified at any addition to our flock."

"And we are glad to receive such a warm welcome," said the man, who appeared to be in his late twenties, dressed in a blue tailcoat of a modern cut and new boots. "I am Thomas Nighthorn, and this is my sister, Mrs. Burgess." The latter was a woman considerably younger than her brother, and nearly as tall as he. She wore a fine chemise dress, though not in the latest fashion; a mass of light brown curls peeked out from beneath her bonnet.

As the pair were the last through the line, we had the opportunity for further conversation. It soon came out that Mrs. Burgess was a young widow, and had moved from London for her health. "The air in town did not agree with me," she said, though she had not the look of an invalid; rather, the smooth skin of her cheeks bore a healthy glow. "I remained only because my husband was stationed at Deptford. But, alas, we lost him in the Glorious First of June."

"Your husband was in the Navy?" asked Mrs. Simmons.

"Yes, he was captain of HMS Eagle, which took many casualties in that great battle."

"Oh, you poor thing," said Mrs. Simmons, "widowed at such a young

age, and all alone here, save for your brother. When will we see the end of these wars? There's scarce a family has not been touched by them. We are missing our Jamie, Miss Elizabeth's brother, who is in the Navy as well."

"And what will you do now?" my father asked.

"We have taken a small house in Leighton," Mrs. Burgess replied. "Unfortunately, Thomas's business keeps him much occupied in London. I will attempt to make myself useful in some way. I'm sure you can recommend charities to me, Mr. Collington."

"Indeed I can, and they will be glad to have your assistance," Father replied. "My daughter also has a passion for aiding the poor, and never fails to make the rounds of our less fortunate neighbors." Father hesitated only a moment before going on. "I hope the two of you will join us for dinner on Wednesday. I am sure we can arrange for half a dozen guests from the neighborhood to expand your acquaintance. Perhaps Lord Burnside and his family will consent to join us." He turned to Anthony, who stood nearby, and gave a slight bow.

That gentleman, always careful of his manners, dipped his head in return. He was of middling height, with blond hair grown shaggy about the ears in the fashion that had become popular since the levying of the powder tax. His fine tailcoat, waistcoat, and breeches were all of muted colors, greys and whites. "As much as I regret missing any opportunity to welcome newcomers to our neighborhood, I must sadly decline, for we will be off to London for the season that very day." His blue eyes, full of earnest regret, slid from Father to me as he finished delivering this news.

"And I must regretfully answer in the negative as well," Mr. Nighthorn put in, "as I return to London tomorrow. But I am certain my sister would be glad of the company."

"Indeed I would," she said. "But you are too kind, Vicar. Please, do not put yourself out to gather a large party on my account. I will be quite content to further my acquaintance with you and your charming daughter." And here she turned to smile at me, leaving me to wonder what I had done that she could have found so charming. We parted soon after.

The news of Anthony's departure for London and its accompanying reflection – that he was likely to be surrounded by dozens of marriageable girls in that city – gave me only a moment's pang of jealousy. Unlike Father and Mrs. Simmons, I had long since ceased to think it likely a match could be made between us. Anthony and I had known each other from a young age, as the Parsonage and the parish church sat on the eastern border of Holbourne, Lord Highdown's ancestral estate. He was a good sort, always the perfect gentleman, attractive in both person and manner, and attentive to my family's needs as a friend and neighbor whenever he was in the country. Two years older than I, he had only recently returned from a sojourn in the Inns of Court. Studying the law was quite unusual for a first son, of course, yet it was no surprise to anyone familiar with Anthony's zeal for making himself useful to his parish and his nation. His father had only allowed him to pursue such an odd course once he was convinced Anthony had no intention of demeaning himself by actually joining the bar; perhaps Lord Highdown felt that some knowledge of the law would be helpful to his son in one day managing the family estates.

As the patron of father's living, Lord Highdown had always humored our friendship, though we were of differing ranks. He even went so far as to tolerate our continued use of each other's Christian names long after it was proper, precisely because a match between us was impossible. Despite the attention he paid to the outward forms of charity and magnanimity, Lord Highdown was of an imperious nature, always conscious of rank and wealth, and confident in his ability to rule his son. The Earl clearly had grander ambitions for his son than an alliance with a vicar's daughter. Whatever Anthony's feelings toward me might have been, a connection with my family could offer neither money nor status; nor did I sense that spark of passion within Anthony that would compel defiance of his father's wishes.

To all of which Father and Mrs. Simmons had counselled patience and a willingness to put myself in the way of Anthony's affections. My future security depended on it, they said, as few other eligible bachelors lived in the vicinity, and opportunities of meeting those beyond our neighborhood were scant. Father regretted not being able to send me to London for the season, but that was for families with better connections and greater fortunes than our own. For her part, Mrs. Simmons persisted in enumerating the qualities of my person that should have given me confidence in attracting a young man such as Lord Highdown: my long black hair, dark eyes, clear complexion, and what she insisted was a fine figure, which she constantly urged me to show off to better advantage. Whereas I felt I was not of such a height as to achieve true elegance, she held that this was all to the good, as Anthony could hardly be considered tall.

And so Father and Mrs. Simmons persisted in believing that a match with Lord Burnside was my best chance for an establishment in life, despite its slim likelihood. In every other respect, Father was a sensible man, yet on this one topic, he persisted in letting his care and ambition for me cloud his better judgment, in contradiction to all he had ever taught about governing emotion with reason. From this I concluded that the cares and demands of parenthood were enough to unbalance even the most composed of minds.

Since our mother's death, Jamie and I had been brought up by Father to meet whatever life put in our way, all of its highs and lows, with equal reserve and composure. With a clear-eyed view of my prospects, I could readily admit how this approach to life could aid me, and I endeavored to follow it, succeeding to a great extent in outward appearances, if not in my inmost thoughts. For, as I looked around me at what life was for women of my state, I could not help but admit a certain restlessness, one which all my self-command was barely sufficient to master. In conversation with the five or six female friends my own age in the neighborhood, I always remained polite and amiable, while inside I chafed at the insipidity of the conversation, the constant talk of the latest fashions, the prospects of any new young men coming to the neighborhood, or which girls had been recently engaged. Surely there must be more to life than an endless list of ornamental acquisitions gained in hopes of finding a match with a partner of indifferent affection. There must be more, once such a match was gained, than shallow conversation and entertainments within a social sphere of six or eight neighboring families, more than endless rounds of visits and balls and good works which did little to relieve the sufferings of the poor.

Nor did an advance in rank offered by a match with Anthony promise a necessary improvement, for not even a young lady of twenty, raised in a small parish in Devonshire, could remain ignorant of the scandalous pursuits by which the higher nobility sought to relieve the tedium of life. Only in those ranks inferior to our own did I see a style of life unmediated by rigid social convention. Perhaps it was a romantic notion of mine, but I imagined that the common people we met in the village and the countryside had a freer form of life than our own.

Thus, if I attended those pursuits by which a young woman makes herself acceptable in genteel society – needlework, drawing, music, and reading – with an air of perfect concentration and enjoyment, this did not always mean that my mind was not engaged elsewhere; for I found I had a knack for making idle conversation or practicing at the pianoforte while my thoughts drifted to exotic scenes from a travelogue I had been reading, or to the moors where I delighted in taking long walks. In inclement weather, I found my composure challenged to the utmost, but on fine days I always took the opportunity to relieve my restlessness with lengthy rambles, during which I delighted in sketching my favorite flowers as the blooming season progressed. Father had encouraged me in this pastime, for he was a botanical enthusiast himself, and when I was young had liked nothing better than pointing out flowers on our walks together. In recent years he had not the energy to accompany me, but he never objected to my walking out alone, for he was always glad to see my sketches and to help identify my discoveries.

But among all my improving pursuits, it was in my riding lessons that I found myself most fully engaged. Lord Highdown had been kind enough to allow me the use of a well-trained mare at any time of my pleasing, along with the expert instruction of his groomsman. I often took advantage of this generosity, relishing the freedom of the wind rushing past my cheeks as we cantered over the moors, wondering how far I might go if I chose to ride in a single direction for an entire day. My favorite were the fox hunts, to which Jamie and I had often been invited. I cared nothing for the fortune of the sportsmen – in truth, I preferred it when the poor fox got away – but I thrilled at the wild chase across fields and over hedges and streams. Of course, riding aside, I could not truly keep up with the men, but I prided myself on my ability to take small jumps. None observing me might have guessed at the joy I felt on these occasions, owing to the reserve which Father had instilled in me.

If, on this Sunday morning, Anthony's announcement caused me little pain, it was no doubt in part due to that same self-mastery. At the same time, my thoughts were engaged elsewhere, as they often had been over the week that had passed since our encounter with the highwayman. The intervening period had given me much opportunity to ponder the loss of the necklace, as well as the feelings the experience had occasioned. It was only with difficulty, and not always with success, that I could keep my mind from wandering back to that event. I did not dwell on the fear and danger posed by the highwayman brandishing his pistol at me, nor on his effrontery in assuming I was Anthony's possession, to be looted as easily as Anthony's purse. Neither, as much as I sympathized with my companions, was I preoccupied with the humiliation Anthony had undergone, nor with the fear Mrs. Simmons had endured.

No, it was to those moments during which the highwayman had so lewdly assaulted my person that my thoughts continually strayed, much as I attempted to draw them back to their proper course. I could hardly admit to myself that his kissing and his roving hand had occasioned something of the same thrill I experienced while riding – that, and something more. It was unthinkable! Every consideration of sense and morality counselled that such feelings should be prompted only by one to whom I had been promised in marriage, and certainly not by a rogue with a pistol. Yet such rational considerations held little sway, for it is a truth seldom acknowledged, that those things which one should *not* want, are the very things one wants the most.

And so it was that I met the prospect of Anthony's departure for London with an equanimity of which my Father should have been proud, though for a reason he could never have expected.

CHAPTER THREE

WEDNESDAY MORNING arrived, and Father sent me into Leighton, but a mile's walk from the Parsonage, to call on Mrs. Burgess and renew our invitation for that evening. I was putting on my bonnet in the foyer when a knock came at the door. Banks, our housekeeper, opened it to reveal Anthony.

"Oh, begging your pardon, I see I have caught you on your way out," he said.

I gave a curtsey. "I was just on my way to Leighton. Will you walk with me?" Mrs. Simmons gave me a knowing look as I passed through the doorway.

Anthony was silent as we made our way out the gate and down the lane toward the village. It was a beautiful morning, with the sun providing unexpected warmth. Our way was bounded on one side by blackthorn hedges alive with the calls of the linnet, while the masses of delicate white flowers gave the air a musky, sweet scent. On the other side, Holbourne's pastures sloped upward from the valley through which the lane ran, shining a brilliant green.

As the silence lengthened, I couldn't help remembering the games Anthony, Jamie, and I would play in those meadows when we were children. Anthony would organize games of pretend in which he played some hero of legend, usually King Arthur, while Jamie was Galahad or Parsifal or Lancelot; I, of course, was Guinevere, or perhaps some maiden in distress, guarded by a dragon. This was all fine for a time, for at that age I could imagine little for Guinevere to do but weave crowns of daisies. As collecting flowers was one of the things I liked best, along with watching the bees and the birds flit about, or any other activity of nature, this did not often trouble me. Yet there were times when I wanted to do more, to pick up a stick and join in the play-fighting, or to imagine we were all tramping off to the Holy Land together – for one of the Earl's forebears had won renown and a title by fighting in the Crusades, creating another scenario for Anthony and Jamie to reenact – but always the answer was no.

"That would make you a camp follower, Lizzie," Anthony would say. "Your father wouldn't like it." He and Jamie, both older, seemed to know what a camp follower was, but would never tell me.

"But what if I were Merlin?" I would demand.

"Merlin was a boy!"

"How do you know? He wore skirts, did he not?"

Anthony would glare at me then, deeply offended; these were but games for Jamie and me, but Anthony took them seriously, as training for his future position as Earl. Lacking a damsel in distress, he could have no opportunity to demonstrate his chivalry.

Later, we put aside such pastimes and Anthony went off to Eton and then Oxford. We saw each other when he was home on vacation, at parish functions, or sometimes when out riding, though on the latter occasions Jamie and Anthony would be far ahead. At the infrequent assemblies in Leighton's village hall, I was careful to allow him two dances and no more, for by this time I had recognized that I would never be Anthony's Guinevere.

Anthony must have been remembering those days of childhood as well, for at last he broke the silence by saying, "Elizabeth, I have been meaning to apologize for my behavior when the highwayman assaulted you."

"Apologize? For what should you apologize? We were all of us in danger."

"Yet I should have prevented his assault on you. It is a moment I will regret for the rest of my days. When I think that we used to play games of chivalry in this very spot, and then when the opportunity for true chivalry arose, I was not up to the challenge."

I stole a glance to see him staring dejectedly at the lane before us. "Perhaps, in such a situation, a woman can get away with what a man could not. Had you provoked him more than you did, he might have shot you. And you did challenge him to a duel."

"Empty bluff and bluster. I knew he wouldn't honor such a challenge.

No, it was my duty to protect you, and I failed. And now Father bids me to follow him to London."

The silence lengthened once more. "You depart today, do you not?"

"We leave within the hour. I wanted to pay my respects before leaving."

"It is most appreciated," I said, employing that cautious reserve through which I had always hoped to safeguard both our hearts, though now my preoccupation with the highwayman also played a part. I was searching for a different subject for our conversation when he went on.

"Elizabeth, is there no chance your father will send you to London for the latter part of the season?"

I allowed him half a smile, careful not to let my gaze linger too long on his bright blue eyes or the smooth skin of his high cheekbones, tanned from his recent outings afield. "I'm sure he's worried that an eligible bachelor would capture my heart and take me far from home." Anthony knew as well as I that Father had not the means to send me, along with Mrs. Simmons, to London. "No, he is happy that I content myself with Devonshire society. It does not trouble me."

He was silent for several moments more, then said, "I wish I could stay in Devon. Town is not for me – too crowded, too many people to know and their ranks to keep track of. I prefer it here in the country. I don't see what London has to offer, and I grow tired of having my every move directed by my parents."

I kept my attention on the lane ahead of me, unwilling to lead him farther into danger. "What is there to occupy you here, now that the sporting season has ended?"

But my efforts were of little use. He stopped in the lane and placed a hand on my arm, his voice low and filled with meaning as he replied, "More than you know, Lizzie."

That was the moment at which, to please Father and Mrs. Simmons, I should have turned my pleading eyes upon him and asked, in all innocence, whatever could he mean? Following which, he would no doubt pour out his heart and kiss my hand, pledging that he would stand up to his father in choosing a mate. But I knew how that would end, for I was sure that Anthony had not the heart to defy his father for long. And even if he did, where could it lead? For it was well known that the bulk of Holbourne's lands were free of entail, and Lord Highdown could dispose of them as he wished, leaving Anthony the poorest Earl in the kingdom when he took the title. Would Anthony commit himself to a life of relative poverty and humiliation in order to marry me? I was certain not. The inevitable result would be heartbreak for us both, the loss of our friendship, and my own reputation sullied as the foolish girl taken in by the frivolous romances of a nobleman.

Now I was glad for all my father's training, as it allowed me to steady myself for what I must do. "Come now," I said, masking my true feelings with more playfulness than I felt. "I haven't a doubt that you will be a great hit in the *ton*. Half the eligible girls will be falling over themselves to capture your attentions. You will make your parents very happy and proud."

For a moment he seemed to consider defying his parents' wishes, proclaiming allegiance to his own heart, but then his expression grew more determined as his upbringing as a gentleman and heir to the Earldom asserted itself. "You have always been my greatest friend, Lizzie. You always have much better sense than I do."

"You sound as if you are off to war! I hope we will be the best of friends for years to come, when our children are playing together on family visits."

I gazed at him as calmly as I could, then we continued our walk, maintaining our silence until we reached the joining of the lane that led to his family's estate, where we bid our farewells. I continued toward town, conscious of a certain hypocrisy in urging my friend to ignore the demands of his own heart, when I could not quiet my own thoughts after one kiss from a stranger, and a rogue at that. I was glad to have the distraction of a new acquaintance to divert my attention as I approached Mrs. Burgess's house in town.

MRS. BURGESS greeted me cordially in her parlor, rising from her embroidery work; again I noticed how tall she was. She wore a white morning dress, with her brown hair done up in a mass of curls at the top and a fringe falling in back to the base of her neck. She mentioned how glad and grateful she was for the invitation to dinner that evening, her smile lighting up her whole face, the skin around her brown eyes crinkling.

I asked her how she had hit upon Leighton as a site for her new abode.

"Oh, I am only a tenant here for now. I had thought of finding a fine house in Exeter – or, that is, my brother had thought of finding one for us – but I found the air unhealthy, and I was troubled by the recent riots. Perhaps soon I will find a house within my means in the country hereabouts. In the meantime, I am glad to find such welcoming and congenial neighbors."

At this point we were interrupted by the elderly housekeeper bringing in the tea things.

"I hope you don't mind," Mrs. Burgess said, as she set about pouring the water. "I know it's not the time for it, but I thought you might enjoy some refreshment after your walk."

I consented, though I thought it an odd time of day for tea, and we continued talking about village life and the weather for several minutes more, until I realized I was in danger of overstaying my visit. As I was making my excuses and rising to leave, Mrs. Burgess reached across the space between our seats and placed a restraining hand on my arm.

"Oh, please, don't rush off. The Captain and I never held with these rules of decorum that require visits of such a length and no longer. If we are enjoying each other's company, why should you not stay as long as you like?" She said it with such energy and affability that I could not deny her. "Besides, you haven't finished your tea, and I have yet to learn what are your favorite books and music, and what beaux are vying for your attentions at present."

"Oh, I have beaux without number," I said with a casual air.

"Well, of course you do! With such a fine manner and attractive – " She broke off as I looked at her steadily. "Oh, you mean you have none! You quite took me in." She smiled, as if pleased to have been gulled in this way. "But you have no suitors? I find that difficult to credit."

I mentioned the light populace of our region of Devonshire, and the surprising plenitude of young ladies compared to gentlemen. I did not mention Anthony. "But in truth, it is not a topic to which I give much thought," I said, hoping not to continue a subject on which I had too much discourse with my other friends.

"I agree. Too much contemplation of one's prospects can be gauche." She offered me a slice of cake, which I declined. "And what of your family? Mrs. Simmons said your brother is overseas?"

"Yes, these past two years. He was in India the last we heard. We are grateful his ship has avoided engagements with the French, though he regrets the missed opportunities for action and renown."

"And your mother?" she asked. She took a sip of her tea, as if she had just asked about the weather.

I looked down at my own cup. "She passed when I was eleven."

"That must have been difficult."

I nodded, staring at the swirling patterns my spoon was making. Thus far I had enjoyed this unusually intimate introductory visit, but now we had entered on a topic hardly appropriate for such an occasion.

The silence between us lengthened. "I lost my own mother when I was eight," Mrs. Burgess said. "It took me some time to realize she was gone forever. Did you find that with your own loss?" She gazed at me with more concern than really proper from a near stranger.

"No – perhaps because I was older." To distract myself from this discomfiting conversation, I turned my attention to a drawing that hung over the fireplace. It showed the mustering of a hunt before a grand manor house. But for the perspective being off, it would have been a lovely scene. This was the price of my education in drawing – instead of simply enjoying another artist's performance, I must always consider its technical merits. The drawing must have come as part of the furnishing of the house, I thought.

I was ready to ask about it when Mrs. Burgess went on. "Nothing can replace a mother's love, can it?"

Really, this was too familiar. "Mrs. Simmons has taken good care of my brother and me," I said at length.

"Of course she has. I could see the love with which she spoke of your brother on the day we met. I had a governess as well, a kind, matronly woman. But it cannot be the same, can it? The loss of a mother at such a young age – it must change one in some irrevocable way, mustn't it?"

I looked all about the room as I struggled to formulate an answer. "I hardly know. Father – Father praised me for bearing the loss so well. If I mentioned her, he would cut me off by exclaiming over the bravery I had shown up to then."

"So it did change you."

I nodded. "I became the brave little girl Father wanted me to be."

"And you never grieved for your mother."

It was impertinent of her to speak as if we were already intimates; yet, seeing the tender look she gave me, I felt none of the impropriety of such familiarity. "No," I whispered, my lip trembling. How quickly she had pierced my reserve!

She reached out to put a hand on my arm. "I apologize. I didn't mean to make you melancholy. It's just that I've grown so used to talking about my mother and her loss; I didn't realize it wasn't the same for you."

It was strange to realize that, in nine years, no one had shown as much concern for my mother's death as this woman of the briefest acquaintance. As unusual as it was, I could not think it wrong. I left her house after overstaying my visit by three quarters of an hour, thinking she would make a welcome addition to the neighborhood.

CHAPTER FOUR

FATHER AND our guests were equally impressed with Mrs. Burgess. The party made nine. In addition to our special guest and Mrs. Simmons, who always dined with us as one of the family, it comprised Mrs. Smith, an older widow with an estate near town; Mr. and Mrs. Ramsay, neighbors with extensive holdings on the other side of Holbourne; and Mr. Graves, a barrister, and his wife. Mrs. Burgess answered all their questions, some of them quite impertinent, with good grace, frankness, and cordiality.

After praising my selection of dishes and the excellence of Jones' potted lampreys and roast woodcock, Mr. Graves turned the conversation to my father's sermon of the past Sunday, remarking on its particularly insightful qualities. Mrs. Burgess agreed, and took the opportunity to question Father on several points regarding Free Will, bringing in the poems of Alexander Pope. She glanced once or twice in my direction as she asked, "Is it not simply human arrogance which suggests we can be other than as God made us, whatever suffering that entails?"

"Yes," Father replied, "that is one comfort for the sufferings mortals endure, and I hope you find solace in it. Others suggest that we suffer due to our poor exercise of the Free Will God gave us."

"I assure you, sir, I chose none of the suffering I have endured."

"No, I believe not, Mrs. Burgess. Having lost a wife far too soon, I find myself in complete agreement. We must bear our lot as we can, for whatever is, is."

It was the one moment of gravity during the course of dinner. After that solemn moment, the conversation turned to lighter topics, and Mrs. Burgess returned to her former vivacity. As she had lived in London, and our guests sometimes spent winters there, she engaged them in a lively discussion of the plays they had seen, with special admiration given to Sarah Siddons' Lady Macbeth and Dora Jordan's Rosalind. She even indulged them by reciting one or two favorite passages from memory and comparing their treatment by different actors.

"And what about you, Miss Collington?" she asked. "Do you enjoy the theatre?"

"Unfortunately, I cannot say that I do, having never seen the best, only amateur theatricals and once or twice a troupe of strolling players in Exeter. In the former, I would often know the players and could never forget having just seen Rosalind or Romeo at dinner the week before, making the whole production seem merely a poor game of pretend. In the latter, if it was a play I knew and loved, I couldn't bear to hear the playwright's words butchered by third-rate actors."

"And you've never been to London?"

I shook my head.

"Well, we must find a way to send you! But did you know Mrs. Siddons also tours? I am certain she has been to Bath, which is not too far. I've heard that in the provinces she has even dared to take on Hamlet as a breeches part – if you can call it that."

"You're quite right, Mrs. Burgess," interrupted Mr. Ramsay. "I've always thought Hamlet a spineless excuse for a man, with all his indecisive philosophizing. It hardly counts as a breeches part, does it?" Here he gave a coarse laugh. "A real man would have just run the usurper through and taken the throne!"

Mrs. Burgess was polite enough to laugh at this vulgarity before saying, "No, Mr. Ramsay, I only meant that Mrs. Siddons is too proper and refined to show her legs in men's stockings and breeches. She has arranged some sort of toga or similar drapery to give the Dane a more classical air while keeping her own person modestly covered. Which, I suppose, is hardly worse than the usual costumery, for who knows what the Danes were wont to wear in that dim past?"

Gazing at her with some admiration, Father asked, "Mrs. Burgess, I am intrigued to know how you came by your extensive reading and education."

"Oh, Thomas's and my circumstances may belie it, but we come from an old landed family in Kent. Father insisted on all the improvements and education for his children: reading, mathematics, sciences, dueling for the boys, music and drawing and needlework for me. He sent our elder brother, Jonathan, to study the law, but a lot of good it did us, for when he inherited the estate, he let it slip away through dissipation and neglect, refusing all of Thomas's advice on its management. Fortunately, I had my portion and had already married Captain Burgess, but poor Thomas was forced to go into trade."

"Such a pity," Father said. "It seems your life has been one trial after another."

"Oh, do not worry on my account. The greatest blow was the loss of my husband, and that was nearly two years ago now. I feel my spirits begin to recover, much as I miss him, and I begin to sense life's possibilities once more." She finished by looking over at me.

With the meal concluded, Father raised his glass to me. "Another fine meal, due to your excellent planning, Elizabeth. I do not know how I will manage without you once some gentleman takes you from me."

"Let us not forget Mrs. Jones, who prepared it," I said. Then, in a more scoffing tone, "And there is little chance of you ridding yourself of me that quickly, Father, as you know well." At which Father and the rest of our guests scoffed in return.

As we women retired to the drawing room, I could not help noticing Mrs. Burgess's uncommon stature, which was not all to do with height alone, for in truth, she was not much taller than Mrs. Graves or Mrs. Ramsay. No, it was something else, her upright bearing and deportment, combined with a sense of vivacity. Not that she had any hint of bubbly girlishness; it was more a sense of energy contained, ready to be unleashed at any moment, and briefly revealed when she stepped toward the drawing room or turned to address a remark from one of our guests with a direct gaze, a frank expression, and a genuine enthusiasm, no matter the topic at hand. She was remarkably unreserved, yet never gauche or impertinent.

How different must her upbringing and parental counsel have been from my own! It was a wonder that her open, hopeful nature had survived the tragedies and disappointments of her life so far; or could it be, I pondered, that her very energy and optimism had helped her bear these hurts in a manner equal to my father's recommended reserve and self-command?

In the drawing room, she paused at a watercolor of the Parsonage hanging above the mantle, showing our home's nine windows arrayed across the front, with dormers and chimneys above, and a bright riot of flowers surrounding it. Bending close, she examined the monogram in the lower right corner. "EC. Miss Collington, is this your own work?"

I had to acknowledge that it was.

"It's so lifelike! And more, you've absolutely captured the spirit of the place. It easily surpasses the accomplishments of many a young lady. Wherever did you acquire such skill?"

"I had the good fortune to be taught by Mrs. Simmons, who herself learned from the great watercolorist, Paul Sandby."

"Lizzie is too modest," Mrs. Simmons put in. "If I had only had her talent!"

"She certainly is full of surprises," Mrs. Burgess said, regarding me with new respect.

Once the card tables were broken out and a game set up, Mrs. Burgess took a lively interest in all the gossip of the neighborhood, paying as much attention to the talk as to the cards in her hand. She seemed eager to hear of the comings and goings of the great families, which ones were making for London for the remainder of the season and which were staying in the country, sometimes putting in humorous remarks. These were never cruel, but showed a wry view of all the quirks and oddities of human nature.

Finally, she turned to me. "Oh, look at you, Miss Collington, sitting there so silent, all reserve and decorum, while we prattle on. You must think me quite the gossip! Or is something making you especially quiet this evening?"

Could she have guessed something of my conversation with Anthony, or that other event that had so perturbed my thoughts? "Oh, not at all," I protested. "I was enjoying the conversation greatly. It is not often that we have such lively and witty discourse."

"Come, now, Lizzie," said Mrs. Simmons. "You know it's not a fortnight since your great shock, and you haven't been the same since."

The other guests had all heard the story, of course, but Mrs. Burgess was innocent of it. "What kind of shock, pray tell?" she asked.

"It was nothing, really," I said, but Mrs. Simmons insisted on going through the story, leaving out the more salacious moments.

"A forward rogue, he was," she concluded.

"It must have been extremely frightening for all of you," Mrs. Burgess remarked, her eyes wide. She turned to me. "And you refused to give him your necklace, with a pistol pointed at you? How ever did you muster the courage?"

"As it was my only memento of my mother, that in itself was enough to carry me forward. But he got the better of me in the end. It is a bitter loss."

"Quite bold was our Lizzie," Mrs. Simmons said.

"Really?" said Mrs. Burgess. "But I suppose I shouldn't be surprised.

You do seem the mistress of your emotions."

"Oh, that is Lizzie, to a T," said Mrs. Simmons. "Reserve and self-command, those are the bywords of good breeding, as Mr. Collington always taught both Lizzie and Jamie. But too much of that is unhealthy, in my opinion, and I sometimes wonder what Lizzie has bottled up inside her. There's more going on in there than she lets on, her mind sometimes wanders so when she should be applying herself to her improvement."

My cheeks grew warm at this frank assessment of my character, and at Mrs. Simmons having caught me out when I thought I had kept my distractions well hidden. Mrs. Burgess saved me by turning the conversation back to the highwayman. "Yes, I've heard of this outlaw. They say he's bold to the point of recklessness."

Just then the men returned to us from the library and Mr. Graves caught the end of her remark. "He'll be caught soon enough, if he keeps wearing that same burgundy coat he's worn so far. One can spot him a mile off."

"Are there plans for his capture?" Mrs. Burgess asked. "I practically fear to leave the village with such outlaws about."

"Oh, I don't think you need worry, Mrs. Burgess," Mr. Graves assured her. "The gang has confined itself so far to robbing the nobility, barons and above. They don't seem interested in the likes of us. He even gave the Marquess of Whinside a lecture as he was robbing him, something about all the good the ill-gotten gold would do the poor in Exeter."

"Isn't that what they all say?" Mrs. Smith said.

"I don't doubt it's a lot of flummery, but this one actually seems to fancy himself some sort of Robin Hood. Has his accomplices call him Lord Rob. Apparently he went on at length about the nobility plundering the commoners, and he views his thievery as merely levelling the field."

"He sounds quite the Jacobin!" Mrs. Burgess put in.

"He made similar statements to us," I said. "Yet he was well dressed and had the manner and address of a gentleman. I wouldn't be surprised to learn he's a person of gentility, or a nobleman who has fallen into debt." I looked around at the gentlemen present and continued in a conspiratorial whisper. "Perhaps he is even someone we would recognize with his mask off!"

Mr. Graves smiled with the others, then said, "But as to plans for his capture – Sir Morris seems wholly ineffectual." Sir Morris Wetherford was our parish's high constable. "There's some talk of involving the militia."

"Oh, the militia can never help," said Mr. Ramsay. "They're too busy quelling the riots in Exeter."

"Perhaps some music would relieve us from this grim subject?" Father offered.

Remembering that Mrs. Burgess had mentioned how much she missed her pianoforte, I asked if she would like to play for us. She protested her lack of practice only for a moment before agreeing. She began with two popular songs, hesitating only slightly here and there, but otherwise playing with a lyricism and taste that would have shamed many musicians of more recent tutelage. Then she invited me to join her in a Bach four-hand duet that she found amongst our stacks of music. I was only glad that I could keep up with her and not shame Mrs. Simmons, who had served as my music teacher. We finished with a piece by Dibdin, Mrs. Burgess accompanying my voice. Our audience was well pleased with us, and Mrs. Burgess beamed up at me from her stool as if she had never enjoyed an evening more.

With that, the party broke up, Mrs. Smith offering our special guest a ride home in her chaise.

When the last guests had departed, Father said to me, "We must make every effort to ensure that Mrs. Burgess feels at home here and receives all the benefits of our notice. It must be a lonely existence, with no relations here but her brother, and him so often away. Elizabeth, I hope you will call upon her often and take pains to be seen in public with her, as this will help to widen her acquaintance in good society, which is the only comfort remaining to her. We must have her to dinner every week."

I readily agreed to this plan, as I looked forward to increasing my acquaintance with such an intriguing character, whose personality was so opposite to my own.

"That is well," Father replied. "I feared that jealousy might prompt you to keep your distance."

"Jealousy!"

"Certainly, for who could blame you for fearing that such an intelligent, lively, and well-bred woman, still in the prime of her youth and possessed of quite an attractive person, could be a rival for a certain young lord's affections once he returns from London?"

"Father, I think you are in love yourself! One evening with Mrs. Burgess and she has captured your heart! When do you plan to propose?"

I let the matter rest with this teasing, having no wish to reveal my morning conversation with Anthony at that moment, and certain Father would not be pleased if I told him the simple truth: Lord Highdown could have even less interest in his son marrying a captain's widow than a vicar's daughter.

CHAPTER FIVE

THE SECOND time I saw the highwayman, I found his gloved hand clasped over my mouth as I came awake in my own bed. I began to struggle, as any girl of pure virtue and good upbringing would, but the thief held a finger to his lips, then whispered, “Be still, for I have no intention of harming you. I come only to return you this.” He pulled out my mother’s necklace and held it before me, the silver cameo catching glints of moonlight shining in through the open window. “Now, if you will promise me not to scream, I will remove my hand and return the necklace to its rightful place.”

It was now five weeks since the robbery, and if the feelings that event had provoked troubled me at all, it was not often, and not greatly. I felt I had nearly forgotten him. Yet here he was, in my very bedchamber. To retain my honor, I should have cried out the moment he removed his hand, whatever promise I had made in nodding my head. To my shame, I did not.

“What do you want?” I whispered.

“Why, you, of course!” He leaned toward me. With the moonlight behind him, he appeared as little more than a threatening shape looming over me, topped by his cocked hat.

I cringed and shrank away.

“No, not in that way,” he whispered. Turning his head, he seemed to realize the dark shape the moonlight made of him. He rose and went around to the other side of my bed, kneeling beside it. "There, now we can see each other equally."

Such a considerate rogue! Now I could see his face, or what was visible of it above his crêpe mask. His eyes were alight with that same energy and humor, as if he never felt more alive than when robbing carriages or breaking into young ladies' bedchambers.

"I said I would not harm you," he went on. "I want only to return your necklace."

"Why would you do such a thing?"

"When I saw you in the carriage, I took you for the daughter of a nobleman. It was only after circling back to follow your carriage home – yes, that is how thoroughly you captivated me! – that I discovered my mistake. I do not make it a habit to rob any but the highest nobility, and so I would rectify my mistake. Will you allow me?"

Again I should have been afraid. Yet his solicitude and his gentlemanly manner reassured me. I nodded, and with the greatest gentleness he secured the necklace in its place.

"But your behavior toward my person in the carriage!" I whispered. "You seem all gentility now, but that was the work of a ruffian. I thank you for returning the necklace, but now you must leave."

He made no move to go. "For my former behavior, I do apologize. I don't often steal kisses while I steal purses, yet I sometimes find myself carried away in my role as leader of bandits."

"Is that what you call it? A role, as with an actor on a stage?" He only looked at me. "Is it true they call you Lord Rob?"

"Some call me that, yes. Others call me Robin. At your service." He tipped his hat.

"So you do take the role of a Robin Hood."

"No, I – " He looked toward the window, and I thought for a moment there was something familiar about his dark eyes as the moonlight caught them. "It was merely a name of convenience."

"But it is not your real name."

"Of course not. No highwayman goes by his real name."

"You say I should trust that you mean me no harm, yet you will not tell me your true name. That is no basis for trust, sir. You have me at a disadvantage."

"Maybe one day I will tell it to you. But for now you must believe me, my conduct toward you was no act. I was so enchanted I simply couldn't help myself."

"What could I have done to elicit such feelings? I'm sure I have never before prompted such lewd behavior."

"I will not take the trouble to flatter your beauty, for you cannot be unaware of your own charms. No, it was the way you gazed steadily into my eyes, even with my pistol levelled at you, the way you calmly denied my request of the necklace. If I could win such a heart, I told myself, what a prize it would be! And so I overstepped the bounds of decency, to my regret. Yet I felt you respond to my advances, I know I did."

He paused, perhaps expecting me to acknowledge those feelings I should never have had. I remained silent.

"You even had the courage to slap me, which was almost beyond crediting. Yet I felt that was only an act, to make your companions believe you blushed out of shock and anger. But I think you blushed for a different reason."

His hand went to my cheek and caressed it ever so softly. I could not help an intake of breath at the tingling this sent through me.

"Yes, I knew it. Perhaps what was wrongly begun can now be carried forward with more honor." Here he leaned down, lifting the bottom edge of his mask at the last moment before kissing me on the mouth, gently this time.

Again I felt a warmth spreading through me, which only increased as his fingers slid along my jaw and down to my neck, sending little shivers down my spine. But he went too far when his hand slid farther down to untie the strings of my gown. I placed a hand on his shoulder and pushed him away. "You are too forward, sir!" I hissed, ignoring the absurdity of accusing a housebreaker and robber of being too forward.

He took my hand from his shoulder and held it. "I will steal no more kisses now, but look forward to the day when they are freely given."

I snatched my hand away from him. "What possible interest could I have in further intercourse with a criminal? You have already placed me in a most compromising position."

"Discomfiting you is the farthest from my wish, so I will take my leave," he said, crossing to the window. He placed one foot on the casement before turning back to me, and I noticed he wore a simple pair of shoes rather than the thigh-high boots he had worn before, no doubt to allow for easy climbing. The pose afforded me an excellent view of his calf outlined in the moonlight; it was shapely and well-toned, but not quite so muscled as men took pride in displaying. "This is not the last we'll see of each other," he said. "Expect me when you see me!" With those last words, he disappeared over the sill.

I could not help going to the casement and peering out to see him scampering down the drainpipe with the agility of an acrobat. Reaching the ground, he turned to look back at the window. I drew back, but I was certain he had seen me looking after him.

CHAPTER SIX

REBECCA – FOR Mrs. Burgess had insisted I call her by her given name after that first dinner – gave a shout of exhilaration as her horse jumped the low hedge separating the moor from the lane that would take us home. Her exultation turned to alarm on the landing, however, as she was jostled in her seat. How she maintained her balance I do not know, for she was pushed forward by the impact, leaning low over the horse's neck, with only the horn of the saddle for a handhold.

"That was a greater challenge than I expected," she panted as she drew her horse up beside my own. This was our first opportunity to ride together in the weeks since we had met, and it must have been even longer since she had practiced her equestrian skills. Yet she seemed thrilled rather than frightened by the experience, her eyes wide and glowing. "I'd almost forgotten the difficulty of riding aside. Would you like to try it again?" She seemed ready to turn her horse around and jump the hedge in the opposite direction.

I politely demurred.

"Lizzie, what is it?" she asked. "You've been even quieter than usual, and you seem distracted."

As well I might, for it was the day after the highwayman's nocturnal visit. Needless to say, I had slept little after his acrobatic departure. At times as Rebecca and I were preparing for the morning's ride, my thoughts had drifted back to the kisses the rogue had boldly stolen from me, and the feeling of his hands against my skin as he replaced my necklace. I had to suppress a shiver at the thought, and Rebecca couldn't help noticing that my thoughts had wandered.

"I am quite well," I said, "but I believe it more prudent to leave such a challenge until you have had more practice."

"Prudence! One can miss much of life through prudence. And how can you counsel me to it, when you just took the same risk as I? Confess it, you found it a thrill, though one could hardly tell by looking at you. You might be sitting in your drawing room waiting for the tea to be brought in."

"I assure you, I enjoyed that immensely."

Rebecca grasped my wrist and pretended to feel the pulse there. "Ah, yes. I believe I can just detect a slight increase in the pace of your heart. Careful, or next your excitement will break through all your sangfroid."

I had to smile at this, and she set off once more with a laugh, no doubt feeling she had won a small victory.

Such teasing had become her favorite pastime as our acquaintance had grown. She liked nothing better than to prick my reserve by making me laugh out loud at a witty remark, or even by provoking me to anger at her impertinence. Yet it was all done with such friendly good humor that I could not long remain cross with her. If I responded with a knit brow and a sharp remark, she would only laugh, saying, "So you are not made of ice after all!" If her teasing managed to provoke a smile, her eyes would come alight with the deepest glow of affection. She simply could not understand the reserve to which I had been so long trained that it now seemed my true nature.

Three weeks had passed since our first meeting, and our acquaintance, begun on such intimate terms, had only deepened. We found ourselves together almost daily, for not only did Father encourage the association, but he had suggested that I assist Rebecca in organizing the Leighton Charitable Society Auction, an endeavor for which she had readily volunteered. She seemed to share my passion for helping the poor, which Father had fostered in me from a young age as part of our Christian duty. Our work on the auction – which involved many hours in the Leighton Village Hall cataloging the valuable but unwanted possessions donated by nobles and gentry from miles around – offered us regular intercourse, added to which were our numerous excursions in the out-of-doors and frequent visits in one or the other of our houses. We were thus afforded all the occasions necessary to plumb each other's characters and find each in the other a most suitable and complementary companion.

On my part, I found her good humor and open nature intriguing, so unlike my own, or that of anyone I had ever known. If there had been anything flighty or silly in her character, as there so often was in the girls whose acquaintance I barely managed to tolerate, I might have been put off. Yet her openness and enthusiasm were grounded in good sense and intelligence. The fact that she was only a few years older than I, but with a much greater wealth of experience, meant she could serve as a guide in those areas neither Mrs. Simmons nor I felt comfortable discussing.

Too, behind her near-constant good cheer there were moments of unexplained gravity. At odd times as we sat reading in our drawing room or her parlor, enjoying that companionable silence with which we had grown so comfortable, I would find her staring abstractedly out a window. "Oh, it is nothing," she would respond to my inquiry. "I was just pondering a passage in my book." Then we might discuss the skill with which the author had produced this sentimental effect, whether it sprang from the inherent natures and concerns of the characters, or seemed rather a mere twist of the plot to entrap the reader's sympathies. The conversation would then turn to other topics, or we would go back to our reading, the moment of gravity apparently forgotten.

Rebecca showed no such seriousness when we were out of doors, and even her near fall had not dampened her spirits. Now, setting off after her as she attempted an unsettled canter, I was curious how she had come to be so bold. I caught up to her as the lane entered a forest of oak and beech and we slowed to a walk, admiring for a moment the sunlight dappling the understory in a pattern of greens and golds. "Have you not always ridden aside?" I asked. "Or is it simply that you have not had occasion to ride of late?"

"Oh, no! You might find it shocking, but once we were married, on those few occasions we had of riding together, Captain Burgess insisted that I ride astride, believing the side saddle a dangerous contraption, no matter the decorum it offered. As for that other reason young ladies are told never to ride astride, it hardly mattered once we were married."

As I absorbed this revelation, two jays began squabbling in an oak nearby, their hoarse, squawking protests piercing the silence of the forest. Then one chased the other over the lane ahead of us, tan streaks with flashes of blue.

"And did you find it easier?" I asked at length.

"Oh, much! I would have asked Lord Highdown's stable master for a man's saddle if it would not have shocked him so. As easily as you and Maggie cleared that low hedge, imagine what you could do if you rode astride! I tell you, Lizzie, you are twice the horsewoman of any man I have seen, you sit your mount with such ease and balance, even at a canter."

"Yet I dare not gallop, or try a high wall. How often did I envy Jamie and the other men as they raced off after the fox, leaving me to the company of a groomsman! The other ladies who chose to ride to the hunt were always far behind."

Rebecca smiled at the unaccustomed fervor of my remark, saying, "Then you have an additional inducement to marriage, for we widows and old married women can get away with much that young ladies cannot."

Marriage had not been a frequent topic of our conversation, for I had too much of it with my other friends, whose opinions ranged from the lack of eligible bachelors in our neighborhood to a determination to attend public assemblies in Exeter in hopes of meeting young men of trade. I had met two or three such men on occasion, and though I felt I had nothing against the way in which they made their living – indeed, it had much to recommend it, in contrast to the dependent nature of Father's income – yet I could not imagine making a match with any of them. For, no matter how refined their manners or attractive their persons, their conversation was as insipid as that of our neighbor girls, saving that the topics were of trade and the price of wool and the vicissitudes of taxation. If any had ever read a book, it was in the long-ago days of their schooling, and if they appreciated music, it was of the sort heard in taverns and on the ships onto which they loaded their goods. Though I told myself I did not hold myself above them, I could not see that we had enough in common to make a happy marriage.

It was here that Rebecca showed tastes broader than my own. Marriage to a man of the Navy had introduced her to a number of sea chanties and tavern songs which she remembered hearing with pleasure. She could even pick out one or two of them on the pianoforte. "Surely you cannot believe that the taste and discernment we show in our appreciation of Haydn or Pleyel are diminished by the simple pleasures of a tavern song, so long as its subject is one of decorum? Even your much-admired Dibdin takes pleasure in naval themes."

Dibdin had been our one point of disagreement. When I mentioned my admiration for that popular composer, she admitted to enjoying his melodies, but stated that she found many of his lyrics odious, looking put out when she said it. Then she appeared to shake off her mood, teasing me with, "Take 'Meg of Wapping' – hardly a fit subject for a young lady, you must admit." I found her attitude surprising, for otherwise she was broad-minded, and even Father saw nothing harmful in that tale of the woman who married seven sailors. But at length I remembered "Tom Bowling," Dibdin's popular lament for a dead man of the sea, allowing me to explain away her dislike as merely a wish to avoid reminders of her own departed husband.

Rebecca's tastes in novels were even broader and less decorous. As a married woman, she had access to those works which society deemed too salacious for unmarried young women, and she readily shared them with me. I blushed when she removed a book from a small *secretaire* she had brought with her from London: the first volume of Richardson's *Clarissa,* which Father would never have allowed in our house, though recently he had spoken favorably of Frances Burney. "You may read it when you visit me here," she said, "and none will be the wiser. I'm sure a girl of your self-mastery will be able to resist the temptations that would threaten a reader of a more susceptible mind." Her eyes crinkled at the corners as she made this statement.

If Rebecca introduced me to a wider range of music and reading, I was the tutor in our walks about the countryside, for she was wholly ignorant of botany, the accomplishment in which I took the greatest pride and interest for its own sake.

"I have always had the greatest appreciation for all types of flowers," Rebecca said. "There's something almost sensual about their beauty, and of course the aroma can be quite intoxicating. But as to their names, and especially those hard Latin ones, I could never get far."

Walks on fine days being exactly what the doctor had prescribed for her, we often found ourselves roving the moors and dells around Leighton together. My solitary walks had been confined to the Earl's estate, but Father was less restrictive when he knew I would have Rebecca's company, allowing the opportunity to visit the wilder tracts farther afield. She proved herself an excellent companion, eager to follow me in my determination not to let a single specie escape my close observation, no matter how awkwardly placed. As we clambered up steep banks or ventured to the edges of soggy bogs, she showed neither a care for the mud splattering the hem of her petticoats, nor for the exertion required. The vigorous exercise seemed to agree with her, and any trace of her former ailment vanished. Only on the steepest crags – where I would often scramble to examine the different mosses and liverworts growing in the crevices – would she show hesitation, sometimes reaching out a hand for help or clutching my arm for balance. This seemed in contrast to the bravado she showed while ahorse.

As spring advanced, more and more of my favorite species showed themselves. If I would speak of the likelihood of seeing the first opening of a particular flower on a particular day, Rebecca would declare amazement at my clairvoyance when my prediction proved accurate. "It is simply paying attention to nature's rhythms and recording them," I told her. "Have you never read Gilbert White's excellent volume on Selborne?"

Despite her professed lack of botanical knowledge, she would show the keenest interest as we crouched together before a flower-strewn bank, peering through my hand glass at the different structures of a bluebell or a primrose as I pointed out the difference between the petals and the sepals, the pistils and the stamens. She even gained some appreciation for the utility of the Linnaean system, as I mentioned the class and order into which each specie was grouped according to its numbers of stamens and pistils. Yet her skepticism remained. "Why can we not simply appreciate flowers for their beauty, rather than classifying and dissecting them?"

I had to smile, for she reminded me of myself only a few years before, when Father had first introduced me to Linnaeus and to Latin on our walks together. I gave her the same answer he had given me then: that in learning of the intricacies and organization of the natural world, we may understand something of the plan of our Creator.

Though she smiled and seemed satisfied at this explanation, her appreciation always returned to the aesthetic when out walking with me, and here her enthusiasm was a match for my own. "How pretty!" she would exclaim, or "What a delicate beauty!" Or, in the case of the marsh violet, "I will not say what that reminds me of!" No matter how I pressed her, she would not reveal what this was, but would say only that it was no wonder the poets speak of the flower of love. She bit her lower lip and turned away, but not before I caught a faint blush rising to her cheek.

CHAPTER SEVEN

IN ADDITION to our work on the auction, Rebecca often joined me on my charitable rounds in the neighborhood. I always enjoyed these visits; what had begun as a chore when I was young had soon grown into a favorite activity, as I came to experience a real joy in the grateful looks and smiles with which the poor greeted us. I had almost begun to think of them as my friends.

If anything, Rebecca's concern for the poor was greater than my own; as much as she appreciated my enthusiasm, she often lamented the likelihood that such charity as we could offer only eased a small measure of suffering, and could never truly raise the poor from their abject condition. Even the upcoming auction, which would raise money not only for the destitute of our parish but also for an orphanage in Exeter, promised to do but little, the need was so great. "So much is out of their control," she would say of the indigent, "or even ours – the wool prices, the shuttered mills, this year's poor harvest, the wars."

"Yet our efforts must count for something," I replied, "since they are always met with such gratitude. It seems we are doing as much as we can."

"So say we, but are we truly? I ask you, Lizzie, if there were any other thing that could be done, even a greater sacrifice than these hours spent on the auction, would you do it?"

I asked her what kind of sacrifice she meant, but as she would not be more specific, I could not answer; still, I assured her that I would go to great lengths to fulfil the duty Father had taught me.

One of the first families Rebecca and I visited together occupied a particularly mean hovel, a place where I had visited often. The yard was all mud, fouled with the droppings of the pigs and chickens the family kept.

"Good morning, Mother Smith," I called from the yard – for that was her style in the neighborhood – and soon the matron of the house appeared, a stout woman in a threadbare smock, with a dingy lace cap covering curls of an indeterminate shade. "Miss Elizabeth," she greeted me, "it's grand to see you, as always."

As I handed over what stuff we had brought – eggs, produce from our garden, a brace of rabbits donated by Holbourne's gamekeeper – I introduced Rebecca, then asked after the family, which included her husband, who made his living as a woodcutter, and four small children. She assured me they all were fine. "And your father?" I asked.

"Much the same, if not worse."

"May I see him?"

We entered the cottage, which was really little more than a hut. If the odor was foul in the yard, it was worse inside, for something about Mrs. Smith's father's skin ailment gave off a putrid smell. The interior had all the appearances one might expect of a home kept by a woman overwhelmed by duties as mother, gardener, cook, nurse, housekeeper, and pieceworker. I was glad to see that Rebecca, if she was bothered by any of this, did not let it show, but took a lively interest in the children running about the single room that served as parlor, dining room, kitchen, and sick room for old Mr. Garner, whose cot was pulled up near the fire.

"How are you today, Mr. Garner?" I asked in a loud voice, for he was nearly deaf.

"Been better, been worse," he responded.

"I brought you a new salve the apothecary recommended." I pulled a vial from the pocket of my walking dress, showing it to Mrs. Smith as I related the apothecary's instructions. The remainder of the visit was spent answering Mr. Garner's questions about certain corners of Holbourne with which I was familiar. He liked nothing better than to reminisce about his youth, when he had run a flock of sheep on those lands, before the current Earl had enclosed them.

As we made to depart, Mrs. Smith exclaimed, "Oh, I nearly forgot, I had hoped to have that panel for your fireplace screen finished by now, but one thing and the other have got in the way."

"Now, Mother Smith," I said, putting a hand on her arm, "I've told you not to put yourself out, you have enough to do as it is."

"But you've been so good to us, dear, and your father, too."

"Father may be generous, but I assure you I have only my own self-interest at heart. Your smiles and your friendly greetings are ample compensation for these trifles I bring you, as is the warm self-regard in which I can then hold myself. I hardly think of myself as generous at all, and neither should you, since I am so well rewarded for my efforts."

"That's as may be, but I aim to have it done while you'll still be needing a fire in your parlor this spring." She smiled and we left her waving after us from her yard.

When we were a distance away, Rebecca took a deep breath. "Did you really mean what you said about generosity?"

"I did. Even now I can feel the warm glow of self-satisfaction coursing through me, and my own self-regard is several notches higher. I call that an excellent bargain. Perhaps I should go into trade!"

"You joke, but there is a real effort involved in visiting such a place and witnessing such misery. Your self-command must have stood you in good stead."

I felt myself stiffening. "Not for all the world would I let Mrs. Smith or her father see me wrinkle my nose or look askance at their condition of life! What is fifteen minutes to me, when they must bear it the year round? And what of you? You bore it equally well."

She dismissed this with a tip of her head. "I have seen my share of squalor. But you! You have led such a sheltered life. It is not many girls of genteel upbringing who could enter that place without some sign of disgust – or who would go at all."

"I suppose I should feel quite smug then!"

"No, not smug, but neither should you undervalue yourself, Lizzie. I – I certainly – " She trailed off.

"Certainly what?" I prompted.

She gave a half smile, but her eyes remained serious. "I certainly do not undervalue you."

I held her gaze for a moment, noticing the flecks of gold in the rich mahogany of her eyes, before shaking my head. "Oh, come, you will turn my head with such talk." I hooked my arm inside hers, and we turned our steps toward the Parsonage.

AS CLOSE as Rebecca and I had become, I had less opportunity to come to know her brother, Mr. Nighthorn, as he was so often in London. On those occasions when he did accompany his sister to a social engagement, he revealed himself a taciturn fellow. On one musical evening at the Parsonage

– for Rebecca loved nothing better than a chance to play our pianoforte, and even better if the parlor was packed with listeners – he sat at the back, remaining aloof from the other guests. During one piece, when Rebecca and I were at the instrument together, I glanced over at him, observing him when he thought himself unobserved. For a moment I thought he was glowering at me, until I realized the look was meant for Rebecca herself, who remained lost in the music. I could not tell whether it was an expression of anger, disgust, or perhaps jealousy. Then his eyes shifted to me and quickly away.

After the recital, I noticed him over by the sideboard, where he was filling his plate from the cold collation laid out there. Mr. Ramsay was in the midst of another story about the highwayman, to which I had been attending closely, though careful to avoid making my interest too apparent. "The rascal and his gang have committed another robbery," he said. "That's the fourth since he accosted you, Miss Collington. He's taken to wearing different coats, so he won't be recognized so readily from a distance. And he always seems to know just when the nobles will be travelling, by what routes, and how much wealth they will have with them." There was much tsk-tsking, but as these events seemed far removed from our social sphere, the talk soon turned to other matters.

I took the opportunity to excuse myself and approached Rebecca's brother. Rebecca herself stood nearby, talking affably with Father.

"Did you not enjoy the recital, Mr. Nighthorn?" I asked.

"No, I found it very fine," he said, unable to hold my gaze.

"It was just that, at one point, when I happened to look up, you seemed – not quite happy, as if you had rather be anywhere else than here."

"You saw that, did you?" His eyes roved the room until they lit on Rebecca. As this seemed to discomfit him even more, he turned completely about, noticing a doorway leading into the kitchen and pantry. He sidled toward it, tilting his head in a manner that indicated I should follow.

This was odd behavior, but I pursued him, unwilling to leave his former attitude unexplained. I advanced as far as the doorway, where he could speak to me in a low voice without being overheard, yet we were still not, in the strictest sense, alone.

"It's – Rebecca, you see – " he began, but then did not seem able to continue. Finally, he began again. "I can see the two of you are becoming close. Only, y'see, she does this, takes up with people, then drops them." I noticed his accent lacked its earlier polish, and wondered if all of his rubbing of shoulders with the London merchant class was wearing off on him. He still couldn't look at me, but took a great interest in the wallpaper of the passageway. "I wouldn't see you hurt, is all."

I was too stunned to speak for several moments. What could he mean by this? Did he intend somehow to protect me by these words, and if so, why should he be so concerned for my welfare? At last I found my voice. "I hardly know what to make of such an impertinent communication, sir. Do you not think me capable of judging your sister's character for myself?"

"No, I didn't mean – it's just – "

"Having come to know your sister well over these past weeks, I find such a statement hard to credit. If it was truly meant as a kindness, then I thank you for it, but I beg you never again to speak to me on this subject. Now, if you will excuse me." I turned to rejoin the other guests.

For the remainder of the evening, I tried to put Mr. Nighthorn's words from my mind, yet I found myself looking at my friend with new eyes, trying to discern her motives as she mingled with our guests. Could it be that she was merely using acquaintance with our family to improve her standing in the neighborhood, and meant to drop us as her circle grew? I noticed she seemed taken with Sally Chisdale, a childhood friend of mine who had married the heir of a large estate in a neighboring parish. As she laughed at some remark of Sally's, she looked over and caught my eye for the briefest moment, then turned away with what I now took for a guilty air. Yet her farewell handshake and kiss on the cheek were as warm as ever, and her reminder of our plans for a walk the next morning showed real eagerness. I tried to put my suspicions aside, but spent a troubled night nevertheless.

CHAPTER EIGHT

OVER THE next weeks, I remained alert for any behavior on Rebecca's part that would confirm her brother's statements, but found none. She continued to show herself as nothing other than a loyal friend, one whose cheerful spirits had gradually begun to pull me out of my habitual reserve. On at least one occasion she turned down an invitation to a much more fashionable house in favor of dining with us and our usual small circle. This hardly seemed the conduct of a zealous social climber. I put Mr. Nighthorn's remark down to sibling rivalry and thought no more of it.

I soon had other thoughts with which to occupy myself, for Rebecca proposed a trip to Bath in May. Not only would this be my first visit to that city, but the famed Dora Jordan was to appear as Rosalind in *As You Like It*, which Rebecca and I agreed was our favorite of the Bard's plays. The trip must needs be short, only a week, for we had much to do to prepare for the auction the following month, but it would allow us to take in the sights of that fashionable city. With Rebecca acting as my chaperone, and even offering to pay for most of the trip out of her pocket, Father readily agreed to the proposal; he and Mrs. Simmons even suggested that this was too short a visit in which to take in all of Bath's wonders – by which they meant that I could hardly make the acquaintance of a suitable young gentleman in such a short period, much less develop the sort of attachment that would lead to marriage.

I found their readiness to have Rebecca escort me in pursuit of a husband, not to mention financing the endeavor, quite mercenary. Too, much as I enjoyed a ball – and what young lady does not? – the prospect of dancing and making polite conversation over tea with complete strangers seemed daunting, even with an introduction by the Assembly Rooms' master of ceremonies to provide a veneer of propriety. No, I was certain that one week in Bath would be sufficient, if not more than I could stand.

ONE DAY early in May, when an unexpected squall had kept us indoors, Rebecca and I sat in Father's library, Rebecca gazing in wonder at the ranks of journals I had filled over the years with drawings and pressed flowers, while I leafed through one of the travel narratives she had brought me, this one of a tour through India. I couldn't help thinking of Jamie as I pored over the illustrations of elephants, tigers, jungles, snow-capped peaks, and the strangely-clad, brown-skinned people who lived there. Was he seeing such sights, and meeting such people? I almost envied him. For me, even the upcoming trip to Bath seemed an adventure; though it would only require a long day's coach journey, it would still be the farthest from home I had ever travelled. But to undertake a journey of years, and see such diverse and wonderful sights!

I tried to imagine travelling to such far-off places, India, or perhaps the former colonies in America, but then I stopped myself when I remembered Father, feeling almost selfish. I was his only daughter, and I had managed his household for the past two years. Who would care for him in his old age? I still remembered the day Jamie left us for the Royal Naval College; he had expressed his regrets at parting, to be sure, but his eyes had still blazed with excitement as he boarded the coach that carried him away. Could I see myself doing the same, watching Father from the carriage's rear window as he receded into the distance, waving his solitary farewell? No, it was more than likely that I would have to content myself, as Gilbert White had done, with intimate knowledge of a few square miles of my home country, and perhaps occasional trips to sample the exotic sights of Bath, or perhaps Portsmouth.

I was interrupted in these thoughts by Rebecca exclaiming, "Lizzie, these journals are wonderful!" She gestured to the one that lay open on her lap. "Your drawings of the flowers are exquisite, as are the scenes in which they are set, and your notes beside them are so insightful and reflect such joy in the endeavor! Why have you not shown them to me before?"

"I didn't think you would be interested, since your enthusiasm for botany was so slight until recently."

"Don't be silly! I would be happy to see anything produced by your hand." She paused, and turned a page of the journal. "It must be gratifying to have a pursuit that not only fills your days in spring and summer, but to which you can return with such agreeable reflections, no matter the weather or the time of year."

I agreed that it was, for this was the only indoor pastime at which I did not grow restless. As I copied a hastily sketched flower from my field journal or jotted down the details of when or where I had encountered it, I almost felt I was back on the moors or hunting along a particularly pleasant stream for a favorite plant, and I found I could work in my journals for hours at a time.

Rebecca bit her lip as I described these feelings, then replied, "Yes, it must be a wonderful addition to an otherwise quiet life. But tell me, as engrossing as these pursuits are, do you not find yourself wishing for something more?"

"What do you mean?" I asked, conscious that I had often felt the same, yet unwilling to acknowledge dissatisfaction with a style of life for which I should be grateful.

"Well, for instance, for all your knowledge of botany, and for all that young women are encouraged to pursue it as a pastime, you would never be allowed to study it at Oxford, and certainly not to teach it. A woman can never become a member of the Royal Society. And I've seen the way you look wistfully at the travel books I've given you, as if you'll never be allowed to see those places. Does it not seem we are as confined by these rules of propriety and our proper roles, as we are by the horns of our side-saddles?"

I had to smile, and told her that I had just been envying Jamie, as she no doubt thought I might, when selecting this volume for me. "It is true, I have begun to think how I might see more and do more than my present circumstances allow; how I might make some mark in the world. As much as I enjoy my rambles, I can foresee the time when the country round about becomes too familiar, and I long for something different. Yet I am not sure that the restraints are necessarily those of our sex; more so, perhaps of my family's state, travel to exotic places being the province of the wealthy. And there is my father to think of; I could not leave him."

"Yet if you were to marry, you would then leave his household."

"Yes, and that is the only reason that could justify such a removal. And even then, I could choose only a gentleman who lived nearby. Perhaps it is better to adapt to things as they are, than to waste effort lamenting them."

At this declaration, Rebecca sat forward like a debater ready to challenge a point she found foolish. Then she checked herself, considering the journal for a moment before saying, "But Lizzie, you have so much to offer the world. Have you never thought of publishing these?"

As often as Rebecca enjoyed provoking my laughter, she did not smile as I laughed now. "Who would be interested in them? They are only the thoughts and sketches of a vicar's daughter, treating a very narrow and unextraordinary part of the world."

"Yes, and who would be interested in the letters of a country curate, musing about a single parish in Hampshire?"

I smiled, knowing she had won this point.

"Your work is instructive without seeming didactic; even your explanations of the Latin names are charming."

I gave a little shake of my head. "Mere notes to aid my own memory."

"And so they would help any novice undertaking a study of the subject, especially young women who are rarely taught the classical languages. Certainly there are few barriers to women publishing novels, or even political tracts. Why not these journals?"

"Even so, I would hardly know how to begin."

"Have confidence in yourself, in the first place," she said, then handed me another of the books she had brought. The volume bore the title, *A Vindication of the Rights of Woman*, by Mary Wollstonecraft. "This author has much to say on the value of women and the contributions we can make to the world when not encumbered by trivialities." I thanked her for it and promised to read it.

"As a first step toward making your skills better known," she went on, "perhaps you can contribute a drawing or a watercolor to the auction."

I gladly assented to this, then asked, "And what of you? Are you satisfied with this village life?"

Since my conversation with her brother, a doubt had begun to creep into my mind – not of the constancy of her friendship, but of the likelihood that she could long remain satisfied in such a quiet neighborhood as ours. And these statements of hers only confirmed this doubt, underscoring her restless spirits. If she thought Devonshire society too confining, what was to keep her here? She certainly had the freedom to live where she would; since she had proposed the upcoming trip to Bath, I had even begun to wonder if she had an interest in removing to that city. It suddenly struck me what a loss that would be.

"Yes, I am quite content here at present," she said.

"At present! And what mark would *you* make in the world? Surely it will be difficult in such a place."

She drew back at this, and I regretted challenging her so bluntly. At last she said, "Having no extraordinary talents, I must content myself with doing what I can. For now, there is the auction. And after – " She paused and looked at me directly. "You see, when I married, I was as trivial a girl as Miss Wollstonecraft so rightly criticizes. I had all the accomplishments to attract a husband, but no great passion, nothing like your own for botanical wonders. A fine figure, a dashing uniform, a gallant manner – these were all I cared for, and I thought they would be enough. And then, to have such a short time with Captain Burgess, and to lose him so soon! I have often wished we had been blessed with a child, as that is the most common cure for a woman's restlessness and proper channel for her ambition. But now I must look about me and see what there is to be done – " Here she broke off and stared abstractedly at the rain pelting the library window.

"I'm sorry. I didn't mean to bring on such melancholy reflections."

She gave a wan smile, and then appeared to make a conscious effort to shake off her gloom, her smile twisting into a mischievous grin. "You mentioned that if you were to marry, it must be a gentleman who lives nearby. Talk in the village is that you have set your bonnet for Lord Burnside, that young nobleman who addressed your father so politely at church the day I met you."

This seemed an unaccountable and awkward change in the course of the conversation, very unlike Rebecca. Though I felt myself coloring, I managed a tolerably composed answer. "If anyone has 'set a bonnet,' as you say, for our neighbor, it is Father and Mrs. Simmons on my behalf. They have lost all sense on the matter." I went on to outline my assessment of my poor prospects in this quarter. I paused when I came to my last conversation with Anthony, for I had told no one of it. Yet if I could not speak of it with a friend as close as Rebecca now was, then I could share it with no one. I told her how close he had come to declaring his feelings for me, and the manner in which I had stopped him before he could expose himself. "Was I right in doing so?" I asked.

Rebecca gave me a look of the greatest approbation. "Indeed, it was well done, assuming your characterization of his parents is accurate – and I'm sure it is, judging by the few members of the nobility I have known. It shows a remarkable forbearance, disinterestedness, and a great regard for the welfare of your friend."

"Oh, he has always been my dearest friend, at least – " and here I had to take a breath before casting my reserve aside, "at least until these past weeks, since your arrival."

Rebecca smiled, even blushing slightly. "Why, how uncharacteristically forthcoming of you! And let me say, how fortunate I find myself in your friendship, for what would my days be without it? You make what would have been a solitary life here tolerable. And more than tolerable, for if I ever contemplated removal to a more fashionable and lively spot, the thought of leaving you would be more than enough to keep me here."

She gazed into my eyes, as we both took a moment to absorb this new level of our intimacy. I felt a curious fluttering in my stomach; perhaps to cover this feeling, I made a joke. "Then we will end up old maids together!"

I laughed at the thought of it, but my joke elicited only half a smile from my companion. "Yes, perhaps," she said.

If Rebecca's customary parting kiss on my cheek was just that much warmer than usual, so too was the deep glow of affection which I carried with me upstairs to dress for dinner. My thoughts drifted toward the future and the growing likelihood that I would never find a suitable match, one that would satisfy both my heart and mind while providing security. Certainly the fact that we had heard nothing from Anthony over the past month was a sign that his family's plans for him were moving forward. If spinsterhood were my most likely fate, surely the comforts of having such a dear friend as Rebecca took much of the sting out of it. Many were the women, and not just those encountered in fictional visions of a feminine utopia, who contented themselves with close friendships with their own sex, even going so far as to combine their resources and establish a household together.

But what if Rebecca were to remarry, a possibility I met with a sentiment bordering on jealousy? In that case, I consoled myself, I could be aunt to her children, assuming they settled locally, just as I would no doubt be to Anthony's, and to Jamie's when he returned from the colonies and settled nearby. It was not such a dismal prospect. I would have the freedom to pursue my botanical studies, and perhaps even publish them. I wondered what kind of income Mr. White had seen with the publication of his letters.

At table, Father noted how happy I seemed, and asked Mrs. Simmons if we had perhaps received a letter from Lord Burnside.

CHAPTER NINE

THE NEXT time I saw the highwayman, I was lost in the fog on Whiddleston Moor. Such a thing had never befallen me, for I was usually conscientious in keeping track both of my bearings and of the weather. But on this day, when Rebecca had been called away to a distant estate to view several fine objects for the auction, I had become so engrossed in my sketching that I had lost all track of time. The pink bells of the bilberry had given me difficulty. I had no trouble with the individual flower, but capturing the structure of the shrub along with its many tiny blossoms had put my skills to the test. I was determined, however, and sat until I was stiff. Only when I felt the chill of the fog blocking the sun's warming rays did I notice that the mists had surrounded the small promontory on which I sat, with only a few other tors and high places poking out of the white sea.

Though I knew the danger of such a situation, I told myself I had been over the same ground often enough that the fog would not matter. I quickly packed my drawing case, slipped my journal into a pocket of my walking dress, and set off in the direction of home. As I made my way down from the rocky promontory and into the dell below, I contemplated our journey to Bath, which was to begin the following day. I was glad my travelling case was ready and waiting in the foyer – I had been so eager for the trip that I had long since packed it and completed every other preparation of the household for my absence. I wondered how the country would differ between here and there, and what sights we would see in the town itself.

An hour later, I was not at all sure I was still on the grounds of Holbourne. I had spent that time walking the same hills over and again, descending into the same vales, dodging left and right around the same bogs and outcrops I had just passed a few moments earlier. At last I found myself in a new place: a featureless moor with here and there a few sheep looming out of the mist only paces from me. I had no idea in which direction home lay. When I came to a line of ancient standing stones, I knew they must be the famous Whiddleston Stones, and realized I had strayed far off course. Despite having discovered my location, I had no idea how I could find my way home from this point until the fog lifted. Knowing it would do no good to continue wandering blindly, I resolved to wait until the fog should lift, or some other means of finding my way should reveal itself. The wind was up, however, and as it cut even through the sturdy gabardine of my walking dress I began to see the fault in my plan.

I had grown cold by the time I heard the sound of hoofbeats coming from down the slope, followed soon after by the sound of laughter. Then there were shouts from farther below, followed by two gunshots from the same direction, and the sound of a ball skittering through the grass and heather to my right.

Instantly I was moving to a position behind one of the standing stones. Strangely, what I felt could not truly be called fear. My heart did not race, and if I trembled, it was only from the cold. The fact that a rifle ball had passed within yards of me seemed to belong to another reality. Yet some instinct of self-preservation bade me move to this more protected spot.

Louder shouts followed the shooting, and the laughter ceased. A moment later three riders emerged from the fog, their faces shrouded in crêpe masks. I was so chilled, I could not think whether to remain hidden behind the standing stone or plead for their assistance. It mattered little, for they had already seen me; their leader, the one in the coat of burgundy velvet, signaled a halt, bringing his black horse within a few paces of me.

"Why, Miss Collington, what a pleasant surprise!" he called to me, seeming not at all alarmed by the shots that had been aimed in his direction.

"Robin," said another of the men, "they won't stay trapped down there forever. Best keep moving!"

"We can spare a moment for a damsel in distress." The highwayman looked down at me with his usual amusement. "Are you well, Miss Collington? Have you become lost?"

I would not show him any fear, though I knew I must appear to be cowering in fright. "How do you know my name?" I demanded, but I could not keep my teeth from chattering.

In an instant, his tone changed to one of alarm. "You are chilled to the bone!" he exclaimed, leaping from his horse. He drew a cloak from a saddle bag and shook it out as he approached me. With the advantage of daylight, I could see that he was of middling height, dressed like any gentleman, his burgundy coat expertly tailored, his fine waistcoat skillfully embroidered, and his thigh-high boots well kept, though now they were splattered with mud. The only thing out of place for a gentleman was the cloth mask.

"May I?" he asked. I nodded, and he threw the cloak about my shoulders, then began chafing my arms.

I drew back. "*Sir*, you are still too forward!" I added an ironic emphasis to his style, for I knew not how to address a highwayman.

"The cold and fog on the moors are nothing to take lightly, as you must know. Can you find your way home?" I shook my head. "Then you must come with us."

I took another step back. "Who are those men, shouting down below?"

"A band of King George's finest."

"Then I will go to them. They will take me home." I turned in that direction.

"I wouldn't do that if I was you, miss," said another of the bandits, the one with the ginger hair protruding from beneath his hat. "They're angry and they're liable to shoot at any shadow what comes at 'em in the fog."

"Jack's right, Miss Collington," the highwayman said. "Now come. We'll get you home, or put you on the right road, at the least." He remounted and held a hand out to me.

"Surely you can't expect me to trust you?"

Some of the humor returned to his eyes. "Has the adage about honor among thieves not spread this far? I have had you in my power twice now, and the only hurt you have taken is a slight blush. And I still owe you a good deed after my former conduct toward you. Now come. Juno can easily bear us both. Jack will take your drawing case."

I handed the case up to Jack, then the highwayman held his hand out and offered me the stirrup. I placed my foot awkwardly in it, took his hand, and finally I was sitting aside behind him.

"Excellent!" he said. "Now, hold on."

"How am I to do that?"

"Put a hand around my waist, otherwise you won't stay on at the speeds we must travel."

We heard the sounds of the redcoats much closer now. The horse lurched forward and I was obliged to do as the rogue suggested. We rode in silence for a time, cantering as steadily as the horses could manage over the rough moorland. I began to feel warmth returning, both from the heat of the horse beneath me and from the highwayman himself. As much as I disdained to touch him, I found I could keep my seat only by clinging tightly to him, and I could not deny the welcome warmth of his body. He seemed to have exerted himself recently, a scent of sweat and damp wool rising from him. He had pulled his brown hair back in a short sailor's queue; it bounced jauntily with our movement, revealing the tanned skin above his high collar.

I knew I should feel frightened. Could I really trust that these scoundrels would see me home, as promised? The highwayman had seemed almost gentlemanly when he had come to my room. But now, with his associates around him, who knew what they might drive him to do? As well, with the redcoats after us and the outlaws pushing their horses in flight, anything could happen: an unlucky shot from a soldier's rifle, or a fall from the horse.

Yet I felt not the slightest fear. The highwayman managed Juno with calm assurance, and though I could not see his eyes, I knew they must be shining with the same joy they had shown when robbing Anthony's carriage. I felt the strength in his torso as I leaned against his back, and sensed the strength in his legs as he flowed with the horse over the rough ground. Occasionally he would reassure me with a pat on my hand where it rested on his midriff, or reach around behind to hold me more tightly as we passed over a rough spot. I could not have felt more safe and secure. And then, unbidden, came the thought of having those arms around me for a different reason, and I forgot my former chill. I struggled to push the thought aside, yet it was difficult, given our proximity.

After a time, with the sounds of pursuit lost behind us, the outlaws slowed their mounts to a walk and took thought for where we were. The same heather and grass covered the moors in all directions, the view cut off by the curtain of fog except where it was temporarily torn to shreds by the wind, revealing farther glimpses of the same featureless landscape. The wind made a lonely sound as it coursed through the heather.

The highwayman pulled a hand compass from a pocket, regarded it for a moment, then pointed at an angle off to our left. "That way, if we haven't come too far north." We continued on, the other two sometimes ranging ahead, unencumbered as their mounts were. The highwayman shouted directions to them occasionally, "A bit left – that's it – now straight on." The two would wait for us when we came upon tors or other obstacles that forced a deviation from the route, then the highwayman would consult the instrument once more.

"Are you familiar with the use of a hand compass?" he asked.

I had to admit I was not, for such things were not often the province of young women.

"Even for those who walk alone across the moors? It seems a foolish proscription. And do you not carry flint and tinder in your reticule?"

Piqued by his criticism, I asked, "Whose carriage did you rob, to set the militia after you?"

"Why, none at all, for today the militia itself was our target."

"Whatever could you want with those gallant young men?"

"Oh, it's great fun to goad them. Today, we led them a merry chase and finally lured them into that bog down below."

"I find it hard to believe you would engage in such foolish trickery for mere fun."

"Stopping them from cracking the heads of unemployed weavers is a further inducement, I must admit."

"Those soldiers are only trying to keep the peace! Surely a mob cannot be allowed to run wild."

He turned to look at me over his shoulder. His eyes, which I had thought black in the poor light of our earlier encounters, I now saw were brown. "Four children were made orphans last week, thanks to your gallant lads' efforts. I don't call that keeping the peace. It is not much, but if we can distract King George's men, and perhaps make laughingstocks of them to cheer the people, it seems the least we can do."

"Still, I fail to see what you could gain from such an endeavor."

"Yes, for what motive could a highwayman possibly have, if not self-interest?" He uttered this statement with such a tone of derision that I saw no way to respond, and we fell into silence.

The highwayman's words greatly disturbed me. I too had glimpsed the squalor of the encampments outside Exeter – shapeless figures in little better than rags huddled before their morning cook fires, men shouting at barking dogs, one or two children hauling water from a nearby stream. I knew Rebecca's and my charitable efforts would do little to relieve such suffering, for these were not orphans, but mainly men. Most had been put out of work not through any fault of their own, but due to the recent downturn in Exeter's woolen industry. However undeserving of their plight, they were nevertheless ineligible for the poor house's charity. The few women and children present had turned down that aid, unwilling to divide their families, choosing instead to live out of doors – a choice I could only view as admirably courageous. No wonder they had resorted to the riot!

Yet, how could I consider such a thought? Father had taught us to respect the laws of God and King, and such lawless behavior threatened the peace and security of our country – which already faced enough threats, with the war in France and fears of that country's revolutionary spirit spreading to England. Such were the counsels of my upbringing, but surely more must be done to aid the innocent poor? I knew not the answer; I knew only that I could never admit such sympathetic thoughts to the rogue seated before me.

After a time, a rock wall loomed out of the fog, a narrow lane running beyond it. "That is Whiddleston Lane," the highwayman said, his tone decidedly cold. "A quarter-mile along it to the left is the village of Whiddleston. I trust you can make your way home from there? Surely you wouldn't want to be seen in the company of outlaws."

I wondered at the feeling of regret his demeanor provoked within me even as I agreed to his plan.

Throwing a leg over Juno's neck, he dropped to the ground, then turned to lift me from my seat. The look he gave me had lost all its humor, and he seemed in fact quite grave and troubled. I tried to ignore the slight disappointment I felt when he turned away to retrieve my drawing case from his accomplice. Then he climbed over the stile and held out a hand to help me follow, all without a word.

I found his coldness provoking. "I assume, in mentioning your motive, you refer to your Robin Hood act?" I looked him boldly in the eye as I alighted next to him. "Yet I can think of many reasons for robbing the wealthiest. And now I discover that you are a traitor as well as an outlaw."

He took a step forward, looming above me. "No, Miss Collington, never a traitor, for I am loyal to England and her people. It is only the decadence of the aristocracy which I detest, leeches sucking the lifeblood of the nation." He turned as if he would leave, but then stopped, one hand on the rock wall next to the stile. "Would you believe that half our income goes to the poor and to those same orphans new-minted by the militia?"

Wondering why he felt such a need to justify his actions to me, I replied, "No, for I find it hard to believe that one who resorts to such villainy could harbor such selfless compassion."

"Is that so?" He nodded at his ginger-haired associate. "Tell her, Jack."

"Aye, it's true, miss. Lord knows I'd be quit o' this business by now if it weren't."

"That's Jack for you," said the highwayman, "always good for a cheery word. In due time, when we have saved enough, all of what we steal from the rich – or my portion, at least – will go to those most in need."

"Yet it is hard to credit such beneficence in a common highwayman."

"Ha!" exclaimed the one called Jack. "Robin, common! That's a laugh."

"Quiet, Jack," the highwayman barked. "Why don't the two of you stand farther off and keep a sharp eye?"

Jack and the other scoundrel rode off a bit, Jack singing a vulgar tune in a gravelly voice. I caught these words before he was out of earshot: "I'm a poor loom weaver, as many a one knows. I've naught t'eat, and I've wore out me clothes."

The highwayman turned back to me. "It is as I told you before – I hope that good works will atone in some measure for the evil I have done. Perhaps if you knew my full story – "

"You are mistaken if you think I have any interest in hearing your self-justifications."

"At the very least, I can promise you a story worth hearing, one equal to any gothic romance."

"I do not stoop to reading romances."

"No? Perhaps you should. They have more of actual life in them than all your Cowper and your Pope. Now, what say you?" His aspect, or what I could see of it above the mask, was one of such earnest pleading that it surprised me, coming from one usually so bold in taking what he wanted. "Will you agree to meet me, if only to hear my tale? I have more than repaid my debt to you, after all."

I should have given him a firm negative on the spot. But he had just saved me much discomfort, if not my very life, and I felt I owed him something for it. What harm could there be in hearing his story? I told myself it had nothing to do with our close contact of a few moments before, or with his earlier kisses.

"There is a great oak tree on the north boundary of Holbourne. Do you know it? You may find me there on any fine day, though of late I do not often walk there alone. If we happen to meet, I will listen to your story." I removed his cloak and handed it to him.

"It is all I can ask," he said. He leaned toward me for a moment, and I did not back away. Then he seemed to think better of himself, turning to step over the stile and leaping into his saddle with great alacrity. He turned back to look at me for a moment, then touched the brim of his hat. "Till we meet again, Miss Collington." He rode off after his companions, leaving me there with an unsettling feeling of regret at his not having kissed me a third time.

Only then did I realize that he still hadn't said how he knew my name.

I DREAMT that the highwayman came to me that night, again climbing in through my open window and again returning my necklace. This time he was no gentleman, stealing a kiss as he shut the clasp at the back of my neck, then letting his hands rove down to my breast, nothing but my thin nightdress separating his hand from my bare flesh. Instead of resisting, I strained against him, my mouth devouring his. Then his mouth moved lower, down to my neck, my throat, his fingers tugging at the neck of my nightdress –

I came awake with a start in the small hours of the morning. This in itself was not unusual, as I had experienced difficulty sleeping for several nights after each of my encounters with the highwayman. If, on those occasions, I had awoken remembering the taste of his kisses in my mouth and the feel of his hand on my breast, this time it was infinitely worse. I was breathing rapidly and my whole body felt flushed and drenched with sweat, though I had thrown back the covers. Worse still, I found my breasts were raw from my having pawed at them, no doubt in imitation of what the highwayman had taught me. One hand was between my legs, though I knew not where I could have learned that, for both mother and Mrs. Simmons had sternly warned against the grievous sin of touching myself there. The thin fabric of my nightdress was soaked through in that spot, though it was not my time of the month.

And yet, this was not the worst of it, for the thing that had made me startle awake was the feeling of bereft abandonment at the highwayman's having ridden away without kissing me. For too brief a time I had felt my body pressed against his, my arm around his waist, the bare skin between hairline and collar so close I could have leant up and kissed it. Only when that was taken away, did I recognize the gap his absence left.

I removed my hand from between my legs, pulled up the covers, and endeavored to calm my thoughts and my breathing. I *could not* be pining for the highwayman! Soon I was overcome with guilt and remorse, tossing and turning for what seemed like hours before finally crying myself to sleep.

CHAPTER TEN

BATH WAS everything I had imagined it, both for good and ill. The famous view of the city on our approach, with its ancient abbey in the center and stately modern buildings radiating outward in crescents and arcs, turning a rich gold in the last rays of the setting sun; the shouts of coachmen and the clatter and clang of carriages in the street before the White Hart Hotel, where our post-coach set us down; the spectacle and bustle of lively people in the streets on their way to the Pump Room; the shops with their dizzying array of wares; the mingled odors of bakers, flower shops, horse dung, and coal fires – it was overwhelming. Best of all was my certainty that I would be free of the highwayman for the next week.

The noise of the city grew less as we made our way to our lodgings in Charles Street. Our apartments were small, a single bedchamber with a sitting room attached that also served as a dressing room.

"I hope you don't mind sharing the one bed," Rebecca said after the porter had set down our luggage and left us alone. "It seemed a necessary economy, as Bath is so expensive."

Surprised at her solicitude, I told her I had shared with Mrs. Simmons on several overnights to Exeter, and occasionally with friends on particularly cold nights. "Why would it bother me?" I asked. "We are both women and the bed is large enough for two."

"I am glad. I only thought that, as an only daughter, you might be accustomed to greater privacy."

As it turned out, of the two of us, Rebecca had the greater need for privacy, as she insisted on closing the sitting room door as she changed her clothes. I found this an unaccountable display of modesty in one of so unreserved a character. She wouldn't even allow me to help her with her hair.

Morning brought a renewal of spirits and eagerness for the delights and discoveries ahead. The first part of the morning was spent finishing our unpacking and looking about our apartments. The sitting room had a charming seat in a bow window, with a view that included a sliver of Green Park. I sat in it as I wrote a letter home, assuring Father and Mrs. Simmons of our safe arrival. These duties accomplished, we set out to explore the town.

Our first visit to meet the Master of Ceremonies and take the waters at the newly rebuilt Pump Room confirmed my expectations of the city. Everywhere such a press of people, and everyone so fashionable! The women in their fine gowns, jewels, and feathered headdresses, even at mid-day; the men in their tall felt hats, finely embroidered waistcoats, close-fitting breeches, and closer-fitting stockings – they were all wonderful to look at, but I almost had to laugh. For, if acquiring a husband *had* been my true purpose in coming to Bath, I now knew I would have met with bitter disappointment. How could I hope to compete with such fashion and finery? My best frock, which I was saving for the theatre, would have served well for any occasion in Leighton or Exeter, but here it would seem hopelessly drab, and more, mark me as a young lady of neither birth nor fortune. The simple gown I had chosen for strolling about amongst the crowd in the Pump Room was something closer to what a serving girl would wear, when contrasted to all the yards of fine muslins, silks, and sarcenets around us. Rebecca's gown and accessories were hardly better than my own, yet she seemed not at all conscious of any inferiority, she always carried herself with such ease. Indeed, with her stature and bearing and easy manner, she turned many heads as we passed among the throng, despite her lack of sparkle and style.

After fifteen minutes of struggling through the crushing and rather impertinent crowd, we arrived at one of several fountains to take a glass of the famous water. Rebecca took a sip and grimaced. "Have you had enough of mingling with the fashionable?" she asked.

I set my glass down, equally repulsed by the unpleasant taste. "Quite, especially as we know no one here."

I was glad when we emerged into the open air of Cheap Street, even if it was city air, with all its mingled odors. "Shall we visit the shops?" Rebecca suggested, and I readily agreed, for there seemed a greater variety here than anything I had seen in Exeter: milliners, haberdashers, bakers, goldsmiths, stationers, and china shops.

Our favorite, of course, were the book shops and circulating libraries. We couldn't subscribe on such a short stay, but we delighted in browsing the books for sale. In Hazard's, Rebecca called me over to a book she had found in the travel section. "Look, Lizzie," she said, holding it out to me.

"*Bartram's Travels!*" Actually, the title was nearly too long to fit on the title page, denoting all the places in the southern American colonies the author had visited. "I have heard of it, of course, but I never thought to see it, unless the lending library in Exeter should acquire it." I turned the pages, marveling at the copper-plate illustrations of exotic turtles and alligators. "It's wonderful!"

"And so you should have it." She took it from my hands and turned to the bookseller.

"But it must be quite expensive!"

"Not to worry, it's my gift to you. I want you to see what is possible. Think, Lizzie, Bartram captured these sketches while facing all the vicissitudes of the wilds of America. What couldn't you do in your own more civilized country, though one not without its own beauties."

"But Devonshire has no true wilds, no fearsome beasts, and certainly no Indians."

"Having lived here all your life, you discount its unique qualities. But to my Kentish eye, it is wilderness enough, and many of our fellow countrymen would feel the same, if only someone would show it to them. And you are that person, Lizzie. You could be the Bartram of Devonshire!"

I had to laugh, but she turned to the bookseller and arranged to have the book bound and sent over to our rooms. "When we get home," she said when she was done, "I will help you select from your journals the best pages to send to a publisher, and plan what else might be needed to make a complete book – that is, if you will approve of such an endeavor."

I readily agreed, glad to have a friend who would support ambitions I had scarcely dreamed of myself.

When we had our fill of shops, we took a turn around the Royal Crescent. I particularly admired the modern architecture of these new developments with their symmetries, clean lines, and imposing stonework, all in the rich yellow stone quarried nearby. They would make a fine study for an artist.

I stopped in the street, turning about to take in the curving line of buildings we had just passed, such a contrast to the greensward below. "I wish I had brought my drawing case and journal with me today," I said.

"Then you must bring them out tomorrow."

"Truly? You wouldn't mind? It could be tedious for you."

"How could I mind, when my fondest wish is that you develop your talents to their fullest? I daresay such a change of subject will be a good test of your skill. Where would you like to start?"

"At Bath Abbey, I believe. Something about the way it contrasts with the new Pump Room caught my eye."

The next day, after taking the waters – an experience I hardly cared to repeat, the liquid had such a foul taste – I set out my portable watercolor case in the plaza before the cathedral, along with my smaller drawing case, and began sketching. I found these buildings quite a different challenge than flowers and nature scenes. Everything was so regular and linear, even on the abbey with all its gothic decorations interrupting the vertical lines; it took only one line to deviate from the strict perpendicular, or the spacing to be off by a hair, for the whole composition to lose its air of reality. I was glad for everything Mrs. Simmons had taught me about perspective drawing, but still found myself frowning at my sketch.

"Are you not happy with it?" Rebecca asked. "It looks perfectly lifelike to me."

"The perspective is off. You see how the Pump Room seems to float in space, while the Abbey is firmly anchored to the ground? I almost wish I had a camera obscura."

"And what is that?"

"A very useful contraption, from what Mrs. Simmons tells me. It uses mirrors to project an image of the scene onto a glass plate, which the artist then traces."

"That seems a bit of a cheat."

"Yes, but it can be vital for scenes with many parallel lines and different vanishing points. Mrs. Simmons had the chance to use one when she studied with Mr. Sandby. However, they are expensive, and I must make do. I will find a vantage from which the perspective is not quite so intricate." I flipped the page of my sketchbook and moved several steps back and to the right, where the angles to the vanishing point weren't as severe. I drew a new horizon line and began again. Soon I felt I was creating something I could take home and develop into a lifelike drawing.

"Yes, I can see how that's better," Rebecca observed before retreating to a bench and opening a book, allowing me to get on with my work.

I was making good progress when I was halted once more by a handsome young couple stopping in front of us to take in the scene. In truth, I think they may have been taking in the strange sight the pair of us made, absorbed as we were in our pursuits while all about us the crowds streamed past on their way to or from the Pump Room. Two people, especially women, so productively employed, while all around us Bath's visitors indulged the far more appropriate pursuits of seeing and being seen, gossiping, and hatching plots either to bring young lovers together or to break them apart – we must have been an extraordinary sight.

These young people were not the first to pause and stare as I worked, so it was something else about them that caught my attention. They were both so handsome, he with a strong nose and chin, his hair left to grow in that wild mass that had become so fashionable since the introduction of the powder tax; she with similar features but more refined, and her blond hair arrayed in ringlets tied with ribbons and topped with a white feather. Their dress even matched, the blue trimming of her white gown echoing the color of his tailcoat.

"What is it?" Rebecca asked, seeing that I had stopped sketching.

"That couple." I nodded toward them. "I would like to draw them – but now they are moving off."

"Leave it to me." Instantly she was up from the bench and striding after them, to my mortification. As they were merely strolling, she caught them easily. They stopped to look at her as she came even with them, and then she gestured toward me; I continued sketching, as if I had no idea I was the subject of their attention, keeping my eyes on my work as they approached.

"Miss Elizabeth," Rebecca said, "this gentleman and lady have consented to your taking their likeness."

I looked at them shyly over my sketchbook and tipped my head. "I thank you." The gentleman gave a slight bow.

"As the Master of Ceremonies is not about," Rebecca went on, "allow me to introduce Mr. Cowley and his sister, Miss Cowley. And this is Miss Elizabeth Collington, whose name you will one day recognize as one of our country's great new artists."

"Mrs. Burgess!" I exclaimed. "I am most pleased to meet you both, but you must pay no attention to my friend."

"It's true," Rebecca protested. "I only persuaded them with the prospect of being immortalized in your early work."

"A woman artist!" Miss Cowley exclaimed with delight. "How extraordinary!" She did not seem to be teasing, but apparently found it marvelous to come upon a woman for whom drawing was more than one of the usual accomplishments. She seemed about my own age, while her brother was a few years older.

"How shall we pose, Miss Collington?" the gentleman asked.

"Oh, do not pose, I beg you. Just stand where you were – yes, that's right – facing each other – now simply take in the scene as you were before, and converse freely."

As I worked them into the scene, they asked me questions, how long I had been drawing, did I have any training, and the like. "But tell me, Miss Collington," Mr. Cowley said at last, "most young women come to Bath in hopes of capturing a husband. Do you not think such a pursuit would be a better use of your time?" He said it in a light way that made me think he too found Bath's social scene as artificial as did I.

"I would far rather capture scenes and likenesses than husbands," I said in the same light tone. "It is a pursuit for which I am far better suited."

"Oh, pshaw!" Miss Cowley shook her head at me, making the white feather of her headgear quiver. I wondered if she could not see my plain dress and calculate from it what my fortune and corresponding value on the marriage market must be.

At last I was finished and the Cowleys came around to judge my effort, giving little exclamations of delight and approval, "Yes, very like," and "You've greatly flattered us!"

"It is just a sketch," I said as I mixed my powders to match the tone of the Pump Room. "I will have to take it home and develop it into a finished drawing, perhaps with a wash of yellow and gold for the stone of the buildings, and blue and white for your garments."

"And what will you call it when it's finished?" Mr. Cowley asked.

"I was thinking to title it, 'Fashionable visitors at Bath'." I repressed a smile as I considered the color I had achieved in the mixing bowl.

"What?" His exclamation startled me, but when I looked up I saw he was grinning. "Not *handsome* visitors? Or better yet, a dashing young gentleman and his doting sister?"

His sister swatted him with her fan. "George! Be careful, or our new friends will think you're serious! Pay him no mind, ladies, for my brother isn't so full of himself as all that." She arched her brow at him. "Though he certainly does dress the dandy."

"That is an astounding assertion, sister, considering the size of your own trunk, full to the brim with new gowns, and you insisted I see my tailor before this visit. If I had thought one new suit of clothes would turn me into a dandy, I should never have gone!" He turned to us. "I have always thought the old saying about the clothes making the man was one of the most foolish ever invented, for much that is unworthy can be papered over in finery."

"Really, George, now you are too serious," his sister said.

"Ladies, I hope you won't be fooled by my sister's fashionable exterior, for beneath it lie a gentle heart, a sweet temper, and a fierce loyalty to any she calls friend."

"Oh, pshaw!" she repeated, then turned to us. "Now that we have embarrassed ourselves by flattering each other, let me ask you, will you attend the ball on Monday?"

"Yes, we intend to," Rebecca replied.

"Excellent!" Mr. Cowley said. "Then may I look forward to dancing with you both?"

"Certainly!" we said at once, and curtsied.

"And our older brother will be there," Miss Cowley said, "and my intended. Perhaps we can all be in the set together, and then take tea in between."

On our way back to our lodgings, Rebecca seemed satisfied. "You see, Lizzie, now you won't have to dance with a stranger – or at least only one stranger; and if their brother is as affable as they are, he will soon seem like an old friend as well."

I certainly had to agree that our prospects for the ball seemed brighter, though it seemed strange that we should advance in intimacy with these strangers so quickly.

CHAPTER ELEVEN

THE DAYS leading up to our night at the theatre seemed to fly by. We spent Saturday in the Sydney Gardens, where I felt much more comfortable and less out of place with my sketch pad. Sunday we spent at church and then on a walk to the Beechen Cliffs. I never drew on Sunday, but found contemplation of Our Lord's creation fitting to the day.

Monday was spent in preparation for the ball. Vanity had got the better of both of us, and we spent considerable time in the shops purchasing ribbons and other adornments for our plain gowns, more time in our lodgings with needle and thread, and then a great deal of time in dressing. As ever since our arrival in Bath, Rebecca rejected my offer to help and insisted on closing the door while she changed her dress and did her hair. Again I found this bashfulness odd in one of such an open nature. She emerged from our sitting room with her brown hair done up in complex strands, held in place by a sparkling jeweled pin.

The ball itself was mostly a success. In addition to the pair with which we were already acquainted, we met their older brother, Mr. John Cowley, an imposing, serious fellow; and Miss Cowley's intended, a Mr. Wentworth, who was older still, near thirty, with a pinched look. For the first set, I was matched with Mr. George Cowley, and found him to be an excellent dancer, one who could carry on a conversation while keeping his step. He remained as witty as he had been on the day we met, and sooner than I would have expected, the pair of dances was over. I felt quite pleased with myself, as I had been familiar with both dances and had held up my end of the conversation without faltering.

At tea, I was eager to learn more of Miss Cowley, and found her to be everything her brother had claimed, though he had omitted her taste in music and literature, and the excellence of her mind. These are qualities in women which men are often prone to overlook, as Mrs. Wollstonecraft had reminded me. Talk turned to the play we were to see on the morrow, Miss Cowley and I mentioning our favorite scenes, and Rebecca reciting a fanciful bit of Touchstone's foolery from memory. As Miss Cowley had taken in Mrs. Jordan's performance the week before, she was able to assure us of a fine evening of entertainment, her descriptions of the production showing excellent taste and knowledge of the demands of acting. "Jaques was especially fine," she said, "for it's a demanding part, and the actor was somehow able to make me sympathize with him. Do you know, as wise as he is supposed to be, Jaques' pessimism is so extreme that I often find him to be my least favorite character in the play."

I was ready to agree with her when Mr. Wentworth patted her patronizingly on the hand. "Perhaps when you are older, my dear, and have faced more of the vicissitudes of life, his character will make more sense to you." She lapsed into silence, her sweet temper showing itself in admirable docility – more docility than even I could have managed were I in her situation. My heart rebelled on her behalf. I was familiar with silly girls whose opinions were worth no more than the breath they wasted on them, but Miss Cowley was not one of them. And to have her opinion so casually dismissed by the one who professed to love her! With such men in the world, I could see why many young ladies kept their opinions to themselves, or pretended to have none at all.

My indignation seemed ready to break through my reserve in some inappropriate remark; I knew similar thoughts must have occurred to Rebecca, and she was just leaning forward to speak when Mr. Cowley turned the conversation to the family estate in Gloucestershire. It was large, he told us, with every acre put to productive use, save for a patch of gardens around the manor house, making for an extraordinary income for the family. Parcels had been carved out and sizeable houses built on them for himself and his younger brother; he already had possession of his portion, along with the independence its lands provided, while Mr. George Cowley would come into his own in a year or two. Meanwhile, Mr. Wentworth had a sizeable estate nearby, meaning the family would not have to face the loss of a daughter and a sister upon her marriage.

"As you can see," the elder Mr. Cowley concluded, "our father has laid everything out on the most rational plan for domestic and familial happiness. The only thing lacking is wives for George and me. Our father is not at all concerned about rank or wealth in our spouses, but has encouraged us, in keeping with his plans, to seek young ladies who know each other well, sisters perhaps, or good friends" – and here he looked back and forth from Rebecca to me – "whose transition into our domestic sphere will be eased by their own acquaintance with each other."

Miss Cowley gave a little start at the presumption of her brother's remark, and Mr. George Cowley gave me an apologetic glance. "That is quite liberal of him," I said. "Your father appears to have the entire family's happiness calculated down to the last decimal place. It seems very – rational, if unconventional." Next to me, Rebecca struggled to suppress a laugh, covering her smile by taking a sip of tea.

"Yes," Mr. Cowley replied, ignoring the tinge of sarcasm in my voice, "our parents are rational free-thinkers in many areas, including equality among their children."

"And this does not pain you, as the first-born?" Rebecca asked.

"It might well have done, had not Father's estate been so large. But my portion is still vast enough to content even the most materialistic of men."

"And what about your future children? Will you further divide your own estate?"

"Should I be fortunate enough to sire a large family, that will indeed be a difficult consideration. But that is to put the cart before the horse, or the chaise before the four, if I may say."

"As is discussing inheritance and marriage plans on a first acquaintance," I was tempted to say, but held my tongue.

We were to change partners for the next set, and I was to take my turn with the elder Mr. Cowley. He was taller than his brother, darker in both hair and complexion, and possessed of a fine figure – exactly the sort of man young ladies are supposed to find attractive. Yet he had no manner, regarding me seriously while remaining silent throughout the pair of dances. I glanced over at Rebecca, envious that she was now able to smile and talk affably with Mr. George Cowley as they twirled about the floor. When we passed each other in the set, she gave me a look of sympathy, and an extra squeeze of my hand to reassure me that it would soon be over.

As even the most tedious and humiliating of experiences must have their end, so did this dance, and Rebecca and I pleaded fatigue when the Cowleys asked if we would stay for one more turn. The brothers gallantly offered to escort us to the street, and even Miss Cowley seemed not unpleased with the early end to the evening's entertainment. Her brothers stumbled over themselves to secure sedan chairs for us, but Mr. Wentworth clung obliviously to her side. In contrast to her former vivacity, she seemed somehow repressed while in his presence, glancing apologetically at each of us. As Rebecca and I got into our separate chairs, she stared after us with regret, as did Mr. George Cowley, while their brother was occupied with arranging for their own chairs.

SOONER THAN I would have expected at the outset of our stay, Tuesday arrived. It was hard to remember that the evening's play was the principal reason for our visit, so entertaining had we found Bath's many other diversions. We spent the day in the usual way, writing letters in the forenoon and reading – *Bartram's Travels* for me, a volume of Shakespeare for Rebecca, though why she needed it I could not guess, since she seemed to have his entire *oeuvre* memorized. Sometimes she would burst out with a speech from *As You Like It*, prefacing it with, "Oh, I'm so looking forward to this!"

"Did you never consider becoming an actress?" I asked.

She gave me a look of mock horror. "How can you ask such a thing? That would have been the height of impropriety!"

At mid-day we visited the Pump Room, where we were pleased to meet Miss Cowley and her younger brother, both of whom seemed apologetic for their sibling's forwardness during the ball. We assured them that we had taken no offence, but Miss Cowley insisted on taking a turn around the room with me alone.

"I truly wish we had met under more fortuitous circumstances, Miss Collington, with more time to become acquainted; but your time is so short, and John has ruined everything."

I assured her he had done no such thing.

"That is well. Then I can trust you not to suspect me of acting on my brothers' behalf if I ask for your card? Of course, you could see George was taken with you, but carrying on a clandestine correspondence for him is the farthest thing from my mind." When I did not respond immediately, she went on. "It's only that I have such limited female acquaintance at home, and we have been here this whole season and I have met none I could truly call a friend. And then to meet you, and Mrs. Burgess too, right at the end, and your stay here being so short! I know we would have been great friends, if given more time. Please say you will write me."

"Yes, of course," I said, thinking how similar our situations had been until Rebecca's arrival in Leighton. I reached into my reticule for a card, the first I had given out.

She handed me her card and I saw that her Christian name was Catherine.

"Thank you," she said, smiling. It was a measure of Rebecca's influence over me that I was able to offer her a warm smile in return. "You know," she went on, "I would love to have a copy of your drawing of us, when it's finished. I suspect Father would even pay you for it, if you wouldn't consider it improper."

At that, my smile only widened. "Would it shock you to know that I hope one day to make my living through my art and writing?"

"How independent of you!" There was open admiration in her voice, though her look had something of that same regret she had shown the night before. We finished our turn around the room, both of us feeling glad of the acquaintance, and I doubly so.

Rebecca and I spent the remainder of the day exploring those sections of the city we had not yet seen, then returned to our rooms to prepare for dinner and the long-awaited play. After arranging my gown and my hair – the latter with Rebecca's help, though she again refused mine – I went to my jewelry box and withdrew my mother's pearl necklace. Of course I had not been able to wear it since the highwayman returned it, for I could find no way of explaining how it had come back into my possession. Though it had not seemed appropriate for the ball, it was the finest piece of jewelry I owned, and I felt I must make some sort of showing at the theatre.

"Here, allow me," Rebecca said, seeing me struggling with the clasp. She stepped up to me, leaning close as she reached around to fasten it. Then she lifted the cameo to get a better look, her fingers sliding along my collarbone to the base of my throat, giving me an unaccountable shiver. "This is pretty. And who is this in the picture?" Her eyes came up to meet mine.

"That is my mother."

"I should have known, she is nearly as beautiful as you are! But I thought the highwayman stole your last memento of her?"

For a moment I considered telling her the truth, but how could I explain my failure to report the highwayman when I hardly knew the reason myself? Whatever that reason was, it could do me no credit, and I hated to risk the disapprobation of my friend. I said the first thing that came to mind. "No, that was another, which belonged to her. This one only bears her portrait, and I save it for special occasions."

She held my gaze for a moment more, then returned the cameo to its place against my breast. I turned away to hide my confusion.

CHAPTER TWELVE

THE THEATRE Royal was not large by London standards, according to Rebecca, but it was the grandest theatre I had ever seen, with three tiers of boxes on either side of the main hall. When we were at last in our box and I had the chance to take in my surroundings, I sat staring at the mural above the stage and all the finely dressed people in the boxes opposite us. I was careful to maintain a cool expression, but on the inside I felt giddy.

My appreciation of the theatre itself was as nothing compared to my feelings for the company when the curtain rose and the play began. On these actors' tongues, the Bard's words came alive with a music and an expression, and at the same time a naturalness, that made me wonder how I had ever understood them before, whether reading to myself, or hearing amateur and third-rate thespians speak them. Never had I been so convinced of a ruler's wrath as when Duke Frederick banished Rosalind, never felt the weight of love between friends as when Celia swore she could not live apart from her dear Rose.

I was surprised when Mrs. Jordan received an ovation on her first entrance, for I had never before seen a star of the stage; when I turned to Rebecca in surprise, she assured me it was quite regular. But when Rosalind entered as Ganymede, "suited all points like a man" and exhibiting "a swashing and a martial outside," the play nearly came to a halt as the audience murmured and some even gasped. The company must have prepared for this disruption, having Rosalind and Celia make a show of their fatiguing trek through the forest before uttering their first lines in the scene, giving the audience ample opportunity to survey them. Mrs. Jordan wore knee breeches that fit her legs like the fingers of a glove, and ankle-high shoes instead of boots, the better to show off the sensuous curves of her calves outlined in the snuggest of silk stockings. Her hair extended just to her collar, making her seem even more like a boy, yet there was also something feminine about her, so that we could never forget that underneath Ganymede's dress was the woman, Rosalind.

The effect of seeing a woman arrayed in such garb, and strutting about the stage in the wide-legged stance of a man, is such as I can hardly describe. Many others in the audience must have felt the same, for the men leaned forward in their seats, and the fans of the women beat the air all the faster. I too found myself craning my neck for a better look, and felt flushed. Only Rebecca seemed unaffected, leaning back in her seat with just a hint of a smile and an appraising look in her eye. Then she turned to me. "Well? Is she everything you expected?"

"Oh, yes!" I replied, though Mrs. Jordan had yet to utter her first line as Ganymede. When she did, her voice was changed. She had made it lower and huskier, to sound more like a man, yet losing none of the energy and affability that made her performance so appealing. Even in her moments of raillery with Orlando, or chiding Phebe, she had such a good-humored nature to her that the audience could not take her for a shrew or a scold. More, on Mrs. Jordan's lips, the words were not like speeches at all, but always had the freshness of a new thought or feeling she had discovered only that moment.

The scene in which Ganymede first encountered Phebe was perhaps the strangest in the play, the director having chosen to play it broadly. When Ganymede asked, "Why do you look on me?", Phebe practically threw herself at him. When Ganymede said, "I think she means to tangle my eyes too," Phebe leaned up for a kiss, only for Ganymede to avert his face at the last moment (sending another murmur of nervous laughter through the audience). And when Ganymede ordered Phebe "down on your knees," Phebe knelt and threw her arms around Ganymede's waist as if she would never let go (to uproarious jeers). I hazarded a glance at Rebecca to see that she no longer sat back in detachment, but was leaning forward, as engrossed as I. She caught my eye and gave me a wink.

When the play neared its end, and all the confusions had been sorted out through Rosalind's "magic," I couldn't help feeling a bit deflated. The four marriages at the end seemed much too neat.

Rebecca must have felt the same, though she sang Mrs. Jordan's praises and had always shown an appreciation for this above all of Shakespeare's works. "As much as I enjoy the play," she said as we made our way into the aisle behind the boxes, "I'm always a little heartbroken for Celia. Here she has forsworn her inheritance, denied her father's wishes, and left her home and place in society, all because she cannot bear to be parted from her dear Rosalind. And no sooner is all this done than Rosalind throws her heart after Orlando and enlists Celia's help to try his love for her."

"Yet surely the love of a friend and the love of a husband are different." I adjusted my fichu as we walked, in expectation of the colder air outside the theatre. "And what is to prevent their remaining the closest of companions?"

"I have seen it too many times, friends drift apart once they have husbands and children. And it happens so quickly! I know Celia must have been hurt, as you saw when she abused Orlando for being an unfaithful lover. She was simply jealous! This business of Celia falling instantly in love with Oliver – it's nothing but a paltry attempt to cover her wounded feelings."

"You sound like Jaques! Do you not believe in love at first sight?"

She turned her gaze on me. "Strangely enough, I do."

I was about to question her further, thinking how alike to Celia and Rosalind we were, though with no Orlandos and no Olivers on the horizon, when we entered the lobby to see Anthony standing with a pair of women. As he was facing our way, he could not help but notice us, his eyebrows arching in surprise. Before I could speak, a single word escaped his lips: "Lizzie!" The pleasure he had on seeing me was as plain as his surprise.

My pleasure at seeing my old friend was equal to his own, though I was better able to remember my manners, giving him a most respectful curtsey and a smile appropriate to greeting an old acquaintance. "Lord Burnside, what an unexpected pleasure."

He recovered himself admirably, proceeding to make the introductions in a more proper style, introducing me as an "old family friend" to cover his faux pas. We learned that his companions were the Dowager Marchioness of Rickenham and her daughter, Lady Mary Dawson. When they learned that I was the daughter of the parish Vicar, the elder lady hardly reacted, giving just a slight nod, perhaps in acknowledgment that I was no competition for her daughter.

Finally he turned to Rebecca. "And may I introduce Mrs. – forgive me, but I have entirely forgotten your name."

"Mrs. Burgess, my chaperone," I put in.

"My profoundest apologies, Mrs. Burgess. I have met such a horde of people in town that I fear my brain has not the capacity for all their names."

Rebecca gave a charming curtsey to all, saying, "No offense taken, your Lordship, for we only met the once."

After exchanging the briefest explanations for each of us arriving unexpectedly in Bath – Anthony was here on a brief visit with friends from London, which had allowed him to wait on the dowager and her daughter – the conversation turned to the play, the weather, and who was in Bath at the moment. I couldn't help noticing the contrast between our two parties. The two women opposite us were got up in the highest style, Lady Rickenham wearing a lavish, layered gown. With its hoop and padding, it must have been fashionable a decade or more previous, and it still served to underscore her importance. She had also retained an elaborate powdered wig that towered above her forehead, and had adorned herself with diamond earrings and a choker of the same stones.

Her daughter was equally formidable, but in the latest style, her flowing gown low-cut in the bodice and made of some sparkly, clinging material, with just the hint of a petticoat beneath. Her blond hair was done up in a complicated mass of curls held in place by a slender diamond-studded tiara. Around her neck she wore a sapphire pendant that exactly matched the color of her startling blue eyes.

In contrast, Rebecca and I made a poor show, I in the same gown I had worn to the ball the night before with slightly different trimmings, and Rebecca in a fine but dated gown and little other adornment. I looked over to see if she too were conscious of this contrast; she seemed at ease, as she always did, though her eyes went back and forth from Lady Mary's circlet to her pendant.

Then I remembered my one piece of jewelry. How glad was I then that I had covered it with my fichu! I could never have explained the reappearance of my necklace to Anthony; it had been difficult enough to explain it to Rebecca, who had never seen it.

The Anthony I had known two months before would have fit in better on our side, but in the intervening period he had turned himself into a dandy. His tailcoat was of that bright blue that was all the rage, high cut in front to show off the exquisite gold-threaded needlework of his waistcoat, while his lavish cravat bore a single diamond stud. He had taken to tying the hems of his breeches legs with elaborate bows that drew attention to the shapes of his calves in their tight stockings. He had let his hair grow longer in a wild rout that touched his high, starched collar.

If his manner of dress could be said to have improved – and I hesitated to call it an improvement – his physical appearance could not. He had a sallow complexion that made me wonder at how quickly he had lost the ruddy, healthful glow acquired from his sporting pursuits when at home. His face, too, had a bloated quality, obscuring the sharp angularity of his high cheekbones, once his finest feature. He seemed so embarrassed he could hardly look at me, though I was still able to note that his blue eyes were bloodshot and bleary with fatigue.

"And how are you enjoying Bath, Miss Collington?" Lady Rickenham asked, interrupting these observations.

"Oh, very well, your ladyship. There is so much to see on such a short visit." How like a country bumpkin I sounded, and I suppose I was.

"You're not here for the season? That explains why we haven't met you until now. You're in luck that the town hasn't emptied out yet, as it often does in May. Mrs. Jordan's appearance on the stage must explain it, despite her lack of respectability – or perhaps *because* of it." Her daughter shifted uncomfortably. "She is the Duke of Clarence's kept woman, and doesn't even try to hide the fact."

Lady Mary coolly regarded her mother. "It's the other way around, ma'am. She keeps him, according to rumor; he uses her money to pay his vast debts. It's why she tours with such regularity."

Lady Rickenham raised an eyebrow. "How modern! At least his debts aren't being paid out of the treasury, unlike his brother, the Prince of Wales." Next to me, Rebecca cleared her throat so quietly that none of the others might have heard.

"But Miss Collington," Lady Rickenham went on, "you really should come at the start of next season. Most young ladies of your age find they can make the best use of their time that way, as it gives them the best opportunity for introductions of consequence."

"We did not make the trip for that purpose, Lady Rickenham," Rebecca said in reserved tones that could have matched my own, "but to show Miss Collington a few of the sights and to see Mrs. Jordan. Tomorrow we will take in the concert at the Upper Rooms, but one can only visit the Pump Room so many times; as we both are in perfect health, we see no need to prolong our stay."

"Quite a long trip merely to see a play," the Marchioness sniffed, "no matter the fame of the actress."

"A pity we did not meet earlier," Anthony said, in tones that meant this as no more than a courtesy. Then Lady Rickenham's carriage was announced. "Miss Collington, Mrs. Burgess." He gave a slight bow to each of us, his glance lingering for an extra moment on me, and then he and his companions left us to await our chairs.

"ARE YOU sure you have no wish to prolong our stay?" Rebecca asked that night as she emerged from the sitting room, tying the strings of her nightcap. "It seems a shame to leave just when you have begun to make new acquaintances – and Anthony seemed disappointed that you were to leave in little more than a day."

"Did he?"

"Yes, he was happy to see you, happier than he could demonstrate before Lady Mary and her mother. And you were happy to see him, I could tell."

"It showed, did it? I thought I had maintained my composure quite well."

"To his companions, or anyone else looking on, I'm sure you appeared as nothing more than old acquaintances." She pulled back the covers and got into bed beside me. "But I know you too well, your dark eyes glow with just that little bit more warmth than usual, and your mouth gives a little twitch when you suppress a smile." Here she placed two fingers near the corner of my mouth, as if to demonstrate its traitorous nature. "Confess it – you still have feelings for his lordship." She smiled as she teased me thus, but there was a certain tension in her voice.

"And if I do, what good are such feelings when there are Lady Marys in the world, with their titles, their fashion, and no doubt their thousands of guineas."

My tone was all cool rationality as I said this, but here again, Rebecca knew me too well. "Ah, you poor girl," she said, stroking my cheek. She was still in a Shakespearean mood, for she went on, "But have no concern over Lady Mary or any of her ilk, for I swear you outshone her, even with that diamond tiara she wore. And your Lord Burnside may have been rather 'point-device in his accoutrements,' but he had not the look of one who loves with any hope; rather, one who has been drowning his sorrows these six weeks, sorrows that no Lady Mary nor any other can soothe, not with all the titles in Debrett's and not with all the gold in the Bank of England."

"But still, Anthony's father – "

"And if not Anthony, what of the Cowleys? Another fortnight here could secure a match with one of them. They were taken with you, or at least George was. You must think of your future, Lizzie."

"It was you who captivated them, if anyone did." Rebecca gave a soft protest before I went on. "And if the older one spoke true, then they intend to pluck us like a matched set at a china shop. What are we to do, draw straws to see which brother each of us will have?" We both laughed at the thought of it. "And if I were to someday marry the younger Mr. Cowley, could you see yourself wedding his brother?"

This made her laugh all the more. "Hardly!" she said. Then, becoming more serious: "No, Lizzie, I know I will never walk the aisle again, for there is no man who could replace my husband."

"And so we would be separated." She nodded. "No," I went on, continuing my former thought, "this parading of young people around Bath like so much merchandise is nothing I can support. If I chance to meet a young man in a more natural way, one who captures my affections without such artifice – and one who will not take me far from my family and everyone I hold dear – then very well. But if not, I am resigned to life without a husband; more than resigned. Father has been putting a bit aside every year for my security, and I know that Jamie will not leave me destitute."

"But this is to leave so much to chance!"

"Then there is my writing and drawing, in which you have encouraged me. I hope to make something from it. But would a husband even allow it?"

"So you really would be content with single life?"

"More than content!" I took her hand in mine. "And can I truly call it single life when I have such companionship?" It seemed most natural then to kiss the backs of her fingers.

While I had never known Rebecca to conceal any thought or feeling behind measures of reserve, now it seemed she did try to contain her emotion. Yet it could not be done – her eyes glowed with gladness and a smile spread slowly across her face, her lower lip trembling slightly. She turned quickly to blow out the single bedside lamp. Turning back to me, she kissed me gently on the cheek and placed her arm around me, as she had done every night after the first.

"Goodnight, my Celia," she whispered.

I smiled to myself as I nestled closer to her. "This is what it must be to have a sister," I thought.

CHAPTER THIRTEEN

EARLY THE next morning, long before sunrise, I awoke to see a dark figure crossing the room toward our bed. Somehow I did not cry out. Light coming in through the window glinted off something he held in his hand, and I knew it was the highwayman, come to return my necklace once more.

"Shhh!" I warned him. "You'll wake Rebecca."

He only smiled and came to my side of the bed, his bare hands sliding around my neck with all the impertinence of his previous visit. This time, however, I lay there rigid, fearing Rebecca would wake, though she seemed fast asleep.

Then, as will happen in dreams, the scene changed, and I was once again on the highwayman's horse. This again differed from the actual event, for I rode astride in front of him, my skirts bunched around my knees. His arm felt strong as it encircled me in a sure embrace, the other hand managing the reins, the horse flowing over the moors so fluidly I hardly felt we were moving at all. So smooth was our motion that the highwayman had little need to hold me, instead allowing his hand its pleasure with me. First it slipped inside my bodice, and I gasped as I realized he wore no gloves, his hand cupping my bare breast. I let out a little groan of delight. Then the hand moved down my body to pull my skirts up yet farther, moving up the inside of my thigh. I leaned backward into him, arching my hips toward that probing hand.

During all this I felt the highwayman's breath hot on my bare neck, but could not catch the words he murmured in my ear. Then I realized it wasn't a man's voice but a woman's – Rebecca's! But if Rebecca was the one who whispered to me, whose arms were around me? I turned my head to look at the face behind me –

Someone was shaking my shoulder. "Lizzie!" Rebecca whispered in my ear. "Wake up! It's just a dream."

I lay absolutely still, a little whimper escaping my throat. I was in much the same condition as the last time I had awoken from this dream, drenched in sweat, my right hand between my legs, my left hand clutching the throat of my nightgown. I knew I must have been thrashing about in my sleep, and I could only wonder how much Rebecca had seen, and how much she had guessed of the nature of my dream. My mortification was extreme. What would she think of me if she knew the wantonness I felt, not to mention the person at whom it was directed?

"Shhh, there, there," Rebecca said, patting my shoulder. "It's all right. You're awake now and you're here with me." She pushed a damp curl back from my forehead and stroked my hair.

"I'm sorry!" I whimpered and turned toward her.

One arm went around me as she said, "You have nothing to be sorry for! Everyone has one of those dreams now and again. Go back to sleep, and you can tell me about it in the morning."

We fell asleep that way and I slept until dawn.

TAKING BREAKFAST in our sitting room, Rebecca could not suppress a smile. It wasn't long before the inevitable question came, the one I had been dreading since awaking in the middle of the night. "Well," she asked, "are you going to tell me about it?"

I looked down at my plate, feeling the color rising to my cheeks.

She leaned forward, placing her hand atop my own. "Lizzie, you know you can tell me anything, anything at all. You need feel no shame."

How much could I tell her? I thought of confiding everything, to have the lie I had told her about the necklace off my conscience, along with everything else. To tell someone about the highwayman and his confounding behavior – what a relief that would be! But I dared not risk it. If she learned I had been consorting with criminals, she would refuse to have any more to do with me. And if I could not tell her of the highwayman, neither could I tell her that the voice I had heard in my dream was hers, for that was perhaps the most embarrassing point of all. But I must tell her something.

"I have these dreams from time to time. I wake in the middle of the night thinking of – a person. I cannot get him out of my mind."

Rebecca smiled. "This gentleman must have made quite an impression on you. Is it Mr. Cowley? Certainly it's not Anthony, given our conversation about him."

"No, it is neither of those. I do not know him at all, and he is no gentleman. His beliefs and practices and way of life are such that I could never support, yet I cannot get him out of my mind. He is – I will say only that he kissed me when he should not have done, twice, and once he placed his hands on my person with no respect to decency. Yet at another time he aided me in such a manner as must incur my gratitude. Oh, what he did was wicked, and it is wicked of me to go over and over it in my mind, reliving feelings I should not have had!"

She took my hand. "My dear, I see you are distraught!"

"How can I take pleasure in such vile actions? But I am sure a woman of your propriety and virtue cannot understand."

"I assure you, I can," she said, smiling. "Everyone feels passion at one time or another, even proper young ladies of remarkable self-command."

"But when I awake, I am – that is, my – " I faltered, blushing deeply. "You saw me. Or, that is, I do not know how much you saw."

"I believe I know what kind of dream you had. But tell me. I promise I won't be shocked."

I kept my eyes on our joined hands. "When I awake, as I did last night, I am touching myself, *down there.* Oh, what would my mother have thought if she ever knew me to engage in such immodest behavior!" I choked back a sob.

She came around the table and took me in her arms. "There, there! You have nothing of which to be ashamed! I cannot speak to this rogue's conduct, but touching yourself in that way, and the feelings it provokes, these are perfectly natural, and nothing to torment yourself over."

"Really?"

"Yes. Take it from an old widow, knowing how to pleasure yourself can be a help in the marriage bed."

I gaped at her, though I knew little enough of what took place in the marriage bed. Seeing my shock, she went on.

"It certainly won't surprise you that some marriages lack passion and romance. Some are made out of mere financial convenience. Others are built on companionship that can grow into love. Mine was more like the latter, for I admired and respected Captain Burgess, and could almost call him a friend, though our time together was so limited it could not grow into love. As to marriages built purely on passion and desire, I cannot speak with any first-hand knowledge, but by all reports they often lead to misery for both parties, for mere physical attraction is likely to wane. No, the best of all is when passion and companionability are combined, though such matches are said to be as rare as a swallow in winter."

After this long discourse, I hardly knew what advice I had been given. "What should I do?"

"First, as to the feelings you are experiencing, keeping them apart from the rogue who incited them, you should torment yourself no longer, for they are common to every young woman. And as for this lout, do you expect ever to see him again?"

"Not at all, but neither did I expect to see him a second or a third time."

"Well, assuming he troubles you no more, he will soon be forgotten, and you can hope to one day meet that person who will excite both passion and friendship. Now, dry your eyes, for we have our last day in Bath ahead of us."

We spent the day paying our last respects to all the scenes with which we had become so familiar over the last week: the Pump Room, Queens Square, the Royal Crescent, and the Sydney Gardens.

While we were thus occupied, I would sometimes catch Rebecca regarding me with a pensive air, as if I had caused her great concern. On our walk back to our lodgings she was unusually silent, and when we came to our door, she turned to me and spoke with unaccustomed gravity: "Lizzie, thank you for confiding in me in such an intimate manner this morning. I know that was difficult for you."

"Oh, but you made it so easy! Are not these the offices of the dearest friends? I thank you for listening, and for your advice. I hope you will likewise confide in me if ever you feel the need."

"Do you mean it?"

"Of course I do."

"Then I hope we can always remain such good friends."

"Of course we will! Why should we not?"

She was solemn for a moment longer, then seemed to shake off the strange mood. "Oh, there is no reason. I was just being foolish for a moment." She opened the door, and we went inside to prepare for that evening's concert.

CHAPTER FOURTEEN

I ENJOYED the concert, but in truth I found Bath's constant round of entertainments rather a chore, and was already beginning to long for the quiet routines of home. I was about to voice this thought to Rebecca as we emerged from the Upper Rooms after the performance, when I spotted Anthony and two other gentlemen in the crowd, moving toward us. They made a distressing sight. Anthony appeared not to have changed clothes since the previous night, and had even slept in them, judging by their disheveled state. His cravat hung limply from his collar, its diamond stud missing. His tailcoat remained unbuttoned, and his waistcoat was only partly fastened. His companions were in a like state of undress. Worse, they leaned on one another and staggered together as if they were under the influence of strong drink.

Rebecca pulled on my arm, whispering in my ear, "This way, Lizzie. Pay them no mind."

But it was too late. Anthony had seen us, and had already tipped his felt hat to us. I could not give my oldest friend the cut direct, no matter his condition. I felt a measure of sympathy for him, and concern over what evils these companions might have encouraged in him.

"Lord Burnside," I greeted him, giving a brief curtsey. I did not smile, but let my eyes show my concern. Rebecca, standing to my left, regarded me for a moment before at last giving her own curtsey.

"Lizzie – " Anthony said with a slight bow. He seemed the soberest of the three. "Miss Collington, I mean." He turned to Rebecca and did the same. "Mrs. Burgess." As he straightened, he tried to stand more erect, and to restore some semblance of propriety to his countenance while fumbling at the buttons of his tailcoat. "I hoped we would find you here." Remembering his manners, he turned to his companions. "Allow me to introduce my friends, Lord Hartwood and Lord Petersly."

Anthony might have recovered something of his gentlemanly manners, but his companions had not. Before either of us could curtsey to them, the one standing next to Anthony, Lord Petersly, exclaimed, "So this is the one you've been pining over. Damn me, Burnside, I can see why!"

Anthony gave him a cutting glare. "Petersly, remember where we are." Around us, the crowd leaving the Assembly Rooms was thinning as sedan chairs carried people away, but we were still in danger of creating a scene.

As Anthony seemed unable to control his friends, I turned to see how Rebecca would manage the situation. She glared coldly at the three, meeting Anthony's apologetic gaze at eye level. She had to tilt her head back to look up at Lord Hartwood, who had moved up to her on her left, returning her glare with his own frank appraisal of her person. "I always did like a tall woman. Mr. Burgess is a lucky man." With an arch grin, he stepped within an impertinent distance of her.

"Stand a pace farther off, my lord," Rebecca said, fiddling with the sleeve at her right wrist. I had never heard her voice sound so grim and hard.

Just then my attention was directed away from her as Lord Petersly grasped my right hand and pressed it to his lips. Never had I been so glad of my kidskin gloves! Even still, I could feel the rasp of his unshaven chin through the cloth. "It is the greatest pleasure to make your acquaintance, Miss Elizabeth," he said.

I pulled back at his use of my Christian name, which he should not have known, but he still grasped my hand in his own. Anthony looked on in mortification, but seemed incapable of the slightest attempt at restraining his friend.

"Burnside may have a family that thwarts his desires," the lout went on, "but I assure you I do not. I would be glad to pay my attentions to a young lady of such blushing manner and attractive person." His eyes roved up and down, taking in every inch of me.

Finally Anthony had heard enough. "Come now, Petersly." He grasped his friend by the shoulder to pull him away, stepping in between us as he did so.

Just then there was a jostling on my left as Lord Hartwood gave a cry. I turned to see him sprawling into the street, Rebecca looking down at him as she rearranged the skirts of her gown. All around us the remaining concert goers gasped and paused to watch. "You're in your cups, my lord," Rebecca said, "and you've trod on my gown." She put a protective arm around me as the fellow got clumsily to his feet.

"You – " he stammered. "She – "

"What?" Rebecca snapped. "Are you saying a woman threw you to the ground?"

"No, of course not! That would be absurd!" He stared around in confusion. "Apologies for my clumsiness, madam, and – for treading on your gown."

Rebecca turned me away from them. "Come, Miss Collington, let us leave the young lords to their entertainment. We have an early start tomorrow." We didn't bother waiting for chairs, but made our way down the square in front of the assembly rooms toward Alfred Street.

We had not gone far when Anthony made to follow. "Please! Wait!" he called after us. "You must accept my profoundest apologies for my friends' reprehensible conduct. Please, won't you allow me to escort you?"

Rebecca froze and turned halfway to him. "Oh, certainly! We never know when we might be accosted by a trio of drunken wastrels." I was surprised to feel her trembling as she stood next to me, and she had a wild light in her eyes.

"Please," Anthony said, "allow me to make amends, to explain – "

Rebecca turned to me. "What say you, Lizzie?"

I looked at her for a moment, then back at Anthony. He stood there in such mortification and contrition, I could feel only pity for him. Something of this feeling must have made its way into my expression, for Rebecca went on in a voice flat with resignation, "Very well then," and the three of us set off together.

"Don't forget to meet us at Mrs. Green's, Burnside," Lord Petersly called after him. "And you had better replenish your purse, as I plan to win more off you." They turned away, but not before one of them said something about a "fine piece."

Rebecca and I walked arm in arm, with Anthony on my other side. For a time we were silent, yet I could still feel that restless, wild energy in Rebecca.

"Noble company you keep, my lord," she remarked. "What are they to be, dukes, marquesses? No lower than earls, I wager."

"You are not far off, Mrs. Burgess. I never meant for them to accompany me. But I had to see you, Lizzie, and they insisted on following along. If I had known they would behave in that manner – " He trailed off, intent on the pavement in front of him.

With every streetlamp we passed beneath, I noticed the stubble on his unshaven jaw and the florid pattern of veins around his nose, marking the effects of too much drink. I couldn't help reaching out to put a hand on his arm. "Oh, Anthony, what has befallen you? Have you been ill?"

He looked up at me, his eyebrows raised, his eyes still bright blue despite their bleariness. But he said nothing, just gave a snort and went back to studying the pavement.

"Why, Lizzie," Rebecca said, her voice high and brittle, "can't you see Lord Burnside is arrayed all points like a gentleman deep in the throes of unrequited love?" For one of such an open nature, she seemed affected, different somehow than the Rebecca I knew. She loved to quote passages from plays, of course, but now it was as if she were playing a part in real life.

"How so?" Anthony asked.

Rebecca would not look at me, her gaze sliding past me to take in all the features of his dress. "Yesterday, you were rather point-device in your accoutrements, as the Bard said, not as one in love, but one set on wooing. Yet your bleary eye and your dissipated features gave you away. And now here you are in the same clothes, but what a change! Your neck cloth looks as if it had been tied by a schoolboy, your shirt is stained, your waistcoat cross-buttoned, your stockings sagging, your shoes scuffed. It appears you have slept in your clothes, my lord. Only, I wonder where? Not at Mrs. Green's?"

"You know of that place?" he asked forlornly, his eyes cast on the cobbles of the street.

"I'm afraid I do."

"I did not sleep there – "

"Few who enter there have sleep in mind."

I looked from one to the other, wondering what kind of place Mrs. Green's was.

"No, what I meant was – after Petersly and the banker emptied my purse at Vingt-Un, I took a place on a couch in the foyer, while my friends – "

"I can imagine what your friends did, being a captain's widow and having heard of such places, but remember you have an innocent listener. I would be no kind of chaperone if I allowed Miss Collington to hear the details of such a place."

"Yes, of course. But what I meant to say was that I might have shut my eyes for an hour or two, stretched out on that couch, but I certainly had little sleep. I would have left my companions there, but I was afraid my lodgings would be shut up at such a late hour."

"And how is your head today?"

"Splitting, despite much recourse to the hair of the dog today."

"You see, Lizzie, this is how fools in love drown their sorrows. Yet I would not recommend it as a cure. I take from all this, my lord, that Lady Mary does not return your affections?"

"I daresay she would have me," he said, though his voice seemed little pleased with this hopeful prospect.

"And I daresay many are the gentlemen who would have her, and gladly. But if not Lady Mary then who is it?"

"Rebecca," I said, squeezing her arm to shake her out of this strange mood. "This teasing is pointless."

She paid me no attention, but regarded Anthony with bright eyes, as if he were her prey. Her trembling had stopped, but her body was tense with pent-up energy.

She clicked her tongue at him. "Ah, I pity you nobles. So much to consider when choosing a mate! So much pressure from parents! How to weigh the advantages of titles, fortunes, estates, entails, bequests, and all the rest! It hardly leaves room for a pleasing eye, a gentle tone, or an affable manner. I'll hazard Lady Mary's heart is as icy as the diamonds in her tiara. It really is much simpler for us common folk, is not it, Lizzie?"

She raised an eyebrow at me, a hint of a smile crooking the corner of her mouth. I could not tell what she was playing at. Something about the encounter with Anthony's friends had spurred her to this raillery, this unnaturalness, but I couldn't guess what. I didn't answer her, but turned to Anthony with a sympathetic shrug.

"Ah, well," Rebecca pressed on. "There are other fish in the sea, and it must be true or it wouldn't be such an old saying." She gave him a wink. "You're a handsome catch, my lord – a little green around the gills at the moment, a bit wall-eyed, and you look as if you spent a night in the hold with the rest of the day's take. But it's not too late to restore your freshness before you go quite off. A new set of clothes, a shave, and a break from the bottle, and you'll see your market price improve considerably. Soon you'll be luring them in by the barrel."

Anthony and I exchanged another glance, and when I turned back to Rebecca she was looking at me, her eyes softening. "Yet, if love be true, it cares not for any other fish in the sea, nor fowl in the air, nor beast on the land. Neither does it care for titles and estates and parents' blessings, but aims at its fair object like an arrow shot from a bow, and none can come between it and its mark."

Our progress had slowed until we were barely moving forward. Rebecca's gaze still held mine, while her lower lip trembled.

Anthony moved a bit in front, his eyes shifting back and forth between us. "I am not without my own devices," he said at last. "I do not depend entirely on my parents, for I have my own independence, apart from the estate and fortune I am down for in my father's will. And the Earldom will always be mine. I can name the woman I would marry, in defiance of my parents' wishes." He paused and glanced around at the nearby buildings, as if they could strengthen his resolve. "Only – "

Rebecca interrupted him with renewed energy. "Then why hide your love, man?" She released my arm and went around to him, grasping him by the shoulders and walking along with him that way. "Be like Orlando and broadcast your love to the world! Let every tree – nay, every lamp post and blank wall know of it!"

Here she broke off from us and went over to a nearby wall plastered with handbills. She tore one down and brought it back to us.

"Here is this broadside, announcing the play we have recently seen, its title, its author – the Bard, of course – the dates and times of its playing, the names of the players and their parts, and all that is needful to advertise the play to the worthy visitors of Bath."

We had stopped in the street, Rebecca roaming around us as she gestured at the handbill and continued her raillery.

"Likewise, advertise your love! Only, give us you the dates and times when you first knew her, when your love for her first grew, when it increased, when it came full to bursting out of you so that it could be kept from the world no longer. Then, instead of the players, list all of your love's best parts, and the roles they played in capturing your heart, whether it be her long black hair or her dark, flashing eyes; her full, creamy bosom; her soft voice; her vivacious wit; her kind heart; or – " and here she faltered as her eyes met mine – "or what have you – " Then, recovering herself: "In short, all that is needful to advertise to the world your love for – But wait – " She stared at Anthony, her tone becoming as hard and flat as Jaques' during his soliloquy. "Wait. Who is it you love? You still have not said."

"Rebecca," I pleaded with her, my hand on Anthony's arm. "Please stop this! It is cruel."

She looked back and forth between us, but mostly at my hand where it rested on Anthony's sleeve. For his part, Anthony just stared at her, his mouth agape. "Yet I will not rest," she said at last, "not until I have plumbed the depths of this gentleman's passion."

Anthony straightened himself and took a step away from me. He gave a bow, now seeming quite sober. "I am sorry, Lizzie, but I cannot stay to be chided in this manner. This is Charles Street. I trust you can make your way safely from here." He turned and walked away from us, returning in the direction we had come.

"Anthony, wait!" I called after him.

"Indeed, wait, my lord," Rebecca called as well, and there was the clinking of coins as she withdrew a purse from a pocket of her gown. Anthony paused to look back. "Your friend dropped this when he fell, and I had no opportunity to return it to him. I'll take a guinea or two to pay for mending the hem of my gown. Perhaps you can use the remainder to recover last night's losses at Mrs. Green's table." She removed several coins, then tossed the purse to him with a sure aim. He caught it and gaped at her as if he did not know what to make of her – as neither did I, in that moment – then turned away once more.

I turned to Rebecca and saw that her wild energy had been replaced by doubt, even fear. She stood with her arms wrapped about herself, though the evening was only cool.

"What did you think you were about?" I asked. "How could you behave with such cruelty toward my friend?"

"You heard him, Lizzie. Such a timid love, he couldn't even name you as its object."

"No, not in front of a stranger! Even in his current condition, he has too much propriety for that."

"And then he said he would forego his inheritance. He cannot put aside his feelings for you, faint as they are. Yet even then he hesitated. Such a feeble kind of love!"

"This is no more than I have already told you. I know he has not the heart for that kind of defiance."

"And you still have feelings for him."

"If I do, to what purpose are they, if they cannot be openly returned? I have only ever tried to safeguard us both from being hurt. But tonight you rubbed his face in it as if he were an untrained puppy. How could you?"

"If you have such concern for him, why not go after him?"

"Was it his friends? What did that one do to you? Did he put a hand on you?"

Her gaze shifted to somewhere past my shoulder, her expression taking on that unexplained gravity I had sometimes seen there before. "Yes, his hand on me. The stale brandy on his breath. It was all painfully familiar. Maybe I will tell you about it someday."

"And did you really knock him into the street?"

She drew herself up straighter, and something of her former fierceness returned. "Not 'knock' him, but I've learned my ways. To any but the closest observer, it would appear he merely stumbled into me and then fell."

"And you took the opportunity to steal his purse. How – how was that even possible?"

She pointed back the way we had come. "Anthony just turned the far corner. You might still catch him."

"Then there was that business with the handbill. You pretended to instruct Anthony in the ways of proclaiming his love, but really you were – you were professing your love for – for – "

"Anthony needs you. I'm sure I wounded his feelings. You had better go while you still can."

She turned and walked down the street in the direction of our lodgings. I watched her receding figure and wanted to follow, but something kept me from it. In the months I had known her, I had never seen her behave maliciously toward anyone. And there was much else I had not guessed about her, not her knowledge of places like Mrs. Green's, not her ability to defend herself against a man with groping hands, and certainly not her deftness in picking his pocket. And her love for me, which had seemed so sisterly, now seemed something more, something not quite proper. I could not sort her out. She arrived at the door of our lodging and paused, looking back at me for a moment before going in.

Half angry and half confused, I was content to see her go. At least I could be sure that a kind word from an old friend would do Anthony some good.

And so I did the most improper thing I had ever done up to that point, in pursuing a single man through darkened streets, in hopes of meeting him alone, without a chaperone. This was far different than a walk to the village in broad daylight. It was the kind of thing from which a young lady's reputation might never recover, yet I cared not. Perhaps something of Rebecca's wild restlessness had rubbed off on me. I could only think that my friend must feel horribly wounded, and I would try to make what amends I could.

I was unsuccessful in throwing my reputation away, however, for I could not catch up to Anthony. After passing several streets, I realized I had no idea in which direction he might have gone. And so I turned back toward our lodgings. Yet here too I was frustrated, for I soon lost my way, spending as much as an hour wandering the streets, looking for the turning that would lead to Charles Street.

A young woman alone in a strange city after dark, with few other souls about, and those not of the best sort – no doubt I should have been afraid. Yet I was not. This was my own little adventure. It struck me that there could be no true adventure if one did not become a little lost, risk a little danger, suffer a little uncertainty as to the outcome – and certainly not, if one did not lose one's chaperone. I had much to ponder as well. So I wandered the civilized streets of Bath, feeling a bit as if I were in the swamps of Florida, and wondering about the evening's strange events, until I recognized first the correct street, then the correct house, and was met at the door by the fearsome figure of the landlady giving me the evil eye, for it was long past midnight.

When I explained that I had become inadvertently separated from my friend, and then had become lost, she relented, saying, "Yes, and quite concerned for you Mrs. Burgess was, too. I'm sure she'll be glad to see you."

But when I entered our apartments, Rebecca was asleep – or pretending to sleep. I undressed and put on my nightgown, then sat at the vanity, brushing my own hair, wishing she would stand behind me and do it. I had become used to the pleasant feeling of her fingers running through the long strands, brushing against my neck as she wound it into plaits, then resting for a moment on my shoulders when she was done. I wanted to go back to the way we had been just that afternoon.

Then I went into the bedroom and climbed into bed, leaning over her to blow out the single lamp. She did not stir, but lay facing away from me. I thought about saying something or putting a hand on her shoulder to see if she was awake – anything to bridge the gulf that seemed to yawn between us. But I was still angry and confused, and so I rolled over with my back to her without a touch or a word. Only then did I notice the bed shaking slightly to her quiet sobbing.

IN THE morning we were quiet with each other. "Did you find Anthony?" she asked at last, her voice subdued, her eyes downcast. "You were gone so long."

"No, I could not find him. Then I became lost."

"I owe you an apology." She looked at me only once before staring back down at her untouched breakfast plate. "You, and your father as well. I was terribly negligent in my duty as your chaperone."

I told her I had viewed it as an adventure, and for a brief moment she smiled. "How brave of you!" But the moment passed, and we had little opportunity for further conversation, as we had to see to our final packing, then get our things down to the White Hart Inn where we would board the post coach. Through it all Rebecca treated me with a reserve that could only match my own. Gone were the vivacity and affability and teasing nature that had drawn me to her. Now she treated me with strict formality, as if she really were my chaperone and not my dearest friend.

The journey home, crammed as we were into the coach's compartment with utter strangers, offered no opportunity to bridge the silence that had grown between us. When we stopped for lunch at an inn along the way, she continued with her distant, repressive demeanor, rebuffing my every attempt to draw her back to her former self. At the same time, my own reserve would not allow me to confront her directly, not in such a public place.

By the time we reached Exeter late in the evening, I was so tired and nauseated from the long, bumping journey that I could barely speak, and so our silence continued for the last leg of our trip, riding in the hired chaise Father had sent from Leighton. We said a stiff goodbye at Rebecca's house as the postilion got her luggage down. Driving up the lane toward the Parsonage, I stared out the window into darkness, all the while remembering my conversation with Anthony in this very spot, on that day when I had sought to safeguard both our hearts.

What little good that had done, I thought, for now I truly knew what it was to have a broken heart, and Anthony had nothing to do with it.

CHAPTER FIFTEEN

I DID my best to hide my sorrow and lack of sleep from Father and Mrs. Simmons at the breakfast table the next morning. If I seemed tired, it could only be from the strains of the previous day's journey; if I recounted our adventure with little animation or delight, it was only what they had come to expect of me. When a village boy brought a note from Rebecca, they naturally inquired whether I would be seeing her that day. They were not at all surprised when I said I would walk out on my own, since Rebecca and I had spent so much time over the past week in close company.

Rebecca's note was such that it was difficult to deny her.

"My dearest Lizzie," she began. "Have you had as little sleep as I have? I am feeling ill and low. Please come to Leighton today and allow me to explain all. I am shockingly ashamed of my conduct toward you, and toward Anthony. Do you remember when you said I should confide in you if ever I felt the need? There is something I must tell you, and when I do, perhaps all will become plain, or perhaps you will hate me. It is partly the fear of how you will react to this divulgence that has made my behavior so strange. My one hope is that when you learn what it is, you will find it within your heart to forgive me and continue as my friend. Please don't keep me in suspense. I've instructed the boy to wait upon your reply. Your dearest, &C, Rebecca."

What was there to explain? She was simply jealous of Anthony, however unfounded that jealousy was, fearful that he would come between us, as Orlando had come between Rosalind and Celia. But why would she not come and speak to me herself? We weren't in the habit of communicating by messenger. Certainly she could feel no worse than did I. No, the matter must not be that urgent, I felt, if she did not come to me directly, instead of taking the time to write notes and find village boys to deliver them. Too, some time away from her would allow me to clear my thoughts. I wrote a hasty reply telling her that a solitary walk was the best thing for me, and that I would see her on the day following, then gave it to the boy, along with a penny.

It was such a fine day, I chose to follow my own prescription, taking my usual route around Highdown. Spring was moving on toward summer, and everywhere Nature was reaching her height of activity. Buckthorn had given way to hawthorn in its turn of blooming, creating large sprays of white in the hedgerows and the woods, giving off a scent that some find objectionable but which I happen to enjoy. Bluebells and ramsons made carpets of blue and white in the forest, and I took the opportunity to pick a bouquet of the former for the vase at home.

The day was like a balm. I felt my sadness begin to lift somewhat, and with it, a growing curiosity about what Rebecca had to tell me. I began to think of circling back around by way of the village and calling on her after all.

After an hour of strolling along the brook that ran through the center of a little valley, pausing along the way to admire the foxgloves that had bloomed in my absence, I came to the track leading up onto pastureland and eventually to a hanging wood where stood the great oak tree. Whether it was the beauty of the day, my lack of sleep, or all that had passed since my last encounter with the highwayman, only now did I remember telling him he could meet me here on any fine day. Whatever the case, I hesitated as I remembered the folly of my having agreed to meet him at all. Rebecca had advised that I would forget him if I kept out of his way, yet here I was, about to arrive at the very spot.

Counter to these cautious considerations, I felt a stubborn resistance to the idea of cutting short my usual walk on account of the highwayman. The oak grew at the farthest extent of Lord Highdown's holdings and therefore was the limit of my solitary ramblings. The hill on which it stood afforded an enchanting prospect of the valley through which I had just passed, and it had always been a favorite spot in which to rest and reflect. What were the chances, I asked myself as I ascended the track leading upwards across the pasture, that the highwayman would be waiting for me today? More than a week had passed since our encounter; certainly he could not have spent a large portion of each day waiting for me there; surely he had coaches to rob and militias to harry.

I was warm and out of breath as I stepped into the shade of the oak and turned to take in the view of the brook snaking its way through the valley, glinting here and there in the sunlight where it shone through gaps in the trees. Brilliant green paddocks rose upward from the valley floor before giving way to the more muted purples and browns of the high moorlands, here and there punctuated by the grey rock of a tor. Above my head, a woodpecker hammered at the bark of the oak.

Having recovered my breath and gotten my fill of the familiar view, I was just ready to continue my ramble when I heard the clearing of a throat behind me, nearly causing me to jump. Turning slowly so as not to betray my alarm, I saw the highwayman stepping out of the forest that grew on that side of the hill, his horse – Juno, I remembered – picketed farther in amongst the trees.

"You!" I exclaimed. "How could you know I would be here today?"

The highwayman stood a few paces off, below the crest of the hill, his eyes twinkling above his crepe mask. He was dressed as usual, in a coat of claret velvet, doe-skin breeches, and high riding boots, topped with a cocked hat. "I did once tell you to expect me when you least expected me." He spotted the posy I held in one hand. "How kind of you to bring me flowers!"

"You are mistaken, for I planned to put these in a vase at home. Is it the custom among thieves for women to present flowers to men? Or for men to neglect to doff their hats in the presence of a lady? You did not do me that courtesy the last time we met."

He laughed at that. "You have me there, although, if my memory serves, I was too busy saving your life to remember my manners." He gestured at a hummock of grass on the other side of the oak. "Come and sit. I will doff my hat and tell you my story and all will be revealed – how I became a highwayman, and a traitor as you named me the other day, and much else besides."

There was something anxious about his manner, and I once again found it a strange contrast to his usual bold behavior.

As I hesitated, he went on: "The view from where you stand is no doubt very fine, but so too is the view from below of anyone standing there with you. I would not further compromise your virtue."

"I am not sensible of having done any wrong."

"Nor have you, yet that is seldom how society looks on such things. Now come – I assure you this is no ruse; I mean you no harm. Surely you know you can trust me by now?" As a further sign of his gentlemanly goodwill, he removed his coat and spread it over the hummock, gesturing for me to have a seat.

It was with less trepidation than I might have imagined that I stepped down off the crest of the hill and approached the seat the highwayman indicated. As I came nearer, he looked on my face with growing concern.

"You seem pale, and you have dark circles under your eyes. Have you not been sleeping?"

"I had a long journey yesterday. But can you blame me if my sleep is interrupted with dreams of mysterious strangers entering my bedchamber?"

He caught up my hand and held it in his own gloved one. "I did not mean to make you afraid. Causing you any kind of pain or torment was the farthest from my intention."

"I did not say it was fear that kept me awake."

His eyes crinkled at the corners on hearing this. "I said I would steal no more kisses, but if I kiss you now, I hope it is no theft." He held my gaze for a moment longer, and I nodded, my lips parting.

Oh, I was foolish! For so much of my life, I had been taught to keep a tight hold on my emotions, but now I was nothing but a bundle of conflicting feelings – confusion and heartbreak over Rebecca, and yearning for the highwayman. What can I say for myself, other than that one moment in the highwayman's arms seemed to offer the only relief? It may be difficult to credit, but I believed that if I kissed the highwayman fully and deeply, this turmoil would end – and if not, I knew no other way to end it. Yet can I be blamed? Matters of love and attraction were never proper subjects in our household, and the mysteries of the human body were left to be discovered on my wedding night. Perhaps I should have read more of those romances good taste had led me to eschew.

As it was, I leaned up toward the highwayman and he leaned down toward me, one hand lifting his crêpe mask only at the crucial moment before our lips met. Then I forgot everything for a time, my whole being absorbed in the pleasure of the meeting of our lips and then our tongues. His arms encircled me and drew me against him, and I felt that warm, tingling sensation spreading down from the base of my spine. I melted against him, my arms around his back, my hands moving up and down the satin of his waistcoat, pressing him closer to me. The kiss went on and on, and instead of being sated, I wanted more and more.

With an effort, I pushed myself away from him. This could not be. What a fool I had been! How many nights would I spend dreaming of this kiss, yearning for a man I could never love and never marry?

"So you do want me," the highwayman said, his breath coming fast, as affected by the kiss as I had been.

"No – Yes – " I walked up and down for a moment before turning on him. "You know it is impossible. You cannot expect me to take up with an outlaw and a traitor. It would ruin me, and destroy my father. You – you are wrong to make me feel this way."

"Oh, Miss Elizabeth, in my experience, we can rarely help how we feel, especially if it is a true feeling of the heart. All your self-restraint is useless against it."

Once again I wondered how he knew my name, but I let it go. "Yet when there is no other choice, self-command can be a great aid in helping us to turn away from those things we should not want. Now I must leave." I turned to go.

"But you have yet to hear the story of how I came to be a highwayman."

I turned to look back at him from the crest of the hill. "As interesting as that may be, I will have to forgo it, for it is now clear to me that any further intercourse between us can only bring me harm. If you dare approach me again, I will expose you to the authorities. Now, I really must go, for I have an ill friend in the village."

In the silence that followed, I turned once more to leave.

"You will not find her there," the highwayman called out after me.

Now I was becoming angry. "You cannot know that." I did not bother to turn around. "Do not toy with me, sir. Now, good-day." I took another pace over the top of the hill.

"Lizzie, wait!" The highwayman's voice changed to one I recognized, though with a pleading tone I had never heard in it before. "I *do* need you. Please, don't go!"

I froze where I stood. How could this be? How foolish I had been for not sooner guessing the truth! Even in that moment the thought crossed my mind that the highwayman had somehow kidnapped Rebecca and brought her here. But of course that was not the way of it.

I turned slowly to face him, not wanting to know the truth. But at last I could deny it no longer. The highwayman had removed his cocked hat and untied the ribbon that held his queue in place, letting his hair fall free, nearly to his shoulders. He had removed the cloth from his face. "He" was no stranger to me. "He" was not even a he. The highwayman was my dearest friend, Rebecca.

Oh, the swirl of conflicting thoughts and emotions that engulfed me then! My mind could not compass it. I could not breathe, and a blackness threatened to engulf me as I felt the world spin for a moment. But at last I mastered these sensations, pacing up and down along the crest of the hill and forcing the breath into my lungs. I would not show such weakness as fainting before this person who now seemed the strangest creature I had ever beheld.

When I had regained some measure of composure, I turned to look at Rebecca, or Robin, or the highwayman – I knew not how to call her. Her face bore an expression of the greatest anguish – that same grave aspect I had seen on occasion in the past, mingled with fear at my likely response. I looked at those eyes, the same eyes that had gazed out at me from above the highwayman's mask. How had I not seen it before? They were surely the same brown eyes with which I had become so familiar over the past weeks. Now those eyes were framed by wavy brown hair worn loose in something like a man's style, and not by masses of brown curls or intricately looped braids, which, I realized, must have been achieved through the use of wigs. No wonder she had refused to let me help with her hair while we were in Bath!

Yet still I could not credit it. How could I have been so taken in by a costume and a mask? Were not the qualities that made one a man or a woman so deeply ingrained that they would show through the veneer of mere dress? But perhaps it was as the old saying had it, that the clothing makes the man. Surely it was her clothing that had tricked me into hearing her voice as that of a man, albeit one with a boyish timbre. Her stature aided in the disguise, allowing her to appear as a man of middling height when in masculine dress.

Still, though she had tricked me as to her sex, how could I not recognize that the highwayman was Rebecca?

And then it occurred to me that I had long known the truth, at least since our meeting on Whiddleston Moor, and most certainly since the encounter with Anthony – the hunter's eyes she had directed at him that night were certainly the same that had regarded me from above the highwayman's mask on the night of the robbery. Perhaps this truth was so shocking that I could never allow myself to admit it.

Many of these reflections came later, of course. As it was, I stood there in stunned silence, not knowing what to think. "Are you a woman or a man?" I asked at last.

During all this time she had been moving steadily toward me, and now she abandoned all caution, stepping up to the brow of the hill where I stood. "How can you not believe I am a woman?" She removed the glove from her left hand and took up my own. "Is not this a woman's hand, that has so often held yours?"

Indeed, it was soft and pale and delicately boned, like my own.

She placed my hand against her bosom. "Is not this a woman's breast, that has so longed to feel the touch of your hand?"

I found it soft and pliant, even through the shirt and waistcoat and the bindings with which she had tried to hide her woman's form. I felt my face flush and my breathing come faster – as did hers, I could feel by the rise and fall of her chest.

I snatched my hand away, taking several unsteady paces away from her. I looked around at the oak and beech trees as if they could solve the mystery of the strange creature before me, and the even stranger feelings I experienced in that moment.

"You are confused and angry," she said. "Of course, it's only natural. But let me explain, let me tell you my story, and all will become clear."

"It is all lies! You have lied to me from the very beginning." I moved another step away. "How smug you must have felt, sitting beside me in the Bath theatre, watching a woman dressed as a man, when you were tricking me, just as Rosalind tricked Phebe!"

"No, Rosalind did not trick Phebe, but Phebe fell in love with Ganymede of her own accord – just as you have fallen in love with me! Don't you see, you are Celia and Phebe in one."

"That night with Anthony, you seemed to be playing a part, like one of the actors on the stage, but now I see it is all play-acting with you – Mrs. Burgess, the highwayman, it is all an act, and none of it is true."

"My love for you is true, Lizzie. Through it all, however changeable you might have found me, my love for you has been the one true constant."

"And then to think of those nights beside you in bed, when all along – "

"When all along I treated you with the chastity of a sister." She came toward me, holding out her hand.

"No, do not touch me!" I stepped back another pace.

She winced as if I had stabbed her. "This is why I behaved so strangely, that night after the concert. Old reflexes took hold of me when that lout put his hand on me, and then I thought I had revealed myself to you, before I was ready. I thought surely then you would guess who the highwayman was, and you would look on me with just the look of contempt you are giving me now. It made me wild and careless – that and everything his pawing hand and drunken breath brought back."

She must have sensed a softening in my posture toward her, for she took another step forward. "But it is not all lies, Lizzie, not at the heart of it. Mrs. Burgess, the captain's widow, is a fiction, I will readily admit it. Yet the truth is, I have loved you since that first moment in the Earl's carriage. Still, I had to know if this were a mere infatuation, or something deeper, for I knew nothing of you other than your beauty and the captivating boldness with which you behaved toward one you had every reason to fear. I created the fiction of Mrs. Burgess so that we might come to know each other, free of all the derision with which you must hold an outlaw. And over these weeks, as I came to know you most intimately, I became only more attached. *That* is real, Lizzie. Equally, I have every reason to believe you love me, though you have not yet learned to name it love."

"But love between women, physical love – "

" – is the sweetest love there can be. All the intimacy and companionship you feel for Rebecca Burgess, you feel for me. And all of your yearning for the highwayman is yearning for me, or do you deny what you felt in my arms just now? Can you say you have ever felt anything like it for a man, even for Anthony?"

I could not lie to her, not when I saw my dearest friend before me, pleading with an anguished expression I had never before seen her exhibit. I shook my head.

"Think of it, Lizzie," she said, taking up my hand once more. "That love of which I once spoke, combining both companionable friendship and the most blissful throes of passion – it can be ours, if only you will stay and hear my tale."

Now I knew why she had made me promise to always be her friend that evening in Bath. It seemed a mean trick, for how could I have guessed that my friend was also an outlaw and a seditionist? Yet how could I have been so mistaken in her character, having plumbed all of its finer points over the past weeks of growing intimacy? Could it be that she was both a traitorous outlaw and the refined, proper, and compassionate woman I knew? Surely the two could not be reconciled?

"How can I be certain this new tale will not also be a lie, as was the fiction of the widowed Mrs. Burgess? How can I be sure you are not a murderess along with everything else?"

She regarded me for a long moment. "I promise to confess all the murders I have committed, which number exactly one. I will leave it to you to judge whether it was justified or not."

"You prove my point! You are no one I can trust."

"I have more to relate that is much to my shame, and much else that will seem far more outlandish and unlikely than Mrs. Burgess's story. When I am finished you may decide whether I have been fully forthcoming or no. As further proof that you can trust me, I have now placed myself and my life fully in your power. You have only to go to Sir Morris, the high constable, to turn me in for many crimes of robbery, and before my tale is done, one crime of murder and many of bribery and extortion. It will be within your power to see me hang. What further proof of my honesty could you need?"

"You could easily run off before I can bring the authorities to you."

"I promise that Mrs. Burgess won't seek to run away, and you will find her in Leighton whenever you wish to bring the constable to her. For it is a mark of my devotion to you that I would rather hang than live without you."

"How can you expect me to run off with an outlaw, and a woman at that?" I truly did not know which was more shocking, my mind was in such a whirl.

For the first time since she had revealed herself to me, that mischievous light came back to her eyes. "If all goes according to my plan, there need be no running off. And, you must admit, I have already swept you off your feet." She smiled that smile with which I had become so familiar over the past months. Much to my chagrin, I felt myself starting to smile in return. I managed to keep my countenance, but I could not keep my heart from feeling her smile's warmth.

"Now come," she said more sternly, holding her hand out to me. "Sit and hear my tale. It is a long one and the day is going forward."

The authority with which she spoke, and the poise and confidence with which she regarded me, reminded me of how strange her energy, her stature, and her comportment had all seemed at first, when I encountered her in woman's dress. But now, as strange as it was to see a woman in men's clothing, this manner of dress somehow suited her perfectly. Did the clothing make the man, or did this woman's character make the man? Yet she was not a man; it was all a muddle. I let her take my hand and lead me to my seat on her claret-red coat.

"First, allow me to introduce myself properly. Rebecca Burgess, though a fiction, is just one of many names under which I have lived. In recent years, the friends who know me best call me Robin, though some call me Lord Rob. But I was born Rebecca Hazelton, daughter of Sir Robert Hazelton, Fifth Baronet of Grimswick, in Kent. Here is the curtsey I gave to King George when I was presented to him on my coming out." She gave a deep, graceful curtsey, her head humbly bowed. "Later, I was Lady Aysgarth, wife of Charles Kingston, Baron Aysgarth." She paused for a moment to relish my surprise. "Now, aren't you glad you stayed? It is an intriguing tale, how I went from that profession to this."

I hardly knew what to say. My curiosity could not have been greater, yet I was too stunned by these revelations to form a coherent thought. At last I could think only to say, "Winning the title of Baroness is not a profession."

"On the contrary, it is the oldest profession, one with which I will have nothing more to do. Perhaps, when I am finished, I will have convinced you of it. Joining the aristocracy is nothing you should want." And with that cryptic remark, she began her tale.

CHAPTER SIXTEEN

THE STORY Rebecca then told was the most fantastical I had ever heard, with all the elements of a gothic romance. She began when she was near my own age, a girl of nineteen, filled with romance, passion, and dreams of finding her true heart's companion, all in a gentleman who would also satisfy her father's insistence on a secure title and income. Her mother had passed away when she was eight, after the last of many still-births; her only sibling, an older brother, had died of the ague when she was fifteen. With no heir, and his health failing, her father's one concern when she reached marriageable age was to see her well settled. As he was himself an only child and he saw the imminent failure of his family line, his fondest wish was to marry her into the most important family that would have her, while keeping some regard for her own feelings.

Two seasons he sent her to London with her governess, herself a distinguished widow with good connections, but at the end of it, her prospects were less bright than they had at first appeared. Though the fortune that would go with her was sizeable, and despite possessing all the accomplishments befitting a young woman of good upbringing, these had failed to attract a bachelor agreeable both to her father and to herself.

"My father could not understand it," Rebecca said, "seeing in me all the talents and beauty necessary to the attachment of any young nobleman; while I thought myself perhaps too tall to suit the vanity of most gentlemen."

In the end, her choices were but two: a superannuated Earl of little charm or warmth, with a greying, balding head under his wig; and Lord Aysgarth. The latter was a man just past thirty and ruggedly handsome. He spoke with a northern accent that hinted of the winds whipping down off the high fells, like something out of a popular romance. His manners were none too polished, but he always appeared kind and attentive, solicitous of her father's health, and of a polite address when in her presence. He talked much of Swanford, his grand estate outside York, with its large manor house and grounds laid out by Capability Brown. He could even show pictures of it in a gazetteer of the northern counties.

"I tried to convince myself I could love Lord Aysgarth, for my father's sake," she said. "In truth I only wanted to marry our near neighbor in Kent, the curate's son, who had followed his father's profession, and whose highest aspiration was to attain his own parish. But father would have none of it. 'My daughter will not live in poverty and make a mockery of our ancient family,' he said. James and I even talked rashly of running away to Scotland together – many are the times I've wondered how my life might have been different had we done so, though I'm not sure it would have been happier."

Rebecca's feelings for her father prevailed in the end, for she was an obedient, loving daughter. He was at the end of his life, and she would not deny him his last wish, making him the happiest by far of all who attended the wedding. Six months after Charles and Rebecca removed to Yorkshire, news came of her father's death. So much had changed by that time, she hardly felt her decision had been worthwhile.

She knew something was amiss the moment they arrived at the estate. The servants all had a cowed look, not just deference for Lord Aysgarth, but outright fear. The house was everything Rebecca could want, save that its very size was overpowering when so often empty. When they did have guests they were not of the best sort – rough men to whom she was not properly introduced, none of whom brought wives to offer her feminine companionship. After dinner they would retire to the parlor for long games of cards and dice, leaving Rebecca to herself. There was society of a sort in York, but she could hardly reach it, as the estate was many miles from that city, and Charles would rarely allow her the use of the carriage. Some of the ladies closer at hand would take pity on her, as they had some idea of her situation, sending their own carriages around to bring her to dinner or a card party or walks in their gardens.

Affairs in the marriage bed were even worse. Rebecca learned on her wedding night what a woman's marriage duty meant – for her, it was more of a nightly trial. Charles would enter her bed-chamber and announce, "Time to get an heir!" He would unbutton his breeches, pull up her nightdress, and a moment later he was done, leaving her with a bruised, burning sensation in her most private parts.

"No, Lizzie, do not blush and look away," Rebecca said after relating this last. "All of this skirting around and avoiding the facts of life, under the name of virtue and decorum, can only lead to a bad end. Much better to know life as it is, to know one's true nature and wants, and how they might best be satisfied in one's choice of a mate. If only I had known more of my husband before our wedding day, I might not have made the worst mistake of my life!"

But the behavior she had so far described accounted only for his more gentle conjugal visits. At other times, when he was in his cups or had lost a large sum at cards, he would treat her person with the most horrid brutality, all the while claiming she was a cold fish who didn't know how to give a man pleasure.

"And how could I," she asked, "when no one had taught me a thing? My governess certainly had not prepared me for these bed duties. Not that it was pleasure Charles was after, but domination. Beasts in the paddock show more love and pleasure in their rutting than anything we had together."

She could hardly credit the change that had come over him since their wedding day, putting it down to the strong drink that was always about the house. In London, he had always been quite abstemious, but now he drank at all hours of the day, and it made him a different man. Sometimes, in his more sober moments, she would catch him looking at her with what seemed like regret, but he never spoke a word of apology or tenderness.

In time, Rebecca took to drinking as heavily as did her husband, and to taking certain medicines the doctor prescribed – anything to keep herself in an almost senseless state while Charles had his way with her. She soon began to sleep at all hours of the day, and was often disheveled and ill-fit for company, so that those ladies who had at first called upon her ceased doing so.

She was left utterly alone, without a friend in the world, with no one who could take pity on her – save one, her lady's maid, Anna. "By rights, I should call her Templeton, according to her rank among the servants, but I can think of her only as Anna," Rebecca said.

Anna came to Rebecca's chamber one evening as usual, to prepare her for bed. "Begging your pardon, m'lady," she said as she unpinned Rebecca's gown, "but I must speak freely, seeing what a state you're in. I know what you're doing, with all this drinking and bottles of medicine. It can only lead to a bad end, and it will make your bedding no easier. But I can show you something that will."

In her drunken state, Rebecca could only look at her blearily. "What?" was all she could manage to utter.

"Now, begging m'lady's pardon, but I must be quite forward to show you, and you must tell me if you want me to stop." Rebecca nodded and Anna stood behind her, sliding a hand up her thigh, pulling up the hem of her nightdress as she went. Then she grasped Rebecca's own hand and placed it between her legs, where her governess had admonished her never to touch herself.

"But it's a sin!" she said, though she did so with a giggle, in her inebriation.

"No, m'lady, the way his Lordship treats you is the sin. We can all hear your screams from downstairs and we're sure you'll be dead within the year unless we can make it easier for you."

As Rebecca described the manner in which Anna treated her, and the feelings thus provoked, I felt myself coloring and my breath coming faster, despite my efforts at self-control. "Ah, I see I've made you blush," she said. "As well you might. For that was when I first learned of the pleasure one woman can give to another – a pleasure I hope one day to share with you."

"I am here to learn how you became a highwayman," I said in my most measured tones, "not to be seduced by stories of such illicit conduct. Please proceed with greater concision and fewer salacious details."

Yet the truth was, those were the details I most wanted to hear; nor was Rebecca likely to oblige my request. "That, I cannot do, for I would have you understand all of me, as I am."

With that, she went on describing the feelings she experienced under Anna's instruction. Finally, the pleasure became so intense that she felt something was about to happen, as if she would turn inside out. Her legs began to shake so that she could hardly stand, and Anna helped her to the bed. "There, m'lady," she said, taking her hand away, "now you're wet enough, things should go easier if his Lordship comes to you tonight. And if you're not, there's always this." She drew a small pot from a pocket of her maid's uniform and showed Rebecca its contents, a smooth, glistening paste. "It's goose grease. Put a finger-full of this inside you and he'll slide in as slick as an eel, no trouble at all."

Rebecca shuddered at her choice of simile, though she thanked her. Anna curtsied and left the room. Later, when Rebecca's husband came in, it *was* easier, though she certainly had no pleasure in it.

Things went on in this way for a time, Anna always seeking to cheer her mistress on those days when she felt especially low, and doing her best to keep her from heavy drink, until gradually Rebecca no longer resorted to it as she had done before, nor to those other sedatives. Sometimes at night Anna would touch her in that way she had done that first time, never to the point of fullest ecstasy, but only so that she would be ready for Charles. Yet these were the moments Rebecca lived for, not just the times when Anna touched the most intimate parts of her person, but when she gave her mistress a secret smile as she went about her duties, or spoke a comforting word as she helped her dress.

"She was my only friend, and I couldn't help loving her, though our stations were so far apart." Here again Rebecca stopped, for she had been pacing to and fro as she told her story, turning to me in a most bold and challenging manner. "Can you blame me?" she demanded.

I looked at her sadly. "No, I do not blame you, but can only pity you."

She raised her eyebrows at that. "No, do not pity me. We'll see if you still pity me by the end." Then she stared off into the trees, as if recollecting her place in the story, before taking it up once more.

Charles' behavior grew worse after her father's passing. Only then could he be certain that none of her father's lawyers would come after him. She had made no mention of the abuse in her twice-weekly letters home, as she had no wish to trouble her father's few remaining days, however bad things were for herself. After her father's passing, feeling himself safe in that regard, Charles began complaining of Rebecca's failure to produce an heir. "I've had you nearly every night these seven months," he declared, "and still your belly's flat as any maid's. What's wrong with you?" Upon the suspicion that she was somehow at fault, he decided that using her more harshly was the best way to get her with child.

"I should have left that house then," Rebecca said, "no matter the consequences to me or my fortune. My father could no longer be ashamed of a daughter who could not maintain her marriage; as for my fate, it could hardly have been worse than it was in the end, though I did not know that at the time. Too, others might have fared better. But I hadn't a friend in the world, other than Anna. How could I leave her? I did have friends and acquaintances back home in Kent, but how could I explain my husband's treatment of me? No one would call his behavior by its proper name, not within the bonds of matrimony. And as for close relations, those who would be bound by family duty, I had none. A distant cousin I did not even know had inherited my childhood home and my father's title. So I remained in the north."

It was around this time that her husband's other fault was revealed, making a matched set along with his drinking, gambling, and brutal treatment of her. One day, when she was in the sitting room, laboring over her work – for at this point she tried to keep as much as she could to her former pursuits, both to remind herself of home, and to keep her mind from the present situation – a knock came at the front door. That was a rare enough occurrence that she listened to hear who it might be. Yet when Stevens, the butler, answered the door, she could hear only a whispered conversation.

Intrigued, she went to see who the visitor could be. The butler and the unannounced guest continued talking as Rebecca approached within earshot, her house slippers muffling her approach.

"I told you, this is all we can spare," Stevens was saying. "It's not safe for you to come here." He held the door only partway open, his back blocking Rebecca's view of the person beyond.

"Stevens," she asked, "who is it?"

He stiffened before stepping aside and opening the door to reveal a girl, three or four years younger than Rebecca, dressed in the drab woolens of a villager. Though she had a long shawl draped over her shoulders and hanging far down in front, it could not disguise that she was with child, and far along at that. She appeared mortified to see the lady of the house, looking quickly back at the ground.

"Nothing to trouble yourself over, m'lady, nor his Lordship," Stevens said, giving her a meaningful look. "Just a beggar from the village."

At that, the lass's head jerked up in defiance. Then she addressed Rebecca, with all the shyness of before. "Begging your pardon, m'lady, but I am no beggar. My father sent me to claim what's due me. He said I got myself into this mess, I can get myself out." She paused, searching for her next words. "As you can see, I'm in a family way, only, there's no father. I mean, that is to say, there *is* a father, only he's – he's – "

"He is my husband," Rebecca finished for her.

She gave a sob and bowed her head. "Only, don't blame me, m'lady, or that is, I'm only partly to blame. He was so sweet, you see, at least at first, and it turned my head, him being Baron and all, and then when he got me alone he – he – " She broke down in sobs.

The girl had no need to finish the tale, for Rebecca could picture it all too well. She felt an unreasoning surge of jealousy that took her several moments to master. Finally she told herself it was silly to feel jealous over her husband's attentions, which she herself did not want. "Stevens, we must take her in," she said.

"M'lady, we cannot. It's not safe for her here."

"What do you mean by that?"

He would not look at her. "I dare say no more, only his Lordship mustn't find out."

Rebecca struggled to parse his words. Had this happened before? And, in that case, what had happened to make Stevens so fearful for the girl's safety?

"Have Anna bring my reticule," Rebecca told him. While the butler was gone, Rebecca questioned the girl about the progress of her condition, whether her parents would support her once the baby arrived, and what were her views for its future.

At last, Stevens returned with Anna, and Rebecca settled two pounds on the girl, as this was nearly all she had (for Charles prided himself on having a wife who would not appear poor when out in public, but by no means allowed her enough money to support this girl indefinitely). She encouraged her to return when it ran out, hoping her own funds would have been replenished by then.

That afternoon, Rebecca steeled herself for a confrontation with her husband, reasoning that introducing the subject at dinner, before he was too much in his cups, would give the greatest chance of persuading him. Adopting a domineering attitude would help drive home the shame that must attend the fathering of an illegitimate child, and allow her to win the day. From then on, she felt, their relationship would proceed on a different basis, for now she surely had a measure of power over him. How wrong she was!

"Dearest husband," she began, not bothering to hide the sarcasm with which she used that term of address, "your secret is out." She held his gaze, hoping her racing heart wouldn't betray her. "A girl from the village, little more than a child herself, is carrying your child. You have betrayed the trust which a husband owes his wife."

He appeared neither surprised nor angry, but merely set down his glass of wine. "Bah!" he exclaimed. "Every lass who finds herself with child by the neighbor lad tries to lay it at the Baron's door. I'll not have it." He attacked his beef with greater energy.

"No, I'm certain she spoke true, for the behavior she described is very like your own toward me. You have a responsibility to this child. When it is born, we will take it into this house and raise it as our own. If it is a boy, he will be your heir, and your conjugal visits to my bedchamber will cease. You may take your pleasure where you will, but no longer with me."

He did not rage, nor did he shout. Yet the footman waiting by the sideboard stiffened and seemed to shrink into himself, as if fearing what would come next, as Lord Aysgarth rose from his end of the long table and walked slowly toward her.

"Leave us," he said to the footman, who made a quick exit. Reaching her seat at the end of the table, Charles took her chin in hand, forcing her to meet his eye as he glowered down at her. Then his hand went around her throat, cutting off her air. "No bastard will ever carry my name. If I find the brat, I'll drown it like a rat in a bag, and its whoring mother with it. You are the only one who can produce an heir, and if you fail in this, I will be rid of you and find another wife. And you will never speak to me in such a manner again. Do I make myself clear?"

By this point Rebecca had nearly fainted for want of air, so that she could barely nod. When he took his hand away, she gasped for breath. The marks of his fingers remained for over a week.

After this, Charles began openly to have his way with the female servants. Perhaps he had been doing it secretly all along, but now Rebecca could be passing along the upstairs hall at any time of day and find a naked maid running from an unused guest room, her husband's rough laughter echoing from within. Soon the day came when he emerged from the servants' quarters with a particularly satisfied, smug expression and a wink for Rebecca. A moment after, Anna came from the same place, her face flushed, still tying her apron strings. When she saw Rebecca's mortification, she bolted upstairs to return to her duties.

"I thought I had come to my last extremity," Rebecca told me now. "My husband had taken my last friend and comfort from me. How could I let her attend me, much less touch me more intimately? I was filled with a jealous rage, for which my anger at the village girl had been but a rehearsal. No manner of rational thought could overcome it."

Rebecca shut herself in her chamber and did not come down to dinner. Later, when Anna came to prepare her for bed, Rebecca was cold and distant with her, forbidding her to brush her hair, or do more than unpin her gown and hand her a nightdress. For her part, Anna could barely look at her mistress.

"M'lady," she finally got up the courage to say, but Rebecca cut her off.

"This is the last time you will attend me, Anna. When you return downstairs, tell Betty that she will be my lady's maid beginning tomorrow morning, and you are to take over her duties." Betty was the scullery maid.

Rebecca's words had their intended effect, as Anna gave a cry and ran from the room. Whatever victory she had gained was cold consolation, for she was now bereft of the last shred of comfort she could hope for in that house.

Rebecca knew she had to leave, and had been making preparations with that intent since shutting herself in her chamber, wrapping in a woolen blanket what few possessions and bits of clothing she could carry on horseback. In truth, she had been preparing for this day for far longer, pondering how she might sneak from the house, steal a horse, and get away with no one noticing. The difficulty would be in the saddling of her horse, a task which had always been accomplished by a groom. With an eye to that problem, she had begun walking down to the stables to watch the process, rather than waiting at the house for the horse to be brought round, until she felt confident in the method and knew where to find her horse's tack.

The last preparation was to ensure that her husband would remain asleep as she stole away. After Anna left in tears, she poured a glass of brandy from a decanter Charles always had at the ready in her chamber. This was often her habit, as she hoped by this show of hospitality to soften his mood – a plan that seldom worked. On this night, however, she mixed in several drops of the medicine that remained from the stock the doctor had given her.

Of course Charles could not omit visiting her, not after she had shown such defiance at dinner. He swallowed his drink without a word, and Rebecca tried not to appear too pleased as he pushed her roughly onto the bed, treating her as brutally as ever. But she was prepared, and she endured it with all the fortitude of one who knew this would be the last such occurrence.

After he stumbled from the room, she put on her gabardine riding habit – awkwardly, as she was not used to dressing herself, and it was quite complicated – set her sturdiest boots by the door, and hauled the rolled blanket from beneath the bed. Then she sat and waited for the house to grow quiet.

She had just decided that everyone was asleep and she could make her escape when she heard the creak of a floorboard outside her door, and then the latch being turned. Could Charles have awakened from his drugged state? What would he do when he found her on the verge of fleeing? Perhaps he would murder her, and she couldn't help thinking of it as a blessing.

Slowly, the door creaked open.

CHAPTER SEVENTEEN

BUT IT was not her husband. The door opened and there stood Anna in her nightdress. She must have crept along the hall in the dark, because she bore no candle. She squinted at the light of the bedside lamp, barely glancing at Rebecca, then turned to close the door silently behind her.

"M'lady, I've come to – " She turned to face her mistress, then at last noticed the dress Rebecca wore. From this sight, her eyes went to the blanket roll on the bed, and from there to the boots by the door. She rushed at Rebecca, throwing herself at her mistress's feet and wrapping her arms about her skirts as a child might have. "No, m'lady, please, you cannot leave," she whispered. "I will die here without you. Or, if you do leave, you must take me with you. Oh, won't you forgive me?" And with that, she broke down in tears, burying her face in the folds of Rebecca's skirts.

Rebecca stared down at her honey-blond hair, at first struggling with too many conflicting emotions to speak. When at length she gained her voice, her first words were far from charitable. "And yet you lay with my husband, and he had a very satisfied air about him when he emerged from your quarters today."

"You must understand," she pleaded, "I have no choice, we are all of us in his power here in this house. And I must be sweet to him, or it goes much harder for me. You of all people must understand that." She continued to sob.

"Oh, Anna, you were my one friend and comfort, and now he's taken you away from me," Rebecca whispered, finding that she too was crying.

Anna stood up quickly. "Oh, no, m'lady. I am still here. I am still loyal and true, in my heart at least. My person is not my own, it belongs to his lordship, but I would give it all to you if I could."

With soft fingers, she smoothed away Rebecca's tears. Then she leaned up to kiss her, on the cheek at first, and then on the mouth.

"That was the first time we kissed," Rebecca remembered, "and I shuddered at the pleasure of it, her lips were so soft and sweet."

Rebecca's tears grew less and Anna drew back to look at her in the lamplight. "He hurt you again, didn't he?"

Rebecca could only nod, choking back a sob.

"Oh, m'lady, I would take all the hurt away, if I could." Then she was kissing Rebecca again, on the face and down her neck, unbuttoning the clasps of her jacket. She knelt before her once more, lifting her skirts this time and ducking under. Rebecca felt soft hands running up her legs to that sweet spot between them, and Anna's cheek pressing against her thigh. "Let me take the hurt away, m'lady," Anna pleaded with her.

And with that Anna began comforting her in a way she hadn't before, pushing Rebecca back onto the bed. "Soon she brought me to that brink of ecstasy where I had been before," Rebecca told me. "This time she did not stop there, but kept going until my whole body was wracked with uncontrollable shudders of delight, and I could not help but cry out in the sheer euphoria of it. I was glad I had given my husband that sedative."

Afterward, the lovers lay together for a time, stroking each other's hair and gazing into each other's eyes, trading little kisses on noses or cheeks or lips. Earlier, Rebecca had been in the greatest affliction, yet now she felt the greatest contentment. It hardly seemed possible.

"I reproached myself for doubting Anna," she said; "we were both my husband's victims; I should have treated her as a friend and ally, not as a competitor for my husband's attentions. I became conscious, too, that I was the one who had taken all the pleasure. Surely Anna needed the same comfort I had received from her. Suddenly all the differences in our station were stripped away, and we were just two women who needed the love and comfort the other could provide. She had comforted me out of love, not out of duty or service, I was sure of it. Should I not do the same for her?"

Yet Rebecca hardly knew how to begin. Without quite knowing what she was doing, she pressed herself against Anna, moving her hips back and forth against her lover's, who responded in kind.

"Here, let us get you out of that riding habit," Anna said, and Rebecca stood up and waited, not at all patiently, as Anna undid the pins and laces securing the gown and stays. Finally, the garments were off, and Rebecca stood there in nothing but a thin shift.

She could wait no longer, and pushed Anna back down on the bed, sliding on top of her and covering her face and neck with kisses. Now Rebecca's thrusting hips found greater purchase through the thin fabric of her shift and Anna's nightdress. But even this was not enough – she wanted nothing to separate them. She tugged at Anna's nightdress until it was over her head and off, and Anna did the same for her, and then they were rolling together, skin against skin, breast against breast, hips against hips, each seeking to enter the other. It was the greatest feeling Rebecca had ever had.

She had always been passive with her husband, lying back and enduring his poking for as long as it lasted. And even with Anna, she had passively received the pleasure that had been offered. But now Rebecca was in command, driving their pleasure forward with every thrust of her hips, feeling a thrill of power as she saw the effect this thrusting had on Anna, the little moans of ecstasy, the gasps of surprise and her eyes opening wide when Rebecca touched on a new spot, or when she put her hands under Anna's buttocks and lifted her yet closer.

"I took such a joy as I had never known in her looks of pleasure, the pleasure I was giving her," Rebecca said. "And she saw the joy in my face, returning it with a loving smile, which heightened my own pleasure all the more. And so the pleasure and the love passed back and forth between us until we shared that most intense moment of ecstasy, our bodies shuddering together as the waves of feeling crashed over us and brought us together in the most perfect union. Though I could not truly enter her in the way a man enters a woman, I felt I *had* entered her, body and soul, as she had entered me, more fully than Charles ever would. We were one. It was a greater spiritual union than that ordained by the pastor who stood before us at our wedding. Nay, I daresay it was as great as the strongest union between any married couple."

With this declaration, she turned to challenge me: "Now, dare you call it a sin?"

I had become so rapt in her story, my heart racing along with those of the lovers, that it took me a time to come back to myself and consider her question in a sober light. All the laws of God and Man would deem her a sinner. She had passed from mere instruction in how better to perform her marriage duties, to a full embrace of Sapphic love, and all outside the sanctity of marriage – though, since two women could not marry, I could not decide if this made it a greater sin or a lesser. She had harmed no one, but had so far only been harmed, and to a most shocking degree, by that man who called himself her husband, but who was no true husband at all. If she had any fault, it was in paying too much heed to the wishes of her father, and too little to those of her own heart – although, how filial duty could be called a fault was beyond me. No, all the fault lay with her beastly husband, whose far greater sin had driven Rebecca and Anna together. In the face of such cruelty, how could any love be called a sin, if it were true love, and not mere lust? If there was an error in my reasoning, I could not spot it.

Still, I felt that Rebecca's sympathetic story had led me somehow into error and so I must exert my independence of thought. "I would dare to declare anything a sin that my heart and conscience deemed to be so. Yet, given all you have told me, I cannot think you did wrong."

She smiled then, as if she guessed what I had not dared to admit: that the more scandalous parts of her story, especially those moments of intimate contact between the two, had excited such feelings in me that I found difficult to disguise beneath a composed exterior: palpitations of the heart, a rapid breath, a warmth in my face, and elsewhere. I tried to imagine Anthony provoking such feelings in me, and could not. Yet it was all too easy to imagine such feelings at the hands of the dashing, bold woman standing before me. All sense and rationality and considerations of virtue cried out against it, but there it was: my thoughts kept drifting back to those moments when we had touched, that strength I had felt in her as I rode behind her across the moor, her arm around me as we slept in Bath, the kiss we had just shared.

It was only with the greatest difficulty that I managed to keep a composed exterior as Rebecca went on with her story, a knowing smile playing across her face – that face which I had always found remarkably handsome.

"Lest you think it was all lust and sensual pleasure between us," she went on, "let me say that the sweetest feeling was yet to come, for after our exertions we lay in each other's arms, and that was the sweetest of all. No one had held me in that way in so long I couldn't remember, not since I rested in my mother's arms, and, as I said, she passed when I was but eight. It seemed that moment would go on forever, and we both wished it could be so; but at length we roused ourselves and considered what to do next."

Rebecca was for continuing with her plan, making their escape that very night, but Anna counselled against it. She was not prepared for such a sudden departure, and they were too likely to be caught.

Hearing the fear in her voice, Rebecca asked, "Anna, what is it you are afraid of? You mentioned earlier that you are all in my husband's power.

How is that so? Are you not free to seek other employment?"

Anna's eyes grew round, as if she had just discovered unknown depths of ignorance within her mistress, and struggled to compose an answer that would not offend. "Begging your pardon, m'lady," she said at last, "but such a choice is not much of a choice at all, even for most servants. I shouldn't expect a noblewoman such as yourself to understand or bother herself with such things." She paused as if this were sufficient explanation.

"Anna, you must tell me, I want to know," Rebecca encouraged her.

"The way it is for most servants, m'lady, is that situations in great houses are few and far between, especially here in the north country. Between situations, many are the servants who resort to crime to support themselves, prostitution for the girls and thievery for the men." Seeing the look on Rebecca's face, she paused before going on. "I didn't mean to shock you, m'lady, but it's the simple truth. The same is true for dressmakers. If you say a woman is a dressmaker in some parts, it's nearly the same as calling her a prostitute or a town-woman, since a dressmaker's income is hardly enough to provide a roof and food to eat. So there you have it: the girls who make your beds or sew your gowns were likely tumbling gentlemen at a half crown a go only recently."

"But their reputations," Rebecca protested, "their virtue, do these have no value?"

"Virtue is one thing, m'lady, having an empty belly is another."

"And you, Anna?" Rebecca could hardly meet her eye. "Have you ever had to resort to such – measures?"

Anna answered her mistress in a most challenging manner. "Not so far, but I ask you – is this so different?"

Rebecca couldn't say that it was. Indeed, she found herself wondering, was her own virtue any better? She had sold herself to a beast for a title and an estate and a life of luxury. It struck her then that all women sold themselves in one fashion or another, and that there was only a fine line between those who were sanctioned by God and King in that trade, and those who were not.

Anna went on. "But that is the situation for most servants. For us, Lord Aysgarth has us even more in his power. With the girls, you may have noticed we are all young. And he makes sure to gain his staff from distant parts, so that the hardship of getting back to our own villages and families is daunting in itself. Then he threatens us that if we leave he'll advertise back home what strumpets and harlots and thieves we are, so we'll never get a situation again.

"For the men, it's different. Either they owe something to his Lordship, or he knows their secrets, some crime they've committed. And so he threatens them with debtors' prison or the gallows. And he uses them to keep the girls in check, to prevent us from running away. You may have noticed that one or two of the rougher footmen always accompany the cook or any of us when we go to the village. That's to keep us from leaving. Oh, some have managed it, but others have been brought back, limping and bruised. It's not impossible to get away, but it's a great risk and most stay. So you can see, we must be careful when we make our escape."

The pair resolved to make plans when they could spare a moment together, and to look out for any opportunities of getting away, and then Anna took her leave, lest she be missed when the cooks began stirring in the servants' quarters.

THE LOVERS had no opportunity to further their plans before an eventuality arose that cast them all into doubt. Lord Aysgarth had always chided Rebecca for the disappointment she had been to him as a wife, not only for her ignorance in performing her bed duties and inability to produce an heir, but also for the size of the fortune she had brought into their marriage. Some might have considered twenty thousand pounds a large sum, yet it had only just covered the Baron's considerable gambling debts. Since then, his losses had only grown worse, to such an extent that the income from the estate could not possibly cover them. In light of this, his creditors had announced they would seize Swanford and all its productive lands at the end of the month. Aysgarth's lawyers could find no means of escape for him, as indeed, they themselves were owed substantial sums, and so deserted him to join his creditors.

Aysgarth now decreed that he would make a rapid removal to his ancient family seat, Kisdon Castle, in a remote part of the Yorkshire Dales, taking with him what few servants and bits of furniture his reduced income could support. All was completed with the greatest alacrity, but with the bustle of the removal, and with Aysgarth's footmen always on the lookout for servants escaping during the upheaval, Rebecca and Anna had no opportunity to pursue their plans.

At first, Rebecca had hoped that Anna would be relieved of her situation, and she even encouraged Anna to beg Aysgarth to set her free. Rebecca would make her escape when she could and meet her in York. But Anna would have none of this plan, insisting on remaining at Rebecca's side until they could escape together. As it happened, Anna was among those servants to be retained, along with the cook, the footmen, and the groomsman. Gone were all the chamber maids, scullery maids, and valets, along with Stevens, who had always been kind to Rebecca, now replaced by one of the thuggish footmen as head of the household.

The journey to Kisdon was a bleak one. The closer they came to their new abode, the more Rebecca doubted that they would ever escape such a desolate and remote spot, until her heart quite failed her. For hours after leaving the comforting confines of the dales, they travelled over dreary moors with scarcely a house in sight, a cold October wind whipping across the brown grass and stunted heather. At last their destination came in view, a misshapen, squarish pile of stone at the top of the moors, hard beneath a yet higher fell that formed the very backbone of this part of the country. To call it a castle would have been the height of charity; it was little more than a crude stone fortress whose moat had long since been filled in, its lone tower's tall, glassless windows peering like black eyes across the moors. A few years more and it would be listed in a travelers' guide to ancient ruins.

As the carriage approached, an old shepherd emerged from a crude lean-to built to one side of the house. He was dressed in what appeared to be rags, with a sheep's pelt thrown over his shoulders to protect from the harsh wind. "Welcome back, Master!" he greeted Aysgarth with a nearly toothless grin. Aysgarth descended from the carriage and surveyed his new domain for a moment before turning to the shepherd and questioning him closely about the number of sheep in the flock, the lambs that had survived since the spring, and the amount of wool that could be expected at the next shearing – for this, the produce of a single flock of sheep, along with what little could be grown at such heights, were to be the sole augmentation to the Baron's reduced income. As Rebecca descended, unassisted, from the carriage, she thanked providence that her father could not see her then, reduced to the state of a shepherd's wife, albeit one who dwelt in an ancient castle. Anna, alighting from the wagon in which the servants had ridden, gave her a mournful glance, then scurried with the rest for the cold shelter of that gloomy place.

Rebecca knew she would never last long there. No fire could warm those cavernous chambers, and no light brighten those silent, unforgiving halls. The stone walls took in all heat and light, reflecting none – more, they seemed to suck at the very life of Rebecca's soul. True, there were no ghosts about the place, no eerie sounds from an empty wing, no hidden door or passage, no drape that moved of its own accord, nor none of the other features that lent a feeling of foreboding to such places in gothic novels – only the grim desolation of the place itself and the presence of her tyrant of a husband. These were enough to make it a place of horror.

Sometimes, to escape her husband – for he was now always about, with few pursuits to occupy him and no gambling partners to visit him – she would sit in that single tower and look out on the moors and the fells, the wind making a doleful sound as it whistled past the glassless windows. How easy it would be, she thought, to simply walk out there in the night and let the cold and the wind end this misery! Yet every time she thought it, a fire of anger would kindle within her breast, and her heart would rebel at the injustice of it. She saw a different life ahead for Anna and herself. What kind of life it could be, she knew not, but anything must be better than this. To win that life, she must act boldly, not sit cowering in a bleak tower.

And so they concocted the only plan feasible in such a remote spot: they would steal out to the stables after midnight and take a single horse, riding double. They would carry what few possessions they could roll in a blanket tied to the saddle. This would take place a week past the full moon, giving them time to get away in full darkness, yet allowing the half-moon to light their way once it had risen. There was much that could go amiss in such a plan, but it was the best they could do.

Rebecca's hopes rose then, only to be betrayed by the very cold and loneliness of the place. One night, when the house was quiet, she felt Anna creeping into her bed. The irony was that they did nothing that night for which anyone could fault them. They merely clung together for warmth and comfort, and Rebecca could not blame Anna, for the servants' chambers were even colder than the rest of the castle, and Charles was stingy with the peat. They fell asleep that way. "Would that I had the sense to send Anna back to her own bed, or to the cook's if all she needed was a warm body! Another fortnight and we would have been free!"

Rebecca awoke in the middle of the night to see a black shape looming over the bed. She gasped, and that woke Anna, who gave a cry of fright, shrinking against her. The only light came from the embers of the dying peat fire, just enough to cast Charles in silhouette. Rebecca could not see his features, but she did not need to, as he stood there stiffly, clenching and unclenching his fists. Something had roused him and brought him there, though Rebecca could not imagine what that was. Nor did she know how he guessed at their true relationship – perhaps it was the way Anna cowered against her, seeking her protection.

But Rebecca could not protect her. He reached into the bed and dragged Anna out by the hair. "What is this whore doing in your bed?" he demanded. He forced her to her knees, twisting the shank of her hair as she begged his forgiveness. "What vile sins have you been practicing while my back was turned? I swear, this is the end, Rebecca. You've never satisfied me, and now I can be shut of you and get a wife that'll please me more." He gave another twist of Anna's hair and shook her like a doll.

Rebecca rushed to the grate not far from where Charles stood and took up a poker, turning on him and demanding that he release Anna.

He laughed for a moment. "Or what? You think you can hurt me with that stick?" Then he brought up short, jerking Anna to her feet by her hair. "So that's the way of it, eh? You love her, she's not just some plaything." He relaxed his grip on her, and Rebecca thought for a moment he would let her go. He looked at Anna, then back at Rebecca, and only then, too late, did Rebecca see the malevolent gleam in his eye, caught in the glow of the embers. Before she could move to interfere, he raised his fist and gave Anna a stout blow to the temple. That might have been enough to kill her outright, but the force of it sent her sprawling toward the grate. She was as limp as a rag doll and could not reach out to stop her fall. Her head hit the edge of the grate with a sickening crack, and she lay still.

"Anna!" Rebecca screamed, dropping the poker and rushing to her side, all fear of her husband forgotten. She gathered her lover in her arms and cradled her head, but felt only the warm stickiness of her blood. "Anna, oh, Anna!" she cried, rocking the limp form in her arms, but she felt no breath from those lips and no beating from that heart.

Meanwhile, Charles paced up and down, muttering to himself: "Now look what you've made me do! Damn her! Well rid of her!" and other such exclamations. Finally, he lit the bedside lamp and brought it over. "Here, out of the way," he grumbled, pushing Rebecca roughly aside. Now in the lamplight, Rebecca saw Anna's eyes open and staring, sightless, and saw too that her head had taken such a wound as no one could ever survive.

"How that blank look on Anna's sweet faced stayed with me for months and years after!" Rebecca exclaimed, breaking down in tears and throwing herself down beside me.

How could I not comfort my dearest friend when she was in such a state? I put my arm around her and she leaned her head on my shoulder, giving herself over to tears for a time. I had heard her recite speeches from plays, seen her put on a show of acting that night with Anthony, but this – this could not be an act, I was sure of it. If she was not genuinely moved at the memory of these horrendous events, then I was no judge of character.

After a time, she regained something of her composure, and sat up. "I'm sorry," she said, pulling a kerchief from a pocket and dabbing at her eyes. "I don't know what came over me, only that it has been long since I have let myself dwell on that terrible night." If this was a ruse, she seemed abashed at showing me a woman's weakness. Straightening her shoulders, she went on with her story, though now in a more subdued voice.

"Now this is a fine mess," Charles said, gazing down at Anna as if one of the servants had spilled a pot of tea. "Ah, well, there's nothing for it," he went on, ignoring Rebecca's sobbing.

"I should have done for him then," Rebecca told me. "The poker was near at hand, and he was preoccupied with the task of removing a sheet from the bed and wrapping Anna's body in it."

But she could do nothing, so overcome was she by shock and grief, especially as the sheet went unceremoniously over Anna's face, and she realized she would never look on her friend and lover again. Her sobbing grew less, and she could only sit there on the floor, absorbed within herself, as Charles lifted the body, wrapped in its white shroud.

"I'll bury her," he said roughly. "You clean up this mess. We'll tell the others she ran away during the night."

He left the room and Rebecca gave herself over to grief. She thought for a moment to walk out on the moors and let the cold put an end to her sorrow; if she could not be with Anna in life, she would be with her in death. But no, that was just a romantic notion, and Rebecca harbored no illusions of seeing Anna on the other side of that great divide. Then shortly, as before, a spark of something else was kindled within her, a rage against her circumstances and a will to live beyond them. Anna was gone, and Rebecca's death would not bring her back. Nothing would, yet there was one thing she could still do for Anna and for herself.

"My husband had already taken much from me – my fortune, my virtue, and my hopes for a secure life. But now he'd taken the one thing I truly cared for, my only friend and companion in the world. I resolved that never again would I be a victim. And the end of my victimhood would begin with Charles."

A calm settled over her then. She had time, because the ground was frozen, and it would be long before Charles could bury Anna so deep no one would ever find her. She went to the bed and pulled the rolled blanket from beneath it, still ready for a quick departure. She put on her riding habit and boots. Then she went to Charles' room, a place where she rarely ventured, though she knew the place where he kept his money, all that he had managed to hide from his creditors, in a locked chest. Breaking the lock was her most dangerous moment; the servants were well used to screams and thumps in the night, but an unexplained clanking coming from the master's chamber could rouse them. At length the chest was open and Rebecca grasped all the gold coins and notes within, placing them in a pocket of her riding habit.

She went downstairs to the castle's great hall, placing the rolled blanket under a divan. She built up the fire, knowing this would draw Charles in when he returned from the cold. From above the fireplace, she took down one of the two rapiers placed there, crossed, over an ancient shield bearing the family's crest. That same crest was engraved in the hilt of the sword. She felt the edge and the point, glad to find them both sharp. She wrapped a shawl about herself, hiding the rapier under it, and sat down to wait, struggling to calm her beating heart for the task ahead, thinking only of Anna, and what she must do.

At last Charles returned from his grim task. As Rebecca had guessed, the fire drew him in; she could only hope he didn't notice the missing sword in the dim light. He said nothing, but went to warm himself by the blaze for a moment. Then, as she had guessed he would, he moved to the sideboard and poured himself a tall glass of gin, brandy being too expensive in his reduced circumstances. He downed it in one gulp. Still he said nothing as he poured himself a second drink, exactly as she had predicted.

"Did you clean up that mess?" he asked, pouring himself a third drink. She did not answer, nor did he notice as she stood up, balling the shawl into a bunch in her left hand, the rapier held in her right. He finished his third drink, then turned to face his wife. "Well – ?"

She threw the shawl in his face, by this means putting him off balance for a moment as he instinctively lifted his hands to catch it. Seizing her one and only chance, she lunged at him, plunging the rapier into his belly, just below the ribcage. His hands came down on the blade, all tangled in the shawl, his face twisted with disbelief and growing fear. He struggled to push the blade out of his belly, but it was no use – the harder he gripped the blade, the more he cut his hands. She pushed it in harder, twisting against the pressure of his hands, until he gave a gurgling gasp. His eyes took on that same empty gaze that Anna's had worn, and she knew he could hurt her no more. She slipped the sword out of him as he fell to the floor.

"Looking down at him," she said to me now, "I felt the power of what I had just done. I felt then that power is the only thing that matters in life, and I vowed to myself, never again would I be without it." Her eyes blazed bright as she said it, showing not a hint of remorse.

CHAPTER EIGHTEEN

AFTER HEARING such a shocking tale, it was only with the greatest difficulty that I could maintain my equanimity. Should I stay to hear the conclusion of her story, or did honor demand that I leave at once? For her part, Rebecca now seemed lost in reflecting on the past.

Could it be true? Had this woman, who always seemed so gentle, really have committed such a cold-blooded murder? And if she had, could I blame her for it, after all her husband's brutality and the murder of Anna? He had received the justice he deserved, I had no doubt – I doubted only that Rebecca should have been the one to deliver it.

Now, having recovered myself somewhat, I was able to consider her story more dispassionately. Several of its points seemed hard to credit. Could any man, no matter of what rank, treat his wife with such brutality and expect to escape punishment, or at least censure? Would a houseful of servants truly submit to treatment as little better than prisoners? That grim castle, like something out of a gothic tale – it lacked only ghosts and hidden passages to make the effect complete. And a young woman of good breeding taking up arms against her husband, and succeeding in his murder – it was the most fantastical of all. Could it all be an invention meant to gain my sympathy?

Yet the expressiveness and earnestness with which she talked of Anna and the grief at her loss – they had all bespoken feelings truly felt. And this was my dearest friend. If I judged her as untrustworthy, then I must distrust my judgment in all things. Then again, I now knew without a doubt that she was the highwayman, and she seemed quite a different person in that garb. Who knew what she was capable of doing in that guise, and what other heinous acts she had committed?

Now Rebecca recovered from her own contemplations and took my hand, looking me in the eye. "You see how you have undone me, for despite my pledge that day, I have placed myself in your power. You now know not only that I am a highwayman, but that I am wanted for murder."

"Why would you risk it?"

"I have asked myself that very question since I first saw you in the Earl's carriage." She reached out for a curl of my hair and wound it around her finger. "Of course, there is your pretty face framed by those black ringlets escaping your bonnet, and your striking figure, which was shown to such good effect in the gown you wore that day. But that cannot be all of it. No, it was the way you spoke so boldly to me in defense of your mother's necklace. And then you slapped me for my effrontery! Your spirit and courage captivated me. I saw in you a kindred soul, one not meant for the cages of genteel society. And everything I have learned of you since only proves me right. I see you chafe at the limits this circumscribed country life places upon you. I see your mind and your heart and your body yearning for more."

"You overstep your bounds, ma'am," I said, rising to my feet and moving away. "You cannot know my inmost desires."

"I know enough that I would prevent my own fate from befalling you."

"Pshaw! No gentleman whom I could ever consider marrying would treat me as Lord Aysgarth treated you. Certainly Anthony would not."

"No, I daresay you're right, but you know my thoughts on that score. Now come, you've only heard half my story."

As great as my doubts were, I had to stay to know the rest of her tale, to hear how she had gone from the wretched creature of her husband to become the bold, self-confident woman standing before me. I returned to my seat, and she continued her narration.

REBECCA HARDLY knew how she made her way out of the house and to the stable, saddling her horse without waking the groom. But soon she was riding away, swallowed by the blackness of a moonless night.

Like many another unfortunate soul, she found herself swept along to London, that great receptacle of the sweepings of the world. With news of her husband's murder beginning to spread, and along with it, the announcement of a reward for any who could discover Lady Aysgarth's whereabouts, she hoped to hide herself amongst the city's multitudes.

And multitudes she found. At first she was drawn naturally to those neighborhoods she had frequented when accompanied by her governess: Mayfair and Portman Square, where members of that rank of society that called itself simply "the World" had their townhomes. Yet a perusal of *The Sun* and other newspapers convinced her that any lodging amongst the ranks of the *bon ton* were far beyond her means. Thus she was pulled inexorably east, past Covent Garden, where men of the City and the rich on their way to the theatre mixed with the poor and the destitute, who filled every mews and lane off the main thoroughfares. The farther east one went, the more varied the populace became: sailors from all over the world, seasonal Irish laborers turned permanent residents, freed blacks from America, remnants of the Huguenot immigration, Polish and German Jews who had fled oppression in those countries, mixed in with English country-folk pushed off the land by the enclosures. All of these strove side-by-side for the few means of making a living – dock work, foundry work, weaving, tanning, flower-selling – in hopes of perhaps saving enough one day to open a print shop or a cobbler's workshop. Failing these, or if the ever-present lure of gambling, gin-shops, and town-women proved too tempting, many fell into those professions outside the bounds of the law. And, everywhere she went, like a grim reminder of her likely fate, women hawked their own persons on the streets, boldly placing themselves before any male passerby.

With an eye to stretching her gold, she took a room over the Hammer & Loom Tavern east of Drury Lane. It was a rough place, frequented by sharps and town-women, with a proprietor who made as much fencing stolen items as from selling drinks. Yet it was far from the roughest she had seen, and there was something safe about it. Perhaps she had grown used to sensing her husband's violent moods, and she felt nothing of that violence here.

She set about discovering how she might make her way in the world. She bought one or two cheap, plain gowns and affected a coarser speech in order to fit in with the Hammer & Loom's inhabitants. She found she excelled in playing a role to suit the occasion, passing herself off as a servant girl who had lost her situation in the north, and was on the lookout for another means to get her living. The women of the town gave her knowing looks, certain she would be one of them as soon as her money ran out, yet she was determined. It was not long before she began to learn the different ways of speaking and behaving among these people, and she soon knew the difference between a queer cove and a harminbeck. In that tavern, she came to know that world of vagabonds, wastrels, thieves, pawnbrokers, fences, usurers, and prostitutes that we in genteel society learn of only in sermons, novels, or perhaps in charitable visits to almshouses.

"To be sure," Rebecca told me, "there was depravity and dissolution and a scant respect for the law, but there was also a spirit of independence among these people, a moral code of sorts, a curious sort of camaraderie, and a freer style of living than I had ever known, one devoid of all our artificial restraints of rank and propriety."

"And did you not think of taking up honest work?" I asked.

"Most certainly. But looking around me, what did I see? Some women earned a few shillings a week running spinning jennies, which would barely cover my room, mean as it was. Some worked as servants, but as I had no means of obtaining references, such situations were closed to me, as was any other position for a respectable woman of good breeding and education, such as a governess. Others sold flowers or oysters on the street, but usually as a cover for selling themselves. Many looked to marry themselves off to a laborer or a sailor, but I had already been down that road, and would not do it again. None of these offered escape from the powerlessness I would no longer endure."

She soon learned much of the various ways of relieving the well-to-do of their extra cash and surplus possessions. Just as the victual trade had its butchers, bakers, fishmongers, and green-grocers, so too did the criminal class, with pickpockets, house-breakers, footpads, coiners, and fences, each with their own apprenticeships, methods, and ranks. At the top were the highwaymen, squiring courtesans about in their fancy coats and spending most of their ill-gotten earnings on their lavish lifestyles or at the gambling tables. The denizens of the H&L seldom saw them, for they held themselves apart from the rest of the rabble, styling themselves gentlemen, as if they were part of the *ton*, their stories legend among the lesser criminals.

Fewer options were available for the fairer sex, yet even the town-women spent more of their time relieving men of their purses than in trading their bodies for coin. Quicker and cleaner to dose a cully's drink, or clobber him with a sap while his breeches were down, than to provide the service he came to the rougher part of town to find. Beyond the prostitutes, there were few other options: playing the damsel in distress rescued by a passing gentleman, providing a comely distraction for the marks of the card sharps, or the jilting game, flirting with a gentleman just enough to lure him into a dark alley where male accomplices waited.

Apart from the violence often associated with these trades, she was most disturbed by the criminals' propensity to prey not on the wealthy, but on the hard-working denizens of those same neighborhoods the criminals inhabited. Shop-keepers, artisans, craftsmen — any who had just barely risen above the lot of the common laborer were vulnerable to having their modest wealth spirited away by a house-breaker or beaten out of them by a footpad. She vowed that she would confine herself to those for whom a stolen purse or a few pieces of jewelry could hardly be missed. A murderess and ruined woman she might be, but she would cling to what shreds of honor she still had.

Thus it was to the jilting game that Rebecca applied herself, as it seemed to involve the least risk to her person and her virtue – or what remained of it. At the same time, it would allow her to select the targets, called flats in the rogues' cant, ensuring they would be men of a certain wealth. She joined with a pair of toughs, Tom and Red Jack, who recognized her skill at mimicking the tones of a gentlewoman and thought her youth and pleasant looks would attract the right sort of gentleman or man of trade. They bought her a stylish yet respectable dress that would allow her to frequent the tea gardens and coffeehouses that men patronized when they weren't necessarily seeking carnal pleasure. "You'll turn their heads, lass," said Red Jack, "and then just bring one with a nice fat purse on a walk past Titus Alley. It'll be easy as pie."

Yet in this world there was always danger, especially for a woman. Mary, one of the older women who functioned as something of a madam and mother-hen to the younger girls of the H&L, took Rebecca aside and schooled her in the ways of protecting herself, showing her the type of small dagger easily hidden up a long sleeve or in a boot, and the tricks of using it. "Most men, seeing a lass with a blade," Mary said, "will soon decide to pursue a less chancy target. But just remember, dearie, once you've drawn it, you must be prepared to use it, and it will end in a mess. And by no means must you let it be ta'en from you." Rebecca heeded her words, and practiced the moves she had been shown in her small room.

At first, the game went well, and the flats were easy to find. There was always at least one man of wealth willing to strike up a conversation, looking past – or perhaps encouraged by – the impropriety of a woman taking tea alone in a coffeehouse. When they heard she was a war widow of some standing and means, they were all too willing to escort her to her door. They were so preoccupied by the frequent smiles and glances she gave them as they walked, and by the flirting conversation she contrived, that they hardly noticed as they passed into the rougher parts of the city. The only difficulty came as a result of the gentlemen's polite habit of giving a lady the wall, to avoid her dress being splattered by passing wagons or filth falling from above. When they arrived at the alley, Rebecca had to stop and then shift around so that Tom and Jack had a clear path to the flat. In a flash, the fellow was unconscious in the alley, and they were headed back to the H&L, arguing over how best to divide his purse and valuables.

Here Rebecca broke off her story. "Oh, Lizzie, I have learned over these weeks to read you well. Despite that cool mask of composure you've put on, I can see this offends you."

"How could it not? To so easily fall into a life of crime! And those poor men!"

"And what did you think was their purpose in escorting me home? Just doing their good deed for the day? It is true, I did encounter one or two gentlemen of real worth who truly seemed to be acting as good Samaritans, and these I led by another way, having them leave me at a respectable door. But the rest soon revealed themselves as interested in one thing only. Well they knew that they were taking advantage of a desperate woman, but one perhaps less likely to give them the pox than a common doxy. For them, I had no remorse. Many of them must have had wives and children, and I viewed our efforts as inducements to avoid such adulterous liaisons in future."

"It seems you always have some excuse for your crimes. Yet whatever wrongs these men may have intended, they do not make your actions any less reprehensible."

Rebecca bowed her head. "It is true, this was near to my lowest point, and I could hardly think of anything other than my own survival. It was with great effort that I spared those few men who seemed worthy. I hoped only to keep what shreds of honor remained to me, while staying true to my vow that never again would I be without power. I ask you, what choice did I have? "

I shook my head, knowing not what to say.

"I told you to withhold your pity, for in the end I have done much that makes me unworthy even of that. But I ask you to withhold your judgment as well, until you have heard all."

I nodded and she went on.

Weeks went by without incident, and the trio had performed the trick perhaps a dozen times. At Rebecca's suggestion, they always shifted from one coffeehouse or teagarden to another to avoid suspicion. Then one job went wrong. The mark was already growing nervous as he and Rebecca approached the alley, the coffeehouse she had chosen being far from that part of town. Then when she stopped in front of the alley and did her little dance to get out of the way – no Tom and no Jack!

"Pardon me, sir!" she exclaimed to cover her odd behavior. "I left my reticule at the coffeehouse. I must return to get it."

The fellow came to his senses and took in his surroundings, his confusion turning to anger. "What kind of chase is this you've led me on?"

When Rebecca made to walk past him, as if heading back to the coffeehouse, he took hold of her arm. "I didn't walk all this way and listen to all your flirting for nothing," he said, then she was the one being dragged into the alley. Soon he had her up against a wall and was trying to lift her skirts.

"Oh, sir," she breathed at him in what she meant to be an enticing voice, running her hand up his thigh as she spoke, "let us return to my rooms, where we may properly enjoy each other."

That made him hesitate, but only for a moment. Then he lifted her skirts higher and said, "I'll have you now and be done with you, you filthy doxy."

In running her hand along his leg, she had gotten the blade into the palm of her hand and now moved it to the inside, pressing the point near his manhood. He froze.

"I don't mean to harm you, sir, but you *will* unhand me," she hissed at him.

He did unhand her, shoving her away and stepping back. She did as Mary had instructed, keeping a tight grip on the blade and turning to face him. He glared at her for a moment, then straightened his cravat, turned about, and walked briskly from the alley as if on an important errand. She departed in the other direction, her nerves shaken.

Back at the tavern, she found Jack and Tom sitting with half-empty mugs of ale. They had grown tired of waiting for her and decided she hadn't found a mark. "I told you louts," she exclaimed, "the coffeehouse was farther out than the rest, and it might take me some time to bring the flat to you!"

The argument became heated, and soon Jack was on his feet and yelling, but Rebecca would not back down. If they were to work as a team, she needed to know she could trust them.

"I may have slipped into my normal accent," Rebecca told me now, "sounding like my mother sometimes had when dealing with the servants."

For that, Jack struck her a blow across the cheek that sent her reeling into a table. "I won't be bossed by a mere lass, no matter how high and mighty you sound," he said.

"Ah, Jack," said Tom. "Now look what you've done! How's she supposed to lure the lordlings in now?" While they fell to arguing, Rebecca took herself to her room to nurse her wounds.

The next fortnight was not easy. She had saved enough from the take to get by while the bruise on her cheek healed, but she felt as penned up as a pigeon in a coop. When her room became too confining, she spent her time in the tavern below, where the working women stared at her with greater suspicion than usual. One evening, when a group of them were fortifying themselves for the night's trade, Sarah, a girl not much older than Rebecca who had grown up in the neighborhood, looked over in her direction. "Then there's tha' un, who thinks she's better'n the lot of us." Her companions gave murmurs of assent.

"What d'you mean?" Rebecca asked innocently.

"Look at you, in your fine gown and your fancy accents. Too good to stoop to whoring. Least we give honest service for our money, so don't you go thinking you're any better."

"I don't think I'm better than you. I know that all women sell themselves to men, in one way or another. It's only that I sold myself to a man once, and I cannot do it again." She told them a changed version of the events at Swanford, putting herself in Anna's place. "He used me horribly and I had to run. I knew I wouldn't get another situation like that. That's why I've stooped to thievery."

"Ah, poor babe," Sarah replied. "Listen, there's none of us but 'asn't got a story just like it. Yet we do what we 'ave to, and you don't see us complaining. It's women's lot is all, and the sooner you learn it, the better."

Rebecca didn't know what to say to this.

Mary stepped in then, coming over to put a hand on her shoulder. "Ah, don't listen to her, sweetheart. Anyone can see you *are* better than us. You're younger, an' you're prettier. I don't know where you get those accents from, but it's plain to see there's something of quality about you. It would be easy to get yourself a couple of young gentlemen, maybe ones fixin' to be married off to very proper young ladies, ones who'll need someone to show 'em real pleasure they won't get at home. Have 'em set you up in apartments, shower you with jewels, take you to their masked balls – it could be a nice life. So cheer up, sweetie, there's fortune ahead for you, if you know how to take it." With that, she gave Rebecca a motherly kiss on the top of the head, and she and the rest of the women of the town left her to ponder her future.

As comforting as Mary had been, it was Sarah's words that rang true. It did seem that a woman's lot was always to be under the thumb of a man. No, Rebecca decided, there could be only one solution to the powerlessness inherent in womanhood – to cease being a woman altogether. It was the next week when she learned how that might be achieved.

CHAPTER NINETEEN

REBECCA SIPPED her tea, pretending to enjoy the view of Berkeley Square outside the Pot and Pineapple Tea Shop, but in reality surveying the crowd for a likely flat. She had chosen this tea room as it seemed a finer establishment in which to encounter a finer sort of gentleman. To shorten the walk, Jack and Tom were waiting in an alley closer to Covent Garden.

Instead of spotting her mark, however, the mark spotted her – or rather, his sister did. A finely dressed young lady of about Rebecca's age approached her table and asked if she would like to join her and her brother over a plate of tea cakes they had just ordered. She pointed to a delicate gentleman a few years older, dressed in an equally stylish fashion. "No one should spend one minute alone during London's gay season," said the girl, who introduced herself as Miss Seaforth. Sensing the possibilities, Rebecca quickly agreed, and was then introduced to the brother.

After an hour of pleasant conversation, during which Rebecca discovered that Miss Seaforth was in town for her first season and her brother was generously escorting her to balls and musical evenings, the young lady startled at the lateness of the hour and offered Rebecca a ride home in their chaise, if it were in the same direction. Sadly, it was not, and as Miss Seaforth really must see to her toilette for a ball that night, she suggested that Mr. Seaforth walk Rebecca home. Rebecca easily overlooked the impropriety of this plan, so neatly did it fit with her own.

The game seemed less likely of success as they walked eastward, for she could not use her usual ruses to distract her companion from the increasingly rough nature of the neighborhood. Feeling her normal flirtatious manner would offer too great a contrast to her former demeanor at the teashop, she inquired instead about Mr. Seaforth's preoccupations, whether he liked the country or the town, sports afield or attending plays. Though the gentleman replied courteously enough, he seemed nervous, or perhaps merely frustrated, glancing back and forth at each new sign of their descent into London's poorer neighborhoods, all the while rapping the ferrule of his walking stick stoutly on the pavement.

At last, half a mile from the appointed alley, he brought up short and regarded Rebecca with a quizzical gaze. "Mrs. Burgess, I am compelled to ask, what sort of game are you playing at?"

"What do you mean?" she returned, adopting a show of surprise.

"Come now, no widow on a captain's pension would find it necessary to live in such mean parts." He no longer seemed nervous, but almost calm, even amused.

"How could you know that?"

"It is my business to know. So what's your game? Did you have a couple of toughs lying in wait farther along, ready to jump out and rob me?"

"Mr. Seaforth, I do not know where you have gotten this idea, but you are mistaken!"

"Please, call me Will," he said, "for there is no need for pretense or formality between us. You are not the only one with a game to play." He smiled at her as if they were both in on the same joke.

"Why? What game are *you* playing?"

"You cannot guess?"

When Rebecca shook her head, he took her hand and drew her to him until their faces were inches apart, Mr. Seaforth holding Rebecca's hand to his cheek. Even through her glove, she found it as smooth as a boy's. From experience with her husband, she knew that men's cheeks, even when close-shaven and not scratchy with a three-days' stubble, bore some trace of whiskers just below the skin, not to mention nicks and a certain rawness from the passage of the razor. Yet this gentleman's cheek had none of these, feeling instead as if a razor had never been near it. Up close, Rebecca could detect a fine, almost transparent down along his jaw.

"You're a woman!" she exclaimed.

"Oh, well spotted." He regarded her with that same quizzical look in his calm, grey eyes. "Or, that is, I was born a girl, but always felt myself to be more of a boy, and since my teenage years I have lived as a man."

"So that's your game, passing as a man?"

"No, that is no game, for it is what I am," he said (and here Rebecca pointed out that Will always insisted on being addressed as a man, even by those who knew his secret).

"Then what is it?"

"Why, wooing well-to-do young women with a romantic bent, especially those who dream of being swept off their feet by a handsome stranger. It's remarkably easy to relieve them of their gold." Here he held Rebecca's wrist to his lips, placing kisses along it while holding her gaze to see what effect this ministration would have. His other arm went around her waist and drew her to him. She felt herself melting in that same way she had with Anna, and gave a sigh. "Ah, so you are not immune to my charms? I confess I was disappointed when I realized you were not the lonely widow you appeared to be, but one has to laugh at the humor of the situation. And perhaps it has possibilities. It's too long since I've had a lover who could appreciate me as I am. Fanny grew tired of me long ago."

"But she is your sister!"

"Oh, heavens, no! I may be a flagrant tommy, but I wouldn't commit incest." He leaned over and kissed the base of Rebecca's neck. "Have no fear. We're still the best of friends and she won't be jealous a bit."

"How can I be certain you won't treat me as one of your marks?"

"Our game is nothing so rough as yours. I capture their hearts and convince them to run away with me, carrying with them a generous portion of the family silver. I've even married them, with their parents' best wishes and their dowries. But now that I've revealed my secret to you, the game is over."

"But the wedding night!" Rebecca protested. "Surely then you are found out?"

"I promise you, save for fathering a child, I can fulfil my bed duties quite capably." Then he kissed Rebecca boldly on the mouth. "Come to my apartments and I'll show you."

Rebecca pulled away. "No! I'd rather you showed me how I too may become a man."

Then it was Will's turn to show surprise. When he had recollected himself, he looked her up and down. "So you want to play the breeches part? Yes, I can see it. You're tall enough, and not too many curves to hide. But why? You make a far better girl than I ever did."

"It is a long tale, but I wish no longer to suffer as a woman at the hands of men."

"You can tell it to me on the way, then," he said, and they set off for Will's apartments in Marylebone.

And so it was that Rebecca fell under Will's tutelage, learning how to dress as a man, carry herself as a man, and to lower her voice to the pitch and timbre of a man's. On her next job with Jack and Tom, she took care to pick a flat of about her height and girth, and not too finely dressed. Once he was knocked senseless, she had them strip him of his clothes as well as his valuables.

Wearing men's dress in public for the first time, she found that people saw what they wanted to see and heard what they wanted to hear. Perhaps her voice wasn't as low and rough as most men's, and her looks not so masculine, but in the right clothes and with her hair bobbed and covered with a man's wig, no one on the street or in the shops took her for anything other than one of the rougher sex.

She reveled in her new freedom, finding she could move with greater ease when no longer confined by stays, a narrow gown and petticoat, or the impediment of thin slippers. Instead, she could walk freely about in boots and breeches. She could even run, if she had a mind, something she hadn't done in years, or climb walls – all skills that could prove useful, as she wanted to leave the jilting game behind. Many were the places she could now go, where she hadn't been able to before, unless escorted by a man: public houses, tobacconists, stables, card parlors, the docks to watch ships come in. She wondered at her former tolerance for the confined life of a fine young lady.

The denizens of the H&L recognized her, of course. "What's this get up, then, Rebecca?" Mary asked her the first time she appeared before them. The tavern was crowded, but it went silent at Mary's remark.

"Please, call me Robin from now on," she said. "And treat me as a man when I am dressed this way, especially when strangers are about."

"Right then," Mary said, speaking for the crowd. "You're not the first, and who can blame you? Lord knows it's not easy living as a woman in these parts." Aye, most chimed in, though some of the other girls gave her jealous looks.

Tom and Jack were not so easily appeased. "What are we supposed to do, eh?" Jack asked.

"I can still dress as a woman for our jobs," Rebecca said, "but I'm looking for a different kind of game, one that doesn't involve brutes beating up the flats. Tell me, why should I include you in my plans after the way you treated me?"

"You see, Jack?" Tom said. "I told you, you never should've treated her rough." Jack stood there looking contrite.

"There is one way you can make it up to me – teach me how to fight. If

I am to live as a man, I must know how to defend myself as a man."

Over the next weeks, Tom and Jack obliged her, showing her all the lowest tricks of street-fighting, whether with a knife, a sap, bare fists, or by means of grappling. Robin, as they now called her, proved an apt student, lacking the strength of many men, but with a good reach, considerable quickness, and surprising endurance. "Wear a lout down, and then you'll have 'im," Jack said, panting, after one particularly long bout.

They acquired a brace of pistols for her, and the trio took the coach west toward Reading to practice shooting in the country. In a matter of hours she had learned the mechanics of loading and priming and had developed a good aim.

At last, she showed them her husband's rapier, which she had brought with her from the north. "Now I want to learn how to use this," she told them.

"Bit old fashioned, that," Tom said. "Not much call for them on the street, and even the fine gentlemen are wearing their smallswords less these days." Robin, however, remembered her brother receiving fencing lessons, and insisted, feeling that her own education in the martial arts would be incomplete without it. "We'll teach you some backswording then, but not with that thing. No one wants to get cut." They practiced with wooden cudgels, engaging in the rough sort of melee common to the lower classes that would have made the Italian fencing masters laugh in scorn.

One morning, as Robin and Will lay together in bed – they had become lovers, Will showing Robin those means by which he had made a convincing man on the wedding night, giving her a type of pleasure she had never experienced with Anna – Will expressed regret at teaching her the ways of playing a man. "For surely now you will want to go into competition with me," he said, stroking Robin's brown hair. "And while naive, romantic young girls and lonely widows are a shilling a dozen, those with gullible parents and portable treasure are not."

"You mistake me," Robin replied. "It's all very well for you to prey on the fairer sex, but for myself, having been one of those girls who fell victim to the wiles and greed of a man, I cannot do it."

"What will you do then? You've said you want no more of knocking men over the head."

The answer came the next time they went out walking together on the streets near Will's apartments. "Pair o' mollies," they heard a man say in a low voice to a companion as they walked past.

Will stopped. "So that's what they think, is it?" He regarded Robin for a long moment. "Yes, I can see it. You'd be quite the lure for a nobleman or wealthy man of trade with a taste for boys. And sodomy is a capital offense, or at the very least, the cause of lost reputations. It has its possibilities."

They hit on a plan for Robin to relieve the wealthy of their gold without resort to violence. With the last of the money from her work with Tom and Jack, she rented apartments near the Vauxhall Pleasure Gardens, where people of all ranks paraded in the evening, indulging in all manner of salacious activity on its Dark Walks, the shrubbery providing excellent cover. She could always sense when a gentleman looked at her in just that way, and when he began to follow her. A quick duck into a dark corner, a hand on the crotch, another at the back of the neck, and a whisper in the ear: "We'll have a much better time at my apartments, my lord, if you'll just follow me. It's not far." Upon arriving at the dimly lit lodging, she let the gentleman take the lead, not letting the proceedings get too far before signaling to Tom and Jack, who would jump out from an empty wardrobe, grasping the mark and searching his pockets for a calling card.

"As far as I'm concerned," Robin would say, "I invited you here for brandy and a pipe, and then you accosted my person with the intent of sodomy. It's certainly a good thing I had friends to hand. You might deny it at court, but think of the scandal, even if the magistrate believed you. Much better to pay us and avoid the trouble." Then they would negotiate terms, the flats having their choice of paying a series of regular small sums or a single large one.

"In truth," Rebecca said to me, "that was my lowest point, for if our former victims perhaps deserved their treatment, these were guilty of nothing other than seeking a mutual pleasure deemed sinful by society. Yet how could I blame them, when I was not so different?"

She paused, fidgeting with the kerchief in her hands, her cheeks coloring. "And here is where I must explain my behavior after the concert. That lout's pawing hand and the brandy on his breath, it brought back those days and the things I had to let the flats do to lure them in – the pawing and the groping, the fingers at the buttons of my breeches, before Tom and Jack would pull them off me. Then too, he reminded me of my husband. It has been long since I have known such fear and debasement. I wanted only to run away from Anthony and his friends, but I felt trapped in my woman's gown and dainty shoes, and besides, how would it have looked? So I reacted out of reflex, pulling an old trick I had learned from a pickpocket I once knew. And then I was even more out of my head with fear that you had finally guessed my secret. You saw how I was, I know you did. The fear made me wild and I lashed out at Anthony, and at you, for I thought I had already lost you. Please, tell me you understand?"

"I believe I do," was all I could say, though in truth my thoughts were travelling in circles, trying to sort the real Rebecca from all the different versions she had presented to me thus far.

In a matter of weeks the trio had so many accounts they had trouble keeping track of them, and more money than they knew how to spend. Robin bought a good coat of burgundy velvet for herself, and a French cocked hat she adorned with a tall feather. The only other things she would spend money on were a book now and again, Radcliffe or Burney, Paine or Wollstonecraft; or perhaps a night at the theatre, seeing Dora Jordan play a breeches part at the new Drury Lane, while she played her own breeches part in the stalls. She frequented The Hive of Liberty bookshop and radical coffeehouses, listening to the political talk and contributing her own ideas as she became familiar with the world of reformers and revolutionaries.

To atone for her guilt over the treatment of their cullies, she began to think how to use her newfound power for something other than lining her own purse. With far more money than she could ever spend on clothes, books, or plays, she set about helping those who had faced as much misfortune as she, lending money to the poor of the neighborhood with no expectation of repayment, satisfying others' debts, or paying for doctors and medicine for ailing children. She even helped keep order by aiding particularly undeserving victims of crime, reclaiming their stolen goods from criminals less selective in their targets than she. Soon she was known from Covent Garden to the East End as Lord Rob, and children would flock in her footsteps, expecting handouts of pennies or candies. "Lord Rob! Lord Rob!" they would squeal when they saw her.

"That was a good time," Rebecca said. "I had never felt so free. I had money enough to feel secure for a time; passing as a man, I felt I had the world at my feet. I would walk boldly about London and feel that I owned the city. My upbringing had been comfortable and secure enough, but so narrow that I had no notion of how the world actually worked. Despite all our notions of nobility, chivalry, and the proper roles of gentlemen and ladies, the only ones who kept to these ideals were those of our class, the lesser nobility and the landed gentry, for our positions were so tenuous that we must adhere to the utmost propriety. For the upper nobility, however, those like my husband, these were a mere tissue of lies, to be thrown away at the whims of lust, greed, or power."

"Yet surely the nobility play a role in anchoring our society, and contribute much to its defense," I protested.

"Yes, if assigning second or third sons to the Navy to lord over press-ganged sailors can be called a significant contribution. And in exchange, they siphon off the wealth of the nation for their decadent style of living. Meanwhile, I came to see that many of the poor become so through no fault of their own. Many among the dregs of London want nothing more than to work the land as their fathers and grandfathers did, but they cannot, for the lords have enclosed the land and driven them into the cities, where they face at best a mean existence in the factories, or if not into the cities, then into the mines, where few live to see old age. And what recourse have they, other than the riot, as the government is in the corrupt hands of the lords? You make a great mistake in seeking to marry into that cesspool of iniquity."

I was nonplussed. "Where did you get such ideas? England wants none of France's revolutionary fervor."

"The City was seething with unrest at that time, before Pitt's Gagging Acts robbed us of our liberty to speak and meet. The coffeehouses were filled with reformers and radicals seeking change. As Robin, I attended meetings of the London Corresponding Society and other reformers. I tell you Lizzie, everyone is shocked at what happened in France, but the day is coming when the people of England will have their say." Throughout all this she had been walking up and down, her voice becoming bolder and more strident. Then she seemed to recall herself to her purpose. "But I digress, and I am nearly at the end of my tale."

The idyllic time could not last. Robin took it hard when Will set off to woo a new mark, for she could not be with him then. "It's for money, not for love," Will assured her. Then Will was caught by the brothers of the latest girl he had convinced to run off with him, tried in court, and sentenced to hang for the crime of fraud. Robin attended the trial and, as difficult as it was, the hanging at Newgate Prison, forcing her way to the front of the crowd. She would not have Will spend his last moments with no friends in sight, and Frances could not show her face for fear of arrest. Robin slipped the hangman's assistant a pound to ensure a quick death.

Though no one asked for his last words, Will stood forth and proclaimed, "There is no fraud, for I am as much a man as any in London. The treasures and the dowries were all freely given."

"That's as may be," said the hangman, "but it is still a crime for a low-born to impersonate a gentleman, as is bigamy." He gave the sign and the floor dropped from beneath Will's feet. Robin's pound was not wasted.

Robin was grief-stricken for a time, yet not so overcome by Will's death as she had been by Anna's – all the denizens of London's underworld lived in the shadow of the gallows. Still, the loss made her consider her own position. While their present strategy insured a steady income – "the flats what keep on paying," as Tom had it – the scheme forced them into too much contact with their victims. It would take just one to set a trap for them, throwing his reputation to the wind out of spite, and they would all be charged with bribery and extortion. Driven by this fear, and still conscious that these men had done nothing to deserve their mistreatment, Robin set about to find a more selective trade.

It was then that she hit on the idea of highway robbery. There needn't be the physical violence involved in the jilting game, and once they relieved the wealthy of their valuables, they would escape into the night, never to be seen again. Some highwaymen were known to assault or even murder their victims, but Robin felt such violence could be avoided through careful planning. With enough intelligence applied to careful preparation, she was confident they could make a comfortable living, with plenty left over to distribute to the poor. Many were the highwaymen who lived in high style, and they kept at it only in order to fund their lavish living and gambling habits. As Robin had none of these, she was sure the trade would support her and her accomplices nicely. Too, they could select only carriages of the highest nobility and Royal Mail coaches carrying the government's tax receipts.

"The government taxes the people, then we tax the government and return the funds to those most in need," she said. "To my mind, that's a much better use than spending it on the Prince of Wales' latest folly."

The chief skills necessary to the highwayman's trade were facility with a pistol, which Tom and Jack had taught her, and skill with a horse, which she had learnt as a child. Only a little practice was necessary before she felt comfortable riding astride, and she marveled at the freedom of it. As to accomplices, Tom and Jack both looked to her as their leader by this point, as her wits had led them this far; for her part, she found them more reliable than she had at the beginning of their partnership, and not subject to those vices that ruined so many in the criminal trade.

Yet three were barely enough to carry off a coach robbery. The carriages of the wealthy had armed drivers and footmen, while the mail coaches were yet more heavily guarded. A fourth partner would add a measure of safety, reducing the need for violence.

Tom and Jack were none too happy when Robin introduced them to the man she said was to be their new accomplice – a former slave from America named Sam. He had fought with the English against the revolution, earning his freedom and passage to England, if no further establishment in life. Robin had met him at a political meeting, finding him particularly eloquent on the hypocrisy of the American revolutionaries who sang the praises of liberty while holding slaves. Through his stories of the war, she learned that he was adept with all types of arms, and knew everything about how to keep powder dry in the rain, and other such skills that would make him a perfect master of arms for the gang. When Jack and Tom saw how fast he could reload and fire a pistol or a musket, any qualms they had about accepting Sam vanished. By the end of a profitable year robbing mail coaches and the carriages of nobles on their way out of London, the four had become as close as brothers.

But their run of good luck could not last. Finding themselves pressed on one side by competitors and on the other by the Bow Street Runners, they knew it was either quit business or leave London. All four had been putting money by, but had yet to save enough to make them independent; moving their peculiar trade to some other part of the kingdom seemed the only alternative.

Then Sam told them he could not come with them. "I fit in here in town," he said, "but not out in the country. It's bad enough, travelling to the outskirts of London for our jobs. But in the country I'd stick out. Dangerous for me and for you."

Robin tried convincing him it would be safe, suggesting he could pose as a servant. She couldn't blame him when he rejected this plan, with some heat. He had made his own vow: that he would never again serve a white man, and wouldn't even pretend to do it now. Robin and her remaining partners said a sad farewell with him when they departed the city.

The three removed to Devonshire, Robin hoping the convoluted landscape of Dartmoor would offer lonely, secluded stretches of road on which to waylay passing carriages, with the frequent fog aiding in their escapes. They had spent two months in Exeter, gathering intelligence, scouting the countryside for sites well-suited for ambush, and making friends with the servants in the grand houses around about before attempting their first job. Anthony's carriage had been only their second.

"And very fortunate I consider myself to have found you within it," Rebecca said. Then she bowed before me, signaling an end to the story.

I HARDLY knew what to think. I had become so engrossed in the outlandish tale that I had nearly forgotten that the person standing before me was the very one who had been brutalized by her husband and who had then murdered him in cold blood; who had been driven by his cruelty to Sapphism and then to dressing as a man; who had fallen from the rank of Baroness to that of a robber, extortionist, and highwayman. And even stranger, this was the woman who had become my closest friend! It was a riddle no amount of rational thought could untangle.

"It is hard to comprehend," I said. "You have always seemed one of the most cheerful and vivacious people I have ever met. How could your humor survive the rough treatment of your husband and everything that came after? It surely would have crushed the spirits of many who experienced it."

"I have asked myself that same question, many times. Was it my cheerful outlook that allowed me to survive such hurts? Or could it be that I would be of an even happier temper, had Lord Aysgarth not abused me in such a fashion? Yet the answer must be neither, for as a child and young woman, I was neither especially lively nor good-humored. Then, under the oppression of my husband, my spirit was next to nothing, it had been so crushed out of me. No, it was only Anna who saved me by showing me love. Even after I lost her, I survived on the strength of what she had given me to arrive in London and begin to make my own way. But it was not until I met Will, who taught me that I could take hold of life and make of it what I would, that I learned to be what I am today – and by that I don't mean merely adopting men's dress. Having suffered in the darkest pit of despair, having thought many times of ending my own suffering, I came to know how precious life is. I learned not to waste a minute of it on doubt, fear, or regret, but to take what happiness and joy I can extract from each moment. Anna taught me to love, but Will taught me how to live. As much as I miss both of them, I would not be who I am today without them. Now, having learned to love and to live, I hope to do both with you, for the rest of my life."

"And what do you propose – that I run off with you and join you in your life of crime?"

"Nothing so precipitous." She sat down beside me. "We can go on as we are, to the eyes of the village and your family as nothing more than the best of friends. None need know that we have become lovers." And here she caressed my cheek as she leaned toward me for a kiss.

I wrenched myself from her and stood up, taking several steps away to stand with my back to her. "You mean we should live a life of deception and lies, all for our own carnal pleasure."

"Not just pleasure, Lizzie – love!"

"Yet many women have shared the most passionate friendships while maintaining their virtue."

She approached me from behind and placed her hands on my shoulders. "But not I, Lizzie. I must love you, body and soul. You don't know what these last weeks have been, to be so close to you, yet unable to reach out and touch you, or give you more than a peck on the cheek." She leaned over me and spoke into my ear, her breath warm on my neck. "Think what it was like for me in bed with you in Bath, when I could only put a sisterly arm around you!"

"Please unhand me," I said in my coldest manner.

She released me and took a step back. After a moment of recollecting herself, she said, "You seem uniquely suited to such a life as we must lead, with all your reserve and self-command. Surely no accidental look or smile would ever escape you, hinting at our true relationship."

"Oh, very kind! Is this what you think of me – that I am a deceiver and a fraud?"

"I think you do not know your true self, and I am trying to show it to you."

"You presume far too much."

"Please, Lizzie, do not do this. Do not shrink away from me. It will kill me."

"I have never heard that a broken heart could be fatal, save in cheap romances."

In response, I heard only her quiet sobbing. I could not help turning toward her; her beseeching look and the tears spilling down her cheeks nearly made me catch my breath. That was the most difficult moment, seeing my dearest friend in such pain, and to know that I was the cause of it.

I took a deep breath, steeling myself against the sympathy that threatened my resolve. "What did you imagine would be my response? What you want can never be, any more than the abolition of the aristocracy. For my own sense of honor, I must have no more to do with you; duty demands that I alert Sir Morris to your crimes. It would be best for both of us if Mrs. Burgess disappeared from the neighborhood and was never seen here again."

With that I turned and walked over the crest of the hill without looking back.

The encounter had taken up so much of the morning that I had to invent my own story upon returning home, telling Father and Mrs. Simmons I had fallen asleep under the great oak tree. The posy of bluebells was quite wilted.

CHAPTER TWENTY

THE NEXT time I saw the highwayman, her hand brushed my own as I examined a fine bolt of linen in the tailor's shop in Leighton. I turned to see her standing next to me, in her usual garb as Mrs. Burgess. I drew back, surprised at her sudden appearance.

Five days had passed since her revelation, three of which I had spent in my bedchamber in a not altogether feigned nervous fatigue brought on by the perplexity of my situation. Though I had pledged to turn her over to Sir Morris, I could not bring myself to do it, and hoped instead that she would simply go away. Yet each day, Mrs. Burgess had called at the Parsonage, and each day I had refused to see her, or anyone. Father and Mrs. Simmons were concerned for me, as I had never before been prone to such unexplained maladies.

As I lay sleepless in my bed, I tried in vain to sort out my contradictory feelings. First, as to her being an outlaw, there could be no question that I must have nothing more to do with her, even if I did not reveal her identity. But harder to explain were my feelings for her as a woman. I had hoped, once I knew the highwayman's sex, that my feelings for that person would abate. Yet they had not, but had grown only more intense. For now I missed not only the rogue's kisses, but the touch of Rebecca's hand on my cheek, the feeling of her body moving next to mine as we walked arm-in-arm, the caress of her soft lips on my cheek as she kissed me goodbye. And worse was missing her laugh, which had never failed to send a warm glow through me, a glow I now knew to name as love.

Of course I had some inkling that women could satisfy each other's desires. My friends who had been away at boarding school had hinted at what their school-mates sometimes got up to, mostly in a teasing manner – no doubt they hoped to shock the vicar's daughter with their more worldly knowledge. This was some of the frivolous talk I could never abide. Yet even Mrs. Wollstonecraft had mentioned the "indelicate tricks" and "gross familiarity" that could sometimes spread at poorly run schools, though she had not mentioned exactly what these were. And there was the Bible, with its passages about men who lay with men. I could not recall any similar passage relating to love between women, yet it was no stretch to imagine that God must disapprove this as well. Still, no matter how rational the argument, I could not reason away my feelings for Rebecca, just as I had not been able to reason away my longing for the highwayman.

And so I remained confined to my chamber in a fugue of uncertainty and shame. On the fourth day, my spirits were lifted somewhat by a letter from Catherine Cowley. It was filled with the usual acknowledgments of the pleasure she had in meeting me, hopes that I had enjoyed a safe journey home, and bits of news about her and her brother's activities in Bath. She closed by urging me to continue work on my drawing of the two of them. Her parents had expressed a desire to own the portrait, if it were fairly executed, since it would include not only two of their children, but the interesting object of the newly rebuilt Pump Room. They were certain it would make an excellent conversation piece in their drawing room, and would be happy to pay me for my trouble.

With this encouragement, I wrote her a hasty note, in which I expressed the real happiness I felt on her interest in continuing our acquaintance, and told her I would get to work on the drawing right away. With more energy than I had felt in several days, I dug my sketchpad out of my partially unpacked travelling trunk, got out my drawing tools, and set to work.

Mrs. Simmons, noticing my renewed energy, insisted that I needed time outdoors. She suggested we visit the tailor's to have a lighter riding habit made up for the summer heat, hoping the fresh air of a walk to town and the diversion of going over patterns would do me good. I had seen no way to argue with this point, and now found myself confronting just the eventuality I had hoped to avoid.

"That linen will make a fine riding habit," Rebecca observed. "Are you planning a long journey on horseback?"

"Only a new outfit for the summer heat." I narrowed my eyes at her. "And what brings you to the tailor's, Mrs. Burgess? Perhaps you have an interest in *men's apparel?*"

"Ah, Mrs. Burgess!" Mrs. Simmons approached us from across the shop where she had been chatting with a friend. "I'm so glad you're here. I've been trying to draw Lizzie out after her recent discomfort. It's so unaccountable, she is usually so healthy and cheerful! As you can see, she is still a bit out of sorts, but if anyone can cheer her, it's you."

"I would be glad to help." Rebecca smiled as if oblivious to the cut I had given her. "I was just on my way to the village hall when I saw you enter here. Perhaps some time spent on the auction will distract you from your troubles."

"I am sure the effect will be quite the opposite," I said, summoning all of my icy reserve.

"Miss Elizabeth!" Mrs. Simmons exclaimed. "What's gotten into you? How can you be so callous toward your dearest friend?"

"You will have to ask her, perhaps she can explain it to you."

As the two gaped at each other, neither having any idea what to do with me, I pondered my situation. If ever I was going to reveal Rebecca's secret, it should be now, when her presence had provoked my anger. She must have felt certain that I would not break her confidence; that in itself was an affront to my honor. Yet, to my shame, I did not speak, telling myself that Mrs. Simmons was as likely to scoff at me as to believe Rebecca an outlaw who posed as a man. As well, three facts cried out my complicity, should any be discovered: I had in my possession the necklace the highwayman had taken from me, the return of which I could never explain; I had met the highwayman on three occasions since the robbery, and had reported none of them; and by now I had known the rogue's true identity for nearly a week. No, Rebecca had already caught me in a web of deceit, and though I hated her for it, I could not, at the moment, see my way out.

I chose to continue my cold manner, hoping she would go away, but Mrs. Simmons practically pushed us out the door and down the lane toward the village hall. "I will see you at the Parsonage this evening, Lizzie. Keeping yourself busy can only do you good."

"Come, dear," Rebecca said when we were out of Mrs. Simmons' hearing. "Take my arm, before our neighbors notice your changed demeanor." Without waiting for a response, she took my hand and hooked my arm in her own; as I didn't want to create a scene, I had no choice but to fall in beside her. It was an exquisite torture, feeling her body moving next to my own, to think of the pleasurable sensations that body had provoked in me, and to wonder about the pleasure she had both enjoyed and provoked in others. Yet this was all wrong. If I was not going to turn her in, at least I should have nothing to do with such an immoral creature. Then again, how could I explain the change in my behavior to my family and those who knew us?

"I have missed your help with the auction these past days, Lizzie," she said as we approached the hall.

"Oh, please, you cannot continue to gull me with that ploy. I know the auction is merely a ruse by which you gain valuable intelligence about our richest neighbors."

"You wound me, Lizzie," she protested, but then her voice faltered. "I will admit – at first that was my main intention. But you cannot doubt my interest in seeing conditions improved for those poor orphans. Have you noticed that none who have given generously to the auction have counted among the highwayman's victims?"

"Still, you should be held to account for your crimes."

"Come now, if you were going to turn me in, you would have done so by now."

"How do you know I haven't?" I looked up at her in what I hoped would be a challenging manner. Then I saw that dear, sweet face wracked with the pain my recalcitrance was causing, and my heart began to lose its resolve. I turned away from her and stumbled on: "Perhaps the high constable has set a watch on you and is waiting until you show yourself as the highwayman."

She laughed at me, though her free hand went to wipe at something in her eye. "Oh, silly girl, I am too cunning for that. We would know if a watch had been set on us. Besides, even had we missed them, they would have had us yesterday. Or did you not hear about the theft of a good amount of silver and gold jewelry from Lord Wetherby, who was on his way to Exeter?"

"You seem pleased with yourself. Confess it, you continue robbing just for the thrill of it."

"Yes, it is a thrill, and I thrive on it. And why shouldn't I be pleased with myself? A moment's fright for Lord Wetherby, the loss of a few items he can never miss with his twenty thousand pounds a year, and excellent punishment for his donation of two paltry candlesticks to the auction. All this in exchange for more food and medicine for the poor of Exeter, and that much farther toward independence for Tom, Jack, and myself, and thus the day when all of our proceeds can go to the destitute. Yet as thrilling and necessary as our work is, I would give it all up to avoid losing you."

I studied her face, wondering if she meant it. I had seen what joy she took in robbing our carriage, and again in taunting the militia; did I mean enough to her that she would give up that excitement, not to mention the income it earned her?

I extricated my arm from hers and stopped in the lane. "If you are serious, then I will have no more to do with you until you fulfil that pledge. As for your other proposal, I – I hardly know how to answer. It is asking much that I throw over everything I have ever been taught as right and proper. Now I must bid you good day." I turned and left her standing outside the village hall.

I FLED Leighton as quickly as I could, avoiding the curious looks of the passersby who knew me. Then, to exorcise my pent-up and confused emotions, I took the long way home, returning to the lane leading to the Parsonage late in the afternoon, wanting nothing more than to be left alone, to lose myself in a book or the perusal of my journals.

Before I could reach the final turning to home, I heard the sound of hoofbeats approaching from behind. Turning, I half expected to see Rebecca chasing after me, but quickly saw that it was a man, definitely a man, and not Rebecca in her highwayman's disguise. As the figure drew closer, I saw that it was Anthony, riding his cream-colored gelding, Caius.

Recognizing me, he drew the horse up nearby and leapt from the saddle, doffing his hat in the next instant. "Elizabeth! Of all people who could have greeted me upon my return – " He drew up short, noticing my serious aspect. "But you look distraught, as if you have been crying. Is anything the matter?"

"Oh, it is nothing." I took the kerchief he offered. "Just a spat with a friend. But it will blow over in time and all will be mended."

"Who is it, if you don't mind my asking?"

"Mrs. Burgess. We had a – disagreement – over the arrangements for the auction."

"Ah, yes," he said, seeming uncertain of himself. "She seemed – strange, when I saw her with you in Bath, most changed from the respectable woman I met that day after church. Her taunting of me, and acting as if she were in a play – it was all quite unaccountable. But then again, my head wasn't in the best state."

I don't know why I still felt the need to come to her defense, but I said, "How would you expect her to behave after being pawed at by your friend? It – it reminded her of something in her past, something horrid, and it put her into a panic. You can hardly blame her for anything that happened after."

"Yet she seemed almost jealous of me."

"Don't be absurd! We had enjoyed a lovely evening at the concert, it was our last evening in Bath, and she hated to see it ruined." He continued looking at me uncertainly, but said nothing. "And what of you? We did not expect you here until July."

"Yes, well, that makes for a long tale." He sounded glad to drop the subject of Rebecca. "Will you allow me to walk you home while I tell it? And I hope it will explain my poor behavior toward you in Bath." I assented to this plan, and we walked in silence for a time, Anthony leading Caius, while he gathered his thoughts.

"As you know, my family, most especially my father, hoped I would make what they deem a suitable match with a lady of acceptable rank and fortune."

"Yes, certainly, everyone expected it of you, as Lord Highdown's first-born son."

"But what I found in London, Elizabeth! Perhaps Father had kept me shielded from his full intentions until he deemed me ready to go into the World. But all of those ideals of gentle manners, propriety, and decorum with which we were brought up – in London, and among the ranks who rule this country, they are but a sham! Of course, I had seen some of this during my time at the Inns of Court, but my studies had kept me so busy then. But now it was as if Father was removing a veil from my eyes. First there were the ways in which he meant to use my knowledge of the law, making it little more than legalized highway robbery – it was as if fair play and honor meant nothing. But that paled next to his talk of buying me a seat in the House of Commons. I knew these practices existed, of course, but I had no idea my father would stoop to such measures for political gain. That led to quite a row on the subject of reform, which I was pleased to tell him I support."

It took all my composure to suppress a bitter smile, so closely did this characterization of the nobility fit that of Rebecca's. To have her assertions about the mercenary and undeserving nature of the aristocracy confirmed by a friend, not to mention one of its members, did nothing to ease the turmoil of my feelings toward her. "This is not the first I have heard of such things," I said at length.

"Yet that was not the worst of it. I mentioned to Father that I had found no very suitable young ladies, none who had captured either my affections or my regard."

"Not even Lady Mary? She seemed a likely catch."

"No, most especially not Lady Mary. Your friend was right – if there is one who can melt that icy heart, it is not I, though I daresay she would have consented to any match that would maintain or improve her standing. But upon hearing of my disinclination to wed any of the women I had met so far, Father took me into his library and explained what he called the facts of life. I was to choose my wife from among the four or five girls my parents had deemed suitable – Lady Mary being one of them – regardless of their persons, their characters, or their understanding. 'There are other women to meet those needs,' he said with a wink, 'and one need not seek to meet all of them in a wife. Be easy, son, for the world is open before you like a – ' Well, I will not shock you with the simile he used."

"I have heard of such behavior among the highest ranks of society, but I had no idea it was so widespread, that even your father – "

"But my story is not done, and I am afraid it grows worse. I fear you will be appalled at my conduct, though I would withhold nothing from you. Father introduced me to a group of young lords who had been in town several years. You met two of them in Bath. They set about showing me all the delights available to a man of means, gaming hells and worse. And all with no hint, not even an inkling, that this was other than as it should be."

"And – did you partake of these delights?"

He looked off at the pastureland and the downs beyond before answering. "I will not lie, or say that it was forced upon me. For some weeks, I threw myself with abandon into dissipation, as if to drown the memory of my poor showing when the highwayman accosted you. If I was to be a creature of my father, then very well, I would be exactly the creature he wanted me to be." He ran a hand over his face, as if to wipe away a bad dream. "But I will make no excuses. What's done is done, and I am only glad that you seem not ready to send me away after this confession. It must be difficult for one of your pure heart to understand." He glanced at me and then quickly away, his face a deep red.

I was tempted to soothe his fears with my own confession, yet I doubted it would be greeted with the same equanimity. From talk with friends who had become engaged, I knew that such unburdenings were almost *de rigueur* for men of a certain experience when plighting their troths. I did not ease his guilt, but said simply, "Go on."

"I was brought part way to my senses when I met you in Bath. First, there was the contrast between yourself and Lady Mary – even with all her finery, she paled by comparison to you. And then there was the conduct of my companions, standing in such sharp contrast to every ideal I hold dear. But the final straw came when they dragged me back to London to visit a particularly vile den of iniquity. There I experienced such feelings of disgust and revulsion that I could think only of returning here, to the happy scenes of home and childhood – and to you. I have ridden night and day to get here before – before – " He looked once again at the green meadows and moors around us. "I must ask you, have you become attached to anyone else while I was away?"

What could I tell him? That my attachment to Rebecca went far beyond that virtuous, romantic friendship extolled by writers of sentiment? That I yearned to feel the highwayman's arms around me? That the two were one and the same? "No, of course not." The lie came easily.

He took up my hand and kissed it. "Then, Miss Elizabeth, you must know, you are the only woman who can ever satisfy all the wishes of both my heart and mind."

If I was surprised, it was only at the remarkable steadiness with which my heart kept its pace. "This is much to take in. You know I have always regarded you as a friend. I would not denigrate the offices of friendship by adding 'and nothing more,' for I value few things more in this world than true friendship. But I have long guarded my heart against anything beyond these friendly feelings, aware as I was that your family would never approve a match between us."

"Nor will they now. I am likely to lose much of my inheritance, and be forced to rely on that independence I mentioned in Bath. It is not all that much, and I may be forced to make my living as a barrister. But I am ready for a life of work and comparative poverty if I can share it with you – and if you will have one of such mean prospects." Here he kissed my hand again.

The esteem in which I held my friend was elevated greatly by this declaration. To turn away from his family and the bulk of his fortune, all on the basis of the soundest principles of honor and propriety – it indicated a steadfast and moral character, one in which a bride could have the utmost confidence and security. And a barrister's living was not so mean. Yet, in my turmoil I could not answer him immediately, but must put him off.

"As I said, this new standing between us will take some getting used to. It could take some time to mend the course of my heart beyond friendship, if it can be mended at all."

"At least may I pay my addresses to you?"

"Of course," I said, looking up at him expectantly, hoping he would allow me the opportunity to more fully gauge my feelings for him. He made no motion, however, other than to gaze into my eyes. I glanced up and down the lane. "We are quite alone. I hope you will not think it too forward of me to suggest a kiss, if you will not take it as a promise of present attachment, but perhaps the beginnings of a future one."

He seemed surprised for a moment, then leaned down and kissed me gently, and briefly, a hand placed in a friendly manner on my arm. No, I thought to myself as he straightened, this intimacy had prompted no change in the pace of my heart, the rapidity of my breathing, or the tone of my cheeks. Nor did I note any such changes in him.

We continued our walk, Anthony bringing me to the gate leading to the Parsonage before going his own way. As he mounted Caius, his coat parted for a moment, and I noticed a brace of pistols hanging from the waist of his breeches. I saw, too, the hilt of a short sword protruding from its sheath lashed to the horse's side.

Seeing me notice these items, Anthony said, "Yes, I travel armed now, for we learned in London of the highwayman's continued depredations in the neighborhood. You should avoid travelling alone, Miss Elizabeth. You never know when this ruffian will be about, and he might show even less restraint in his behavior toward your person if he catches you out. In fact, I mean to make it my occupation to apprehend the lout. After my failure that day in the carriage, and these months wasted in dissipation and idleness, I feel it is the least I can do. If few of my peers fulfill their duties to their people, it does not mean I must follow them in their dereliction."

It had been a trying day, and I must have lost my countenance at this last statement.

"You seem taken aback," he observed.

Taken aback hardly compassed my feelings at the moment. If ever there was a time to reveal Rebecca to the world, it was now. He had already taken note of her odd behavior in Bath, and would readily believe that she had taken on the role of the highwayman. A few words, and I would be out of my predicament.

But an image came to me of Rebecca swinging at the end of a rope, and I could not do it. Then I knew I was truly lost – no matter that she deserved punishment, no matter that it made me her accessory, I would not be the instrument of her downfall.

Yet still she was not safe. Were Anthony any other gentleman, I could have put his words down as idle boasting. But if he really had returned to his sense of duty and his commitment to the ideals of *noblesse oblige,* then I had no doubt he would spend hours patrolling the countryside, or perhaps shadowing mail coaches and the carriages of his fellow nobles, all in an attempt to protect those he imagined his retainers – and me most of all. I could not feel sanguine about this gallantry; I neither wanted nor needed his protection. Most of all, I feared what would happen were he and the highwayman to meet.

"I most certainly am taken aback, for I am concerned for your safety," I said at last. "You must be careful. Cannot the militia see to the highwayman?"

"They have done little thus far. I assume you've heard what happened on Whiddleston Moor? But I am not so foolish as to go after three armed rogues on my own. I mean only to track them to whatever lair they hide in, then bring in the militia. So have no worries on my behalf."

With that, he made his last farewell and cantered off down the lane, all unaware that my worry was not mainly for him.

CHAPTER TWENTY-ONE

THE NEXT time I saw the highwayman, she swept me off my feet. I was out walking on the third day after our encounter in the village, trying to disentangle my confused thoughts and feelings for Anthony and Rebecca. Then I heard hoofbeats on the lane behind me. Half-expecting Anthony, I turned to see Rebecca, or I should say Robin, in her highwayman's guise. She made no greeting, instead drawing Juno in near me, circling around and around me until I grew dizzy. Reining yet closer, she reached down with her left arm and lifted me to a seated position in front of her. I must have assisted her in some way, without ever being aware of it, for how else could she have lifted me to her horse? Yet to ride off with her was the last thing I wanted. I struggled against her as we cantered down the lane, but she held me tightly with one arm around my waist.

One may imagine how little I had slept by this point. Two days of rain followed by a day of waiting for the lanes to dry had kept me indoors, giving me ample opportunity to ponder my predicament. Had I ever thought Anthony capable of defying his father, I might have held out hope for a match with him, believing as I did that friendship formed the soundest basis on which to build a marriage. Yet, now that the lessons afforded by his season in London had pushed him to go against his family's wishes, it was too late, for in that time I had been given my own lesson. I now knew how much more was possible than a mild attachment. *His* were not the kisses that haunted my dreams.

If Anthony had met in me the one who satisfied all the wishes of his heart, as the saying went, then I had found that same satisfaction in another. And yet that person, the person who now held me around the midriff and whose warmth I could feel through my thin morning dress, was wrong in so many ways – a woman, in the first place, and an outlaw, who had lost all connections and reputation. How could my heart have made such an error? Yet, having made it, how could I extricate myself from my heart's demands? Surely I *must* extricate myself – mustn't I? To defy my father, my church, and the laws of our king by following Rebecca – it was impossible – wasn't it?

With such perturbed thoughts as these I had wrestled over the last three days, showing an ill temper and weak eyes to Father and Mrs. Simmons. "Anthony back at home, and you unfit to receive him!" the latter exclaimed. "You are wasting the best chance you will ever have, Miss Elizabeth." Still, much as I struggled for self-command, my thoughts *would* stray back to Rebecca and all those little moments in which she had prompted my attachment to her, though I could not then name them for what they were – the kisses on the cheek, the smiles, the teasing, the way she would caress the inside of my wrist as we walked arm in arm. Most of all, the warmth of her body in bed during our trip to Bath. Every time I thought of it, my throat would go dry, and my heart would beat faster with desire – and how much more so, as I remembered melting into her arms as she kissed me, before I ever knew she was a woman!

Try as I might, I could not train my mind back to its proper pursuits, whether reading, playing at the pianoforte, or working in my journals. The only activity that could hold my attention was working on my drawing for Catherine. Nearly a fortnight had passed since that day in front of the Pump Room, yet it already seemed to belong to a simpler, more idyllic time, when my dearest friend had not also been the highwayman, and when I had not known what it was to feel impure thoughts for her. And so I threw myself into that drawing with a concentration almost bordering on obsession. I hoped only to achieve a more fully developed sketch that I could send to the Cowleys for their approval before proceeding to the final work, yet I labored over the minutest details, discarding several attempts I deemed failures. Finally I had an acceptable copy and packaged it for mailing, rolling it up inside one of my sketches of the Sydney Gardens, and included a note suggesting that the final work should be done in watercolor.

If drawing could occupy my mind during my waking hours, nighttime offered no such relief. Fleeting images of Rebecca in her morning dress alternated with those of Robin in her highwayman's garb, creating a whirl of sensations: flesh and smiles and kisses and flashing eyes. Worst was the remembered sound of her laugh. I would hear it in my dreams, then awake feeling happy, only to remember that I would never hear that laugh again, if I were any sort of proper and virtuous woman. And then my future without her would stretch before me, as desolate as the last leaf falling from a tree that would never know another spring.

In such a state I had wandered out that morning, not even bothering to change out of my morning dress, hoping fresh air and exercise would clear my thoughts, or at least distract me from them; for it was apparent to me that in Rebecca, or Robin, I had met with a conundrum that no amount of rational contemplation could solve. And so Robin had found me, my thoughts and feelings no clearer than they had been when I set out.

"Sshhh," she hushed me as Juno cantered beneath us. "We need to talk, and out of the way of prying eyes and ears. I have been quite out of my mind with missing you."

"What are you going to do with me?"

"Come now. You know you need not fear me."

"Then set me down! I told you I would not see you until you give up your life of robbery."

"Not until we reach our destination. Then I will have my say."

As I ceased my struggle, she urged the horse into an easy gallop. She rode astride, of course, and though I rode aside in front of her, I felt secure with her arm around my midriff. Juno's smooth gait added to the feeling of safety – Juno, protector of women. How fitting, I thought, and gave a laugh. Hearing that, Robin urged the horse to greater effort, and I lost myself in the thrill of a speed which I had never before experienced, the moors and fields and stone walls blurring as we passed them. Our speed, combined with the power of the horse beneath us, Robin's arm around me, the light in her eyes – my breath caught in my throat and tears flooded my eyes, and not just from the wind of our pace.

Our speed was such that it took only a few moments to reach the shelter of a wood, where Robin slowed the horse to a walk, turning onto a climbing track. I struggled for recollection, chiding myself for becoming so carried away with this attempt at wooing me. If her kisses had not ravished me, perhaps the thrill of a breakneck ride on horseback would, or so she must have believed.

"Why did you kidnap me in this way?" I demanded when I could speak calmly.

"You must know I called on you at home several times, but Mrs.

Simmons said you were too indisposed to see me. And I wanted more privacy than the Parsonage can provide. But truly, as Robin I feel more able to press my suit."

We neared the crest of the hill, and I saw that we had come to the great oak tree, approaching it the same way Robin had come when first we met here. She dismounted, tugging her crêpe mask down to look at me, and now she was Rebecca, the person I had come to hold dearest in all the world – yet not Rebecca, for she was still Robin in her man's dress.

"May I help you down?" she asked. I nodded and slid forward as she placed a hand on either side of my waist and gently lowered me to the ground.

The action brought us within inches of each other. She straightened, still holding my waist. Leaning closer, she said, "Do you remember that kiss we shared in this very spot?"

I twisted out of her grasp before she could lean down and kiss me again, taking several steps away before turning back to her. "Of course I do – to my regret. That was forward of you, and a mean trick, as I had no idea who you were."

"I remember that you gave your assent before I kissed you, and that you responded warmly during the course of it."

"If that is so, it is only because I thought I was being kissed by a man. I could never respond in such a way to a woman."

"But you did, Lizzie. In your mind you may have thought me a man, but your senses could not lie, not when you felt my arms around you, and certainly not when I placed your hand on my breast. I know what you felt."

She had stepped nearer to me as she spoke. I made no answer and she took another step, her eyes flashing as she grasped me by the shoulders. "Stop this, Lizzie. You know you love me, and you know you are mad with desire for me, or why would your sleep be troubled? Yes, I know what those circles under your eyes mean, for I too have slept little." She leaned down to kiss me, but I pulled away once more, turning my back on her.

"Yet it cannot be helped," I said. "What you want is impossible."

"It is all possible, if you will only reach out and take it! I am offering you a world you have never known, and could never imagine from the confines of a Devonshire village. We can go anywhere, do anything. Travel abroad, live in London, or anywhere else in this country we choose. I know that under all your reserve you crave adventure as much as I; and you can have it, if you join us. Together we can help to change the world! Or, if you demand it, we could have a quiet life together, living as friends and companions, with no one knowing the intimate details of our attachment. We could even stay here. There is no reason for you to desert your father and all your friends. I cannot believe you would throw all of this aside in favor of life as a lonely spinster."

I turned on her. "That is no longer my only choice. Anthony has returned from London, and now seeks my hand in marriage, in defiance of his father's commands." I did not tell her of the remarkable accord between his opinions of the nobility and her own.

"How bold of him!" she scoffed. "You cannot tell me you love him."

I remained silent.

She reached out and caressed my cheek. "He cannot make you feel the way I do." Her fingers moved down to my jaw, and along it, then to my neck.

The lack of sleep, the tumult of my mind, the images and sensations with which I had tormented myself over the past week – all of these conspired to undo my self-mastery. I could not suppress a shudder at her touch.

"I thought not. Of course it's impossible for you to marry him – safe, bland Anthony, with no more passion than a piece of dry toast."

She went on to abuse him in a similar fashion until I could bear it no longer. "Stop!" I exclaimed, pushing her away from me with all my strength. Her eyes opened wide in surprise. "You will not speak of him in this manner! He is a good friend and a fine gentleman of a more truly noble character than you can ever know! If it is impossible for me to love him, it is because you have made it so!"

She smiled. "Why, Lizzie, what has become of all your self-command? Have I achieved victory at last?"

"You're a devil!" I shrieked at her. "You put these feelings in me, and now I demand that you take them back!" I was out of my mind with rage. I flew at her, striking at her face and neck and shoulders with my open palms, grasping at her hair and her eyes with my nails, emitting the most hideous shrieks all the while.

With her greater height, longer reach, and trained reflexes, Robin rebuffed these attacks for several moments, all the while smiling at me, the light of victory in her eyes. At last she grasped me by the wrists and, with a sweep of her leg, had me on my back, throwing her body on top of mine, pinning my hands to the ground on either side of my head.

"Careful, Miss Elizabeth. Do not forget I am the highwayman, and prone to take what I want when provoked to anger."

I don't know how I did it. Remembering a trick I had seen my brother use while wrestling, I twisted first one way, then quickly the other, surprising her and pushing her over until I was on top. Only later did I realize that Robin must have expected such a trick and had allowed me to get away with it.

Now I had her pinned, sitting astride her, with my hands holding her wrists to the ground. We glared at each other for a moment.

Then she relaxed. "Now I am in your power," she said. "Do with me what you will!"

How could she be so infuriating? I raised my hand to strike at her smiling face, thinking to wipe away that triumphant expression. She did not flinch or raise her free arm to ward off the coming blow, but merely gazed back at me in curious expectation.

I hesitated then, telling myself this was the only way to relieve my feelings and drive her away for good. Seeing me hesitate, her eyes softened and she became Rebecca once more, *my* Rebecca. I lowered my hand, knowing I could not do it – I *did not want* to do it. Instead, I caressed her cheek with my fingers, then her lips – slightly parted and no longer smiling – then down her neck as far as the top of her high collar.

"Yes, my love," she breathed.

She had been right all along – I did love her, and not only in that chaste, sentimental way so fashionable in novels. I wanted to unite with her, body and soul.

Suddenly I was kissing her, on her mouth at first, and then all over her face, her eyelids, her neck, with a frenzy equal to that with which I had attacked her a moment before. I still held one hand pinned above her head, as my other roved down her body, pushing aside the flaps of her open coat, grasping at the buttons of her waistcoat. Finding this operation difficult while wearing gloves, I paused to remove them, while Rebecca regarded me with a knowing look.

"My, Lizzie, you are like a tiger when you cast off your reserve!"

I threw my gloves aside and pinned both her hands back once more, exulting in my power over her. "Do not mock me," I said, glaring down at her. My hair had come partly undone, and long strands hung down in her face and over her breast.

She laughed. "That is no mocking, for I love this change in you; your feelings are now so like my own! Now, come to me, my darling." She extricated her hands from mine and ran her fingers through my hair, pulling me down toward her for a long, deep kiss.

Yet still I was insatiable. My hand went back to unbuttoning her waistcoat, driven on by the kisses she was placing down my throat and farther down to that valley between my breasts peeking out from the bodice of my gown. Pushing the waistcoat aside, I began tugging her shirt from the waistband of her breeches. Finally the tail was free and my hand slipped beneath it, feeling for the first time the sweet soft woman's flesh of her belly, taut with straining toward me. Never, in my waking moments, had I touched myself in such a manner, yet now I could not understand how I had not. My hand moved up and found that she had not bothered to bind her breasts before riding out, meeting with soft flesh surmounted by a hard nipple. She shuddered with pleasure, and I couldn't help giggling at the power of my touch over her – at that, and at the surprising pleasure of touching a body so like my own.

"Now you are the one who is mocking me," she said.

"No, I am simply giddy with delight."

"Yes, yes, my dear, now you see how it can be between us."

Still I was not sated. I wanted to know all of her, to be inside her, and have her inside me, until we went through and through each other, and were one. My hand went to the waist of her breeches and attempted to slip under. Finding it quite snug, I tugged at the many buttons closing them up the front. At last two or three were free and my hand slid under, down and down to that velvety patch just above the parting of her legs. But I could get no farther, so tight were the breeches.

I went back to tugging at the buttons, but Rebecca grasped my hand and held it to her lips, kissing it over and over. "No, my love, this is not how I would have you the first time, or have you have me, pawing at each other while half undressed. I would see all of you and have you see all of me, that we may know each other, skin to skin, and you may fully experience how it can be between two women – not like this." She kissed my hand again.

I sobbed with frustration. "You cannot leave me like this; I will die of yearning."

"Shh, shh," she hushed, stroking my hair. "I know, my sweet, I know. You cannot imagine how I have yearned for you these past weeks, sitting next to you at the pianoforte, or walking beside you – or in bed next to you in Bath! You cannot imagine the depths of composure it took to keep from throwing myself at you at any moment. And the last days away from you have been a torture."

Still I would not be put off. "Please, having brought me this far, you must satisfy me." I grasped her hand and placed it between my legs.

"Very well, but I must hold you, and look at you, your first time. Come over to the oak tree with me."

We rose and she led me over to the oak. She removed her gloves and then her coat, rolling the latter into a pillow and placing it against the trunk, then sat with her back to it. She drew me down after her, one hand pushing my skirts above my knees as I sank down with my back to her, her arms around me. With one hand she tilted my chin up to kiss me tenderly. The other moved with the lightness of a feather up the inside of my thigh, working its way toward the parting of my legs, eliciting shudders of pleasure.

At last her hand reached the vital spot. "You're wet already," she said.

"Is that good?"

"The greatest good." Her fingers continued their work. When they dipped inside I caught my breath and looked up at her in surprise. She returned my gaze with the most tender smile, taking delight in the pleasure she was giving me.

"Is this what Anna showed you?"

She nodded. "In some ways you are very like her," she said, never stopping her gentle stroking. "You are petite, like her. I could lift her with ease, and take all of her in my arms, as I can you."

But I was beyond attending these words, as my eyes closed and I concentrated on the waves of pleasure coursing through my body. I found that my hips, all on their own, were thrusting back and forth to meet that stroking hand, and from my mouth there emerged moans and cries of pleasure. Whenever I could open my eyes, I would find Rebecca looking down at me with the greatest love, intent on the effect her efforts were having, and with an expression of rapture, as if she were experiencing a pleasure as great as my own.

"Yes, my sweet, that's it," she whispered to me, then kissed my neck or nibbled at my ear, her free hand stroking my breast.

Finally, just when I felt the pleasure could grow no greater, that I must lie suspended on this plateau of ecstasy and hope to stay there forever, Rebecca's stroking became more intense. I lost all control, my hips bucking into her hand, and my legs closing around it, crushing it. I cried out in the most intense agony of ecstasy, as wave after wave of rapture shook my body.

At last the shudders subsided and I lay back in her arms as she let her hand rest between my legs. "There now," she said, kissing the top of my head and stroking my hair with her other hand. I looked up at her face to see the greatest expression of happiness there. How could giving me this pleasure give her such joy? Thus far I had received all the benefit of our encounter.

I turned sideways in her arms and ran my hand up and down her thigh. "Surely I must return the favor," I said.

"Hush now." She took up my hand and kissed it. "These moments after ecstasy are the sweetest you will ever know. Relax and enjoy it while it lasts."

We lay there for a time; on my part I felt only bliss, a bliss in which Rebecca seemed to partake equally. For the first time that day I noticed the sound of the breeze through the trees, heard the call of a song thrush from the bushes nearby, and noticed the beauty of the sunlight filtering through the leaves. It was as if all my senses had been opened to the world. What's more, I felt no sense of shame, which Father had always taught was the surest sign that one had sinned.

At last we came out of our mutual reverie, and talked of our situation, and the future.

"This is just the beginning," Rebecca said, "for you have experienced only a little of what we can have together."

"Yet what I experienced was sublime. I never knew such a feeling was possible."

"No one does, until they experience it for themselves. And no one will tell you about it beforehand for fear of exciting immoral and illicit feelings in young ladies, leaving them to discover it – or not – on their wedding nights. I never would have discovered it, if not for Anna."

"Yet now, having experienced it, I cannot call it immoral."

"Nor can I. Many call it so only to keep women as the property of men." She clasped me tighter to her. "But now the highwayman has stolen you and you are mine!" Then she held me at arm's length. "But not mine, for I have stolen you only to give you back to yourself."

"But I want to belong to you, and you to belong to me."

She regarded me for a long moment, as if judging whether I was in earnest.

"I want that too, but it is a decision of the greatest consequence, and even greater for you than for me. We will talk more of it later, after you fully know what it means to be with a woman. I would have you make no choice before then. Do you know the Old Inn at the crossroads?"

"Yes, it is a place of ill repute, and no respectable person would go there."

"All the better for us, for it is likely that none who know you will see you there. Jack and Tom and I use it as our base in this neighborhood. Come to me there tomorrow morning, telling your father that we plan to go into Exeter and won't be back until late."

"And what will we do there?"

"Why, share even greater delights than we have today. That will help you decide whether you truly want a life with me. And it will bring me luck to win the prize we're after tomorrow night. Then we will make our plans for the future, whether to run away for a life of excitement and adventure, or to stay here, for all appearances the friends we were before. And if you still believe I should desist in my highway robbery, I will be ruled by you."

I looked at her and wondered if she meant it. I knew the thrill she took from the risks of her highwayman's life; would she give those up for me? Could I ever replace the joy she felt in bold actions and daring deeds? And if she could not, what would I give up to be with her?

At length we rose from our languor, straightening our clothing, Rebecca giving me one last kiss before covering her face with her mask and becoming Robin. She mounted Juno and pulled me on in front of her, and down the hill we rode.

CHAPTER TWENTY-TWO

IF ONLY I had never forced Rebecca to chase me down in the guise of the highwayman! If only she had let me follow my own way back home! But as Robin she was bold, and insisted on carrying me at least partway back to the Parsonage. And perhaps we were still so absorbed in each other that we were less alert than we might otherwise have been. Whatever the cause, we struck the lane and turned along it, and did not hear the sound of hoofbeats approaching until it was too late. A rider appeared around a corner ahead. We both quickly recognized him as Anthony, and just as quickly, he recognized us.

Both parties reigned to a stop, not twenty paces apart. "You!" Anthony exclaimed, drawing a pistol. "Robbing carriages wasn't enough for you, and now you have proceeded to kidnapping ladies! Set her down immediately, then I will turn you over to the authorities."

Rebecca – Robin – was having none of this, of course. I could see by the light in her eyes that here was but another opportunity for adventure. Quicker than Anthony could react, she had drawn her own pistol and trained it on him. Neither had cocked their weapons, but now each did.

"No, Anthony, ride away!" I exclaimed. "Have no fear for me!"

"Do as Miss Collington says, for I have the advantage of you." It was Robin speaking, for she had lowered her voice that half octave that made her sound more mannish. "You dare not fire for fear of striking her." After which, she whispered in my ear, "Never fear, I will not kill him."

"You are such a rogue that you would use her as a shield?" Anthony demanded.

Robin turned Juno to one side, so that her right shoulder was turned to him and I no longer shielded her from Anthony's pistol. "This will only improve my aim. But are you such a good shot that you can be sure of hitting me and not the young lady?"

Anthony's voice was full of doubt as he responded: "That may be so, but you will have to shoot me down to get past me. If you attempt to flee, I will shoot you in the back. That much I can risk without hitting Miss Collington."

The two eyed each other for a moment, then Robin's eyes darted from side to side, looking for some means of escape, but finding only dense forest on one side and a steep slope on the other. Yet I believe she did not truly want to escape, she was having too much of a thrill, and she still thought she had the upper hand.

"As neither of us would see the young lady harmed, I will set her down, if I can trust your word that you won't shoot me as I do so. Then you may take her to safety."

Anthony nodded, and Robin used her left hand to lower me to the ground.

"Elizabeth, to me!" Anthony commanded.

"That's right," Robin said, her pistol still trained on him. "Take her and go. I promise to harm neither of you."

But she hadn't reckoned on Anthony's sense of duty. "You will not leave here unless it be under my control or in the undertaker's cart."

"Don't be a fool, man! Surely Miss Collington's safety must be your first concern."

Anthony kept his weapon aimed at Robin as I drew even with him. "Elizabeth, into those trees. You'll be safe from errant shots there."

"No, Anthony, please!" I begged him. "Let us away, and leave the rogue for another time." Then I said what I should not have done, but my desperation to have these two parted drove me to it. "Think of our future together. I could not live if anything happened to you."

His gaze did not waver from Robin. "I am thinking of it, for how could you ever feel safe with a husband who had shown cowardice before such a villain? This ruffian has besmirched your honor as well as my own, and has put the whole neighborhood under a constant state of fear. It is a lord's duty to protect and defend the people who come under his care. I mean to carry out that duty, to whatever end. Now, please, make yourself safe."

With a sob, I retreated into the trees as Robin replied, "Oh, very fine words indeed, but you know as well as I that only you lordlings, and not the people, have aught to fear of me." The two glared at each other, and I feared that one would shoot the other at any moment. Robin went on: "Lower your weapon, sir, for I still have the advantage of you. Had I wanted to injure you, I would have done so by now."

"I cannot."

"Very well, then, let us try the steadiness of your horse." With that, she turned her pistol toward the sky and fired. Juno remained calm, no doubt having been trained to such explosions of noise, but Caius whinnied and bucked. Anthony's pistol went off, discharging into the ground, causing his mount to rear all the harder and spin about. As he struggled to control Caius, Robin drew her second pistol, cocked it, and levelled it at him.

"Run away, you fool!" I screamed. Anthony was too busy with his horse to notice that this was directed at Robin. She glanced over at me, her eyes burning with that same thrill that had been there when first we met, only brighter.

At last, Caius was under better control, and Anthony had drawn his second pistol.

"You are making it remarkably difficult to spare your life," Robin said. "You must know you cannot hit me while your horse is skittering about like that."

"Turn and flee and you will discover whether or not my aim is poor."

Robin regarded him for a moment. "A fine pickle we are in. Neither of us can flee, yet I have no wish to kill you. How will we sort it out?"

The two eyed each other for a moment more; in the silence, a raven cawed from a nearby tree.

"If this is a matter of honor, as you say," Robin went on, "then let us settle it in the time-honored manner. I see that smallsword lashed to your horse. Will you match it against my rapier?" She dropped Juno's reins, held in her left hand, and drew her sword from its sheath on the horse's left side.

I gave a low sob as Anthony considered the rapier uncertainly. This was madness, each trying to outdo the other in displays of bravado for my benefit.

As he still hesitated, Robin went on, "Come now. Surely you have had fencing lessons, and with the best swordmasters money can buy. Thrust, parry, *riposte,* disengage, all that? You'll have the advantage of me there, for I only learned to fight in the street; yet my weapon will give me the longer reach. What say you?"

"I say that a gentleman doesn't abase himself by accepting a challenge from a commoner, much less a base rogue such as yourself."

"Ha!" Robin's exclamation was more a groan than a laugh. "You noblemen and your code of honor! Yet I remember a day when you challenged me; how convenient that the code now appears to support your side."

"Appears?"

I did not need to see beneath her mask to know that she was smirking at him. "What if I told you my father was a Baronet?"

Anthony narrowed his eyes at her. His horse had grown calmer, while I grew yet more fearful that he would take the opportunity to shoot Robin without warning.

"Why would I believe such a thing?" he demanded. "A Baronet's natural son – *that* I could credit, though it does you no good."

"Given my current profession, I am sure you will pardon me from providing you proofs, even were I to have them. But I swear to you I am of noble birth, though circumstances prevented me from acquiring a nobleman's training in such matters as dueling and the code of honor. Now, how much longer can this go on? Or will you suggest another way of settling our impasse?"

Anthony hesitated a moment longer but finally nodded.

"I will be quite satisfied with first blood, if you will retreat once I draw it," Robin said. Anthony shook his head. "To the death, then. I would not let you take me to gaol for a mere nick."

"No, stop this madness!" I wailed. "Anthony, what can you hope to gain?"

"A dead highwayman. That is much to gain."

"We have no seconds," Robin said, "but perhaps Miss Collington can assist us by holding our pistols while we duel."

They dismounted, each keeping a watchful eye on the other as they stepped toward me, setting their pistols down at the same time a few paces away, then backing off. I collected the weapons as the opponents saw to their horses, took off their coats, and prepared their swords.

As the duel began, I could hardly tell what I was seeing, for I am no expert in fencing. At first, they merely stood there, their swords inches apart, the tips making small orbits about each other, while Robin made cutting remarks about the excellence of Anthony's form, posture, and technique. Anthony tried her once or twice, lunging forward, but each time she repelled the attack and held her ground.

"I see all those lessons have not gone to waste," Robin said. I knew she was smiling under her crêpe mask, there was such humor in her eyes. Anthony was silent, his face grim with concentration.

As the fight went on, it seemed to me that he had more style and elegance, while Robin fought with the agility and fierceness of an alley cat. As their exchanges became more frenzied, she thrust and parried like a tom swiping with its claws, but then had to dart out of the way of Anthony's more sophisticated counter-moves. Once or twice, it seemed that only the greater reach provided by her long arm and longer weapon kept her from being wounded, perhaps mortally.

If I knew little of what I was seeing, I knew even less of what I was feeling. I was afraid for both, as I wished neither of them harm. But beneath this fear, I felt excitement, and even pride that they were fighting over me. The instant I recognized these feelings, I hated myself for them; it was wrong for these two to treat me as the prize in a contest, or as some bird before which they were enacting a courtship display. Even so, though I was far from wishing either of them dead, I could not help wondering which I would choose as the winner, if I could. Having wondered, I knew instantly what my choice would be; the question remained whether I could live with the outcome.

I was awakened from this reverie by Robin drawing first blood. She had parried a thrust of Anthony's and when he stepped back, he grunted in pain, a line of red showing on the sleeve of his shirt just below the elbow of his sword arm.

"Now, having yielded first blood, will you relent?" Robin demanded. "You gave it your best try."

Anthony stood there, breathing hard, sweat pouring from his brow, trying to stanch the bleeding with his free hand.

"Anthony, please," I begged. "You have done what honor and duty demanded. No one will blame you for having been bested by a highwayman. Now let us leave."

"Shoot him!" Anthony shouted at me.

"What?"

"You have two pistols – shoot him!"

Robin laughed. "Oh, by all means, let a young lady finish your fight for you. What of honor then?"

"To blazes with honor! The point is to stop you and your gang from continuing your marauding! Now, do it, Elizabeth, for the love of God."

"I cannot. I – I have never shot a pistol before."

"They're both cocked; simply point one and squeeze the trigger. He's close enough, you won't miss."

"Yet I cannot. You cannot make me kill a man. It is not – proper for a lady." These were the best excuses I could conjure in the heat of the moment.

"You see?" said Robin. "If anyone is going to finish me, it must be you. I can tell by the way you hold your sword that your arm is tiring. Have you not been training regularly? Too much dissipation, perhaps? Or is it the blood loss?"

Her taunting sent Anthony at her in a fury. She was forced backward, using all her agility and reflexes to deflect and dodge his thrusts. Finally, with a great lunge, he thrust at her chest, but she was able to deflect the blade upward, toward her face. It looked for an instant as if the blow had struck home, and I shrieked in fear. Then I saw that she had parried the thrust while pulling her head back just in time. But the weapon was caught up in the cloth of her mask, and as she thrust it violently to the side with her rapier, the mask came with it.

Anthony danced away from her backstroke, and then could not take in what he saw. He stared in disbelief at Robin unmasked, then glanced over at me and back again, his sword dangling at his side. His first words were so incoherent as not to form an intelligible thought. Finally he managed to stammer, "You – you are Mrs. Burgess!"

"That is one of the names I am known by." Anthony's sword must have grazed her after all, for her neckcloth was turning red with blood. She withdrew a kerchief from her waistcoat and pressed it to the spot.

"And you are also the highwayman, who robbed us and many another over the past weeks."

"I cannot deny it."

He turned to me. "Elizabeth, how could you not know?"

From the anguish on my face it was plain that I had been well aware of my captor's identity. His expression was indescribable.

"And she – she did not kidnap you?"

I shook my head and sobbed. He could only look back at Robin, then at the sky, trying to make sense of all this. "So it is as I suspected – the two of you are – " He paused, unable to describe our relationship. "I would never have guessed, had I not seen – " Again he trailed off.

"What did you see?" My heart raced faster, though that hardly seemed possible. If he had seen us – but how could he have?

Robin slashed idly at the air with her rapier. "Are we going to continue this, or will you stand down, my lord?"

"When I returned to London last week, my friends insisted on taking me to a place, a secret club, where women go to meet other women, to – to – "

"Yes, I know of it," Robin snapped, "though I have never been. It is exclusive to ladies of the *ton*."

"What none of them know is that, attached to the rooms where they meet, are smaller rooms where men are allowed to view the – the proceedings – through cleverly concealed spy-holes." He gave me a sidelong glance, and I felt almost naked before him, as if he might as well have been spying on Rebecca and me just an hour before.

"Such excellent company you keep, my lord," Robin said. "By God, does the depravity of these nobles know no bounds?"

"You must believe me, I would never have gone to such a place if I had known what was in store. And when I realized what the nature of the entertainment was to be – and that these women had no idea they were being watched – and that men should take their pleasure from watching them – I left the place as quick as I could. I told Petersly and Hartwood I wanted nothing more to do with them and their debased ways."

"How noble of you! Yet I think their conduct in Bath should have been enough to put you off them."

"But the point is, after seeing those women kissing, and – "

"Spare us the details, my lord." Robin's rapier slashed the air between them.

"Then I couldn't help wondering – you seemed so jealous in your behavior toward me that night in Bath, as if I were your rival for Lizzie's affections." He gave a short laugh.

"You find that funny, do you?"

"No, only that your goading had an unintended effect – for it was your taunting that bolstered my resolve to declare my love for Lizzie. But then that night in London made me wonder if you hadn't somehow seduced her. With that thought in mind, I returned here as quick as I could, and it turns out I was right. Now I have even more reason to stop you." He lifted his sword and Robin did likewise.

"Wait!" I wanted to step between them, but dared not, as I held the pistols. Anthony was in such a desperate rage that I could not trust him. "Would both of you please stop this madness? I would have neither of you harmed, for you are the two people I esteem most in the world – as strange as that may sound to your ears, Anthony."

"I do not know what to think, Lizzie." I could hardly bear the depths of despair in his voice, but this was not the time to show weakness.

"Yet you both must know" – and here I turned my gaze on Robin – "that neither of you will have me if the other should die of this encounter."

"You would let this outlaw go free?" Anthony asked.

"I would. I believe I can convince her to stop her life of robbery, if you let her go."

"Then you have fallen completely under the spell of a rogue and a flagrant virago. Step back, Elizabeth, please."

"Now the game really is up," Robin said. "I am ready to quit the field. Lizzie, if you will just discharge both pistols into the woods, I will be on my way."

I stepped toward the trees and did as she said, flinching with each report and feeling the sting of the recoil in my hand. The smell of sulfur was thick in the air.

Robin backed toward Juno, sword still pointing at Anthony. "Come no farther, sir. You are nearly spent, and seeking to detain me is useless."

"I will not be beaten by a woman – or hermaphrodite – or I know not what!" Tired as he was, he raised his sword and advanced on her.

"You see with what derision we are held, Lizzie. But I will overlook that remark and spare your life, my lord, if only you will relent. I beg you, Anthony, don't make me do that which I shall regret forever." She backed away, parrying and dodging each of his thrusts, yet refusing to attack in turn. Finally she was backed against Juno, who blocked the lane. The horse stood there placidly as the fight went on.

"I can go no farther, sir; I would turn and ride away, if I could trust you not to stab me in the back. I give you one last chance to desist."

Yet he kept coming at her and with a roar she bashed his weapon to the side and pierced the soft flesh beneath his shoulder. She did not drive her rapier deep, but it was enough; Anthony's cry of agony was terrible to hear. He staggered backward as Robin withdrew her weapon, its point dripping blood.

"I warned you, you fool!" she snarled.

I rushed to Anthony as he sank to his knees.

Robin knelt next to me. "You saw, Lizzie! You know I did my best to avoid giving him a mortal wound. Here, use my kerchief to bind it. Do you know how? Let me help." She tugged at his shirt to expose the wound.

I pushed her away. "Just go, before anyone else sees you!"

"But I – " She broke off with a sob.

"Go, before you make it worse. It was your boldness that led to this."

"Come with me."

"I cannot. I must care for Anthony." I pressed the kerchief against the wound.

"Then meet me where we agreed. I will await you there." I looked up at her and our eyes met for an instant. Then she collected her things, leapt astride Juno, and dashed off.

"What did she mean, meet her?" Anthony asked, his speech slurred. "What did you plan?"

"Shhh. I must bind this up, then get you home." Still he rambled on, increasingly incoherent, as I tore a strip off the hem of my dress and used it to bind the kerchief in place against the wound.

Then he grasped at my arm with renewed vigor. "I would forgive you, you know," he murmured. "I can only guess what kind of attachment you have formed with this woman, but – if you will come back to your senses and – consent to marry me – none need learn your secret."

I hushed him again. "You are delirious. You are not making sense." He said no more. "Can you ride?" He nodded.

With a great effort I got him over to his mount, then guided his boot into the stirrup and boosted him up. It was awkward with just the use of his left hand, but finally he was seated. I took the reins and led Caius homeward.

CHAPTER TWENTY-THREE

I DARED not look back at the Parsonage as I shut the gate and stepped out into the lane, the light of the westering moon casting long shadows behind me. My resolve might have been altogether undone had I allowed myself to contemplate what I was about to leave behind: Father, Mrs. Simmons, Anthony; any possibility of seeing my brother again; the only home I had ever known; most of all, my reputation. Only my single-minded purpose to be reunited with Rebecca, to the exclusion of all other considerations of duty and attachment, had impelled me thus far.

The decision to leave my home had been forced upon me much sooner than either Rebecca or I had wanted, and by her own boldness. Once she was unmasked, there could be no doubt that she must quit the region. Nor did I have any doubt that I must follow. My only thought was to be with her, to satisfy the yearning that had welled up within me these past weeks, one which no amount of self-mastery could subdue. But more than this, Rebecca had become the dearest companion of my heart, and I could not lose her. From the moment I recognized which of my suitors I would choose as the victor, no matter if the other lay dead, I had known what I must do.

This one desire had been my only thought as I led Anthony's horse home, related his injuries and their cause to the family's horrified housekeeper, waited in the drawing room to hear word from the doctor, and learned that Anthony would make a full recovery, though he must remain sedated until morning. It stayed with me as I made my way home, where

Father and Mrs. Simmons, distraught with worry for me, forbade me to walk alone, even into the village, until the highwayman was apprehended. Even as I retired early, pleading exhaustion from the events of the day and bidding each a fonder goodnight than usual, my thoughts strayed to my impending flight.

It was only as I sat waiting for the house to quiet and all within it to be abed that I felt the first quaver in my resolve. Perhaps I could wait and join Rebecca in a less precipitous manner, I thought. Yet if I failed to meet her at the agreed upon time and place, and she quit the neighborhood without me, how would I ever find her again? As well, Mrs. Burgess's disappearing at the same time as the highwayman would throw suspicion on her, even if Anthony did not reveal her identity. In that case, leaving Leighton to live with my friend would be as hurtful to my father as eloping with a highwayman.

Yet I thought I saw another way, if only I could convince Anthony to keep our secret. For, even as I made ready to run away with Rebecca, to follow wherever she would lead me, I thought I saw a different path, a way forward that would spare Father and Mrs. Simmons much pain. To put my plan into effect, I must join Rebecca while putting no suspicion either on myself or on Mrs. Burgess. And to do that I must make everyone believe the highwayman had kidnapped me. I told myself that Father would take this no worse than my having eloped with the rogue. Yet the plan would work only if Anthony kept our secret.

Hoping that our friendship was worth that much to him, I set about making it appear I was a victim of foul play: a hastily scrawled note in a disguised hand, in which the highwayman warned that it would be no use to pursue him and his captive; all the valuables in the room gathered into a cloth parcel; the bed-chamber's remaining objects thrown into disarray; the room's one window left wide open. Finally, a thought of what I was to wear. I had planned on donning my riding habit and sturdiest riding boots, but it seemed unlikely that the highwayman would offer me either as he dragged me from the house, or walked me out at gunpoint. No, I would have to leave wearing only my nightdress and slippers, perhaps with a cloak grasped at the last moment thrown over all. Fortunately, it was a warm evening.

The house had grown quiet, but I had one last task. I sat at my writing desk and composed a letter to Anthony, attempting to explain myself and my love for Rebecca. I told him something of her history and her treatment by her husband, and that she had long viewed the aristocracy in that way he had only recently come to recognize. I told him of the benefit the poor received from the highwayman's looting, and that I was certain I could convince her to stop even these robberies and return to a life within the bounds of the law. I told him how our friendship had grown and become intimate, even before I learned she was the highwayman; how alike our minds were on many points; and how happy she made me. Finally I begged him, telling him that if he truly loved me, he would let me have this happiness, and do nothing to reveal the highwayman's true identity.

With this letter written, I crept from the house and into the lane, and did not look back. Nor did I let doubt creep in as I walked along the moonlit lanes, over moors and fields and past dark woods. I made my way by the most direct route to Holbourne, approaching with considerable trepidation the imposing manor house with its twelve sets of windows in orderly rows across the front. I had been to the house itself only a few times, during the annual parish dinners, spring festivals in its park, and the few social occasions to which I had been invited since my coming out. I approached the servants' entrance, hoping no dog would bark, and slipped the sealed letter under the door. No one within would recognize my hand, and I had to trust that none would break the seal before handing it to Anthony.

Then I turned my steps toward the Old Inn, all of the self-command I had ever been taught bent on reaching Rebecca. If regret made itself known at all, I diverted myself with listening to the calls of the nocturnal animals and contemplating the unexpected beauties of the moors at night: the looming shapes of the trees and the moonlight illumining the mist gathering in the dells, turning it all to silver. Such beauties had been denied me, as I had never been allowed to walk out at night, but now these, and many more, would be mine. And one person would lead me to them – that person who had shown me that life could be much more than I ever expected or dreamt.

DAWN WAS breaking as I arrived at the Old Inn. Even in the warm morning light, it was a dreary place, decrepit, with whitewash peeling from its walls and old carts and pieces of unrecognizable equipment strewn about its yard. From one side came the sound of an axe splitting wood, and I beheld a strange creature, whether boy or man I could not tell, clad in what seemed to be a dun-colored sack that might once have contained seed. He did not notice me.

Once, when these bumpy lanes had been the crossroads of highways leading east to Exeter and south to Dartmouth, the inn had been a thriving establishment. Then the authorities had routed the turnpikes elsewhere, and travelers seldom visited. Unwilling to subsist on the meager local trade of farmers roundabout, the innkeeper began catering to rough sorts, those willing to pay extra for a room for various dark and devious purposes, no questions asked. No respectable person had been seen near the place in years.

With this unpleasant scene before me, my first misgivings began to creep in. Yet I summoned my courage and went up to try the front door, finding it locked. I took a deep breath and gave it a rap. At length it was opened by a haggard old man with several teeth missing.

"I am here to meet..."

The man leaned out the doorway as he hawked and spat into the yard beyond me. "Aye, been expecting ye, though not at daybreak." He stood back and let me enter, giving a vague wave toward the stairs. "Upstairs on the left."

The place was worse within than without, with many years of grime and grease covering its surfaces and a sour smell, as of unwashed bodies and spilled ale, filling the still air. Almost worse than these was the evident lack of propriety of the innkeeper allowing me to make my own way upstairs, with no announcement or introduction. I supposed it didn't much matter whether Rebecca had taken her room as man or woman, these goings-on must be common in such an establishment. I shuddered, wondering if I would often find myself in similar places in future. I consoled myself with the thought that Rebecca would be waiting for me at the top of these stairs; then all would be right, no matter the surroundings.

I ascended the steps, the boards creaking and uneven, but I was reluctant to place a hand on the rail for balance. Reaching the door, I did not knock, fearful of waking the inn's other inhabitants; surely there could be none here I would care to meet. I tried the door, surprised to find it unlocked. Rebecca was asleep in a canopy bed with the covers thrown back; she wore only a long man's shirt. I caught my breath at the sight of her bare legs emerging from its tails, lit by the warm morning light streaming through the open window.

Closing the door behind me, I surveyed the chamber. It was a corner room, and had windows facing south and west. An attempt had been made to clean it, and everything was tidy and in order. Robin's breeches had been folded neatly and set on the chest at the foot of the bed, with her boots standing nearby, cleaned and polished. The shirt she had worn the day before had been washed and hung up to dry. A stack of books stood on the nightstand, one of them lying open, along with her workbag. I was much comforted by this scene. Despite her bold recklessness, and even in this mean outlaw's refuge, she was still Rebecca: sensible, energetic, and fastidious.

I approached the bed, and as my shadow crossed her face, she leapt up in alarm, reaching for the pistol slung in its holster at the head of the bed. Then, seeing me, she relaxed, a smile spreading across her face. "You came!" she said, replacing the pistol and reaching a hand out to me.

But it was too late. I had seen the alarm and fear in her eyes, those eyes I should never have expected to reveal such a weak emotion. Was this how we were to live – hunted, afraid, starting at each shadow and footfall? All the regret and doubt I had kept at bay throughout the night now overcame me. I let out a sob and fell to my knees next to the bed, burying my face in my hands.

"My love, what's wrong?" She jumped out of bed and knelt next to me, her hands on my shoulders.

I looked up at her through tear-filled eyes, seeing nothing but concern in her own. "This place – " I said. "The fear you just showed me – The sword fight yesterday – Father – Father awaking even now to find me gone! What have I done?"

"Oh, my sweet! This is my fault. Damn my recklessness! I did not count on Anthony's doggedness in pursuing his duty. He is a remarkable man, far worthier than any lordling I have ever known."

"This hardly helps."

"Will he recover?"

I told her of the doctor's prognosis.

"I am glad." Her look of relief turned grave as she took up my hands and held my gaze for a long moment. "If you wish it," she said at last, her voice subdued, "I will saddle my horse and carry you back home as quick as may be. We can hope they haven't yet discovered your absence."

"You would do that for me? You would give me up?"

"It would break my heart to do so, but I cannot bear to see you so distraught. I would not be the one to cause you such pain. And what good is it to win your love if you feel nothing but bitterness and regret, and blame me for it?"

For a moment it was as if I were seeing her for the first time, and my chest suddenly felt much too small to contain my heart. "I do not blame you. It is my choice, and I make it freely. I cannot turn back now."

"Then come to bed. You must have had less sleep than I, and I had but little." She drew me to my feet, and then down beside her in the bed, pulling a sheet over us. I felt her unpinning my hair and stroking it and then I knew no more.

THE SUN was high when I awoke several hours later. Rebecca held me in her arms, and I lay with one hand resting on the bare skin of her hip. I turned my head toward her. She was looking down at me, her head propped on her elbow, a smile of contentment on her lips. The light coming in the window lit her eyes, black pools at the center surrounded by a rich mahogany – I thought I could gaze into them forever. Then she leaned down and gave me a long kiss, and that was even better.

"Good morning, my love," she said. "You are quite beautiful when you sleep. Your mouth parts halfway, and I could kiss it again and again." She followed her own suggestion, her free hand slipping around to my breast. As the kisses went on, I ran my hand from her hip down to her thigh and back again. I felt none of the frenzy of the day before, but rather a languorous, sensual pleasure, and the deep delight of having my lover's arms around me.

"I want you," she whispered in my ear. "Do you want me?"

"Of course I do." I turned to face her more fully, taking her face in both my hands. "I want every inch of you."

"Then we will do this properly." She sat up, drawing her man's shirt over her head. For the first time, I saw her as she truly was: her collar-length brown hair framing her wide cheekbones, small nose, lively brown eyes, and thin, delicate lips; the whiteness of her throat and neck, marred where Anthony's sword had grazed her; her pale shoulders and the expanse of smooth skin above the curves of her round, pert breasts; her flat belly, with a patch of hair disappearing between her closed legs.

She pulled me to a sitting position and tugged at my nightgown until it was over my head and off, looking at me with a hunger that would not wait to take all of me in. "You're so beautiful!" she said, reaching for me and pulling me down on top of her so that I felt the softness of her skin with the whole length of my body. She was right: the feeling of the two of us lying together, skin to skin, was infinitely greater than anything I had felt the day before. We remained in such a manner for a time that stretched on, kissing each other over and over, our hands exploring up and down.

At length, we found other spots to kiss and other places to explore, trading nibbles, caresses, tastes, strokes, nuzzles, and thrusts, the love and the pleasure passing back and forth between us. Her body was a strange country to me, yet familiar; like the dells and moorlands where I loved to ramble, it was a well-known place, but never failed to offer a new encounter or unaccustomed delight.

And then there came that most important discovery, the moment when I first saw her most intimate part. At first it was a mere slit; then she showed me how to touch and caress it, and it bloomed like the prettiest blossom of

May. The petals, hidden beneath the silkiest brown hair, were formed in two parts, outer and inner, the latter a rosy shade of pink.

"Ahh!" I gasped in delight. "It's so pretty – *you* are so pretty, like a flower!" I grinned at her.

"The flower of love, my love," she said, beaming back at me. "I told you, I appreciate some blooms above all others."

I did not smile at her joke, for I was too engrossed by the sight before me. How infinitely more alive was this blossom than any I had seen – for when I touched these petals, Rebecca responded with shivers of delight. And more so when she guided my fingers to that spot which, when she had touched the corresponding spot on my own body, had driven me into such flights of ecstasy. It sat at the upper opening of her cleft, hooded, with a nubbin of pink flesh poking out, reminding me of nothing so much as the hood and spadex of the Arum plant if viewed from a certain angle. That this suggestive inflorescence is commonly known by the name, "Wake-Robin," struck me as more than a happy coincidence.

Suddenly, I found myself bursting out in tears.

"Lizzie, what is it?" She sat up, stroking my shoulder.

I wiped my eyes and collected myself for a moment, struggling to express the most scandalous thought of all. "It's just that, all this time, since you first told me of your love for women, I could think only that it was a sin. That, in large part, is what held me back from you. Even after yesterday, I thought I was throwing my own soul away by coming here. I dared such a sin, if it meant I could be with you. But now that I've seen you, and seen for the first time how women are made, I cannot help but wonder why Our Lord would fashion our most intimate parts to look so much like the most beautiful and wondrous works of His creation. Why would he give us such a great attraction to the flowers of field, forest, and stream, and bar us from that same attraction in each other?"

"And your answer is?"

"Our Lord must approve our love; it must not be a sin; we have His blessing."

"Oh, Lizzie, yes!" She took my face between her hands, gazing at me through her own tear-filled eyes.

We returned to our passion with even greater fervor. At one point, when I had become engrossed in pleasuring her, she reached a hand out to tip my face toward her. "I must see you. You must look at me as you do it." Our eyes met, and I felt an even greater love for her than I had before, if that were possible. I felt wholly absorbed in her, as if I could crawl inside her and never come out. At her moment of greatest pleasure, I saw her in all the nakedness of her extremity, and I knew her more deeply than I had ever known anyone. I saw into her soul, and she saw into mine, and we were one.

Afterward, sated, drenched, we lay in each other's arms, sharing the deepest bliss. The question I had pondered the day before, how Rebecca could have gotten as much joy as she had given, was now answered, for I felt fully compensated for my efforts, as if I were the one who had received all the pleasure. Yet, more than pleasure and lust, what we had just shared was the sweetest expression of our love. Rebecca was my truest friend in the world, the one who knew me as I truly was, who had brought out those parts of me I did not know existed. If there was anything wrong in uniting with her in this way, I could not find it. Father had always taught that, except in the most extreme cases, sinners were conscious of the wrong they did, the sin making itself felt through guilt and shame. Yet I could detect none of these, only a profound sense that we belonged together, doing exactly this, sharing exactly this joy.

"One kiss, my bonny sweetheart, I'm after a prize to-night,
But I shall be back with the yellow gold before the morning light;
Yet, if they press me sharply, and harry me through the day,
Then look for me by moonlight,
Watch for me by moonlight,
I'll come to thee by moonlight, though hell should bar the way."
– Alfred Noyes, "The Highwayman"

CHAPTER TWENTY-FOUR

WE DOZED for a time, then Rebecca nuzzled me awake. She was kneeling on the floor beside the bed. "Yesterday you said you wanted to bind yourself to me forever. What say you now?" She opened her hand to reveal a gold ring resting on her palm. "Miss Elizabeth Collington, will you make me the happiest of women, for the rest of our lives?"

"You know I haven't changed my mind. I only hope I can make you happy."

"How can you doubt it? But if you are willing, then let us make this a proposal and a wedding in one." She took my hand and held the ring before it. "Wilt thou love me, comfort me, honor, and keep me in sickness and in health; and, forsaking all other, keep thee only unto me, so long as we both shall live?"

My lip trembled as I tried to speak. "I will," I said at last.

With great solemnity she placed the ring on my fourth finger, then kissed me.

"Wait," I said, and got out of bed, retrieving the parcel of valuables I had brought with me and withdrawing from it a dull gold band of my own.

I knelt before Rebecca. "I lied to you that day in the carriage, when I told you I had only one memento of my mother. This ring was hers. She gave it to me before she died, to wear on my wedding day. Now I would have you wear it. Will you be my – " I stopped. "I don't know how to call you."

"I will be your wife or your husband or whatever you would have me be."

"Then, Rebecca Hazelton, will you be mine, till death do us part?"

"I will." I slipped the ring onto her smallest finger, the only one that would fit it. We collapsed in each other's arms and remained in that attitude for a time.

At length Rebecca sat up. "And now it must be time for the wedding breakfast. Are you hungry?"

"Famished!" I said as Rebecca got to her feet and pulled on her shirt and breeches.

"This place has no servants. I will descend into the depths and see what I can find that won't turn our stomachs." She returned a short time later with a tray laden with hard cheese, harder tack, pickled eggs, and mugs of ale. "The beer is not too sour," she said.

As rough as this fare was, I ate it with relish. We sat on the bed, the tray between us, trying not to spill the beer, I in my nightgown and she in her man's clothes. She reached over the edge of the bed and pulled a small dagger from a sheath hidden in her boot, casually using it to slice the cheese.

"Is that the knife you used to protect yourself in London?"

"One very like it, though I have had no occasion in recent years to use it. Most in London, and even in Exeter, know better than to challenge Lord Rob." Her voice filled with pride as she said it, before growing more serious. "But I have not the same advantage when dressed as Rebecca Burgess. I nearly used it on that lout in Bath, I was that startled by behavior I thought was long in my past."

I looked at this bold woman who had become my one true love and wondered about her. Where did Robin end and Rebecca begin? Surely it was Robin's boldness and boastfulness, her strength and sense of mastery, which had drawn me to her in the first place, making me yearn for her with an intensity I could never have imagined. But it was Rebecca's more feminine qualities which had drawn me yet closer to her – her tastes, opinions, and interests, some in accord with my own, and some so different they had forced a change in my views. Was she one person in men's clothing, and another in women's dress? I could not help questioning her on this score as we ate.

"Oh, my dear!" She laughed, setting down her mug of ale. "It is not that complicated. Rebecca and Robin are one person. It is the world that treats me differently when I wear men's garb. And when I dress as Robin, my boldness and bravado – what you might call my masculine qualities – have a freer expression, simply due to the freeing nature of the garments. But I would say there are no masculine and feminine qualities, save that our education and our dress make them so, but only fine ones and poor ones. For what woman can do without bravery, fortitude, and endurance, given what we often have to bear? It is only the confining stays, the slippers, the narrow skirts – and when we go on horseback, the awkward side saddles – that cut us off from a physical expression of boldness and vigor that should be as much the province of women as it is of men. And for a man to become a true gentleman, he must mute the rougher, more brutish aspects of his nature with gentler qualities often considered the domain of the fairer sex. If only my husband had learnt that!"

"And which guise do you prefer? Which do you adopt most often?"

"In London and Exeter, I was always Robin, so difficult are those cities for single women who are not well guarded. But in Leighton, where I could walk about in feminine dress without fear, I must confess that I enjoyed living as a woman and returning to those pursuits I enjoyed as a girl at home. In future, we will have to see which is most fitting."

"I love you as Robin, of course, for that is how I was first taught to desire you – you are so strong and masterful in that guise. But I hope you will still wear a gown sometimes, for me."

"I will," she said, grinning, "especially one of those sheer gowns with a deep bodice that have become so fashionable."

From this, we turned to more practical matters: how we would make our escape from Devonshire, where we would go, how we would live.

"I suggest London," Rebecca said, "at least at first, as it will be easy to lose ourselves there. I know a neighborhood that is not too rough where two women can let apartments and attract little notice. Then we can plan where to settle, under what guise. After gaining tonight's prize, we will have many possibilities."

I told her of my letter to Anthony, and my hope that he would keep our secret, perhaps allowing us to return to Leighton. Her brow knitted together at this, and even more so at the news of my feigned kidnapping. "It is dangerous," she said. "Ah well, they'll be looking for you anyway, and I trust the inn-keeper not to reveal our presence, as I pay him well enough. With luck I'll be back before dawn and we can plan our next move. But how will you know if Anthony chooses to keep our secret?"

I had to admit this was a flaw in my plan, for I was not accustomed to such machinations.

She seemed doubtful for a moment, then said, "We will take that as it comes, but first I must complete tonight's job."

"And you *must* commit one more robbery?"

"For our security, yes. The mail coach will be carrying a particularly large sum of gold. With this prize in hand, after dividing half to the poor in Exeter and allotting Jack and Tom their shares, my income will come to five hundred pounds a year. It will allow us to live as we please, though perhaps not in London, which is expensive."

"I could easily live on less. Father's income has been three hundred a year, and we have had no difficulty."

"We may live as economically as you wish, but this is the goal I have set. I would not see us reduced to poverty by unforeseen events, for gold is power. I told you already, I will not be without power ever again."

"But what – " I could hardly voice my thought. "What if you are captured?"

She put down her mug and pushed aside my empty plate, taking me by the shoulders. "Of that you need have no fear, for I will fight until the end if I must. I would rather go down in a blaze of gunfire than allow myself to be captured. I will never put myself under the power of any man ever again, and I would not have you see me hanging from a gibbet." My eyes must have gone wide at this, for she continued in a bright voice: "But not to worry. We have robbed the mail coaches before, and we have our ways."

"Your boldness will be the death of you! You saw what it got us yesterday, and yet you persist!"

She placed a finger over my lips. "I promise you, Lizzie, I will return, though hell should bar the way."

It was with great trepidation that I relented, seeing no way to dissuade her. I watched silently as she set about cleaning her pistols and reloading them. As evening drew on toward a late sunset, she turned to dressing in a fresh shirt, a dark waistcoat, doe-skin breeches, clean stockings, and her thigh-high boots. I helped tie her cravat with its bunch of lace, then pulled her hair back in a short tail, tying it with a black ribbon. Going to a wardrobe, she looked through the coats hanging there, before pulling one out.

"The coat of claret velvet for the highwayman's last ride, don't you think?" She put the coat on, then turned to show it to me. "We'll need to see about clothes for you. There are a few gowns in the wardrobe. I'm sure they're much too long for you, but you'll burst out of the bodice in a most enticing fashion." She gave me her devilish grin as she put on her cocked hat, becoming the highwayman once more. With her dashing figure before me, I felt that same tingle of excitement that had run through me on first seeing her.

"Come, give me a kiss, for I will need luck to win this prize." She bent down and kissed me long and hard on the mouth, then straightened and regarded me more seriously. "If only I could tell what you were thinking. But I see your mask of reserve has descended once more. If that is what helps you bear the hours while you wait for me, so be it."

She went to the window and looked out, scanning the evening sky. The first stars were out, just visible in the glare of the waxing moon. "The mail coach travels at midnight, an unusual schedule meant to throw off bandits. Fortunately, I have a well-placed informant. If all goes well, I should be back before dawn. But if the militia takes our scent, we will have to lead them a chase, and in that event, expect me by the light of tomorrow's moon. But remember – nothing will keep me from returning here. Now I must go!"

She kissed me once more on the cheek and stepped to the door, calling for Jack and Tom as she opened it. Through the doorway I saw two men emerge onto the landing from the bed-chamber opposite. One was the ginger-haired Jack, and the other was the man I had known as Thomas Nighthorn, Mrs. Burgess's brother, now dressed in coarser clothing.

"Good evening, Miss Collington." He grinned in at me, tipping his hat.

"You two have met, of course," Robin said. "Tom was a good sport to play my brother, considering he never approved of the risks involved. And now, away!" She shut the door behind her and they were gone.

A few moments later, a whistle came from the yard. I went to the open window to see Robin astride Juno, about to throw a pebble at the casement.

"I just had to see you once more and say one last farewell for luck," she said, reaching up to me.

"Farewell then." I felt unable to say more with her accomplices nearby.

"So cold! Lean down and let me touch you, at least."

My hand could not reach hers, but in leaning out the window, I saw that my long hair would. She twirled a lock around her fingers for a moment as she gazed up at me. "You *will* be here when I return?"

I tried to ignore the hint of doubt I heard in her voice. "You know that I will."

She released the lock and turned her horse. "Till the dawn!" With that, she joined Jack and Tom in the inn-yard and they thundered off down the road.

Then a gate hinge creaked and I turned to see a dun-colored shape disappearing around a corner of the building.

They had tied her up to attention, with many a sniggering jest.
They had bound a musket beside her, with the muzzle beneath her breast!
"Now, keep good watch!" and they kissed her. She heard the doomed man say –
Look for me by moonlight;
Watch for me by moonlight;
I'll come to thee by moonlight, though hell should bar the way!
- Alfred Noyes, "The Highwayman"

CHAPTER TWENTY-FIVE

REBECCA DID not return at dawn. She did not return at noon. I tried to quell my growing fear by remembering her words: I was to look for her by the light of that night's moon. Yet this counsel did little good. I could only think of her, shot down in the road by the mail guard's blunderbuss, a red stain spreading across the front of her white shirt.

To take my mind off my worry, I put on one of the gowns in the wardrobe, then went downstairs, the gown's long hem trailing down the steps behind me. Seeing no one about, I poked around in the larder, finding but few scraps of wholesome food. It hardly mattered, for I had little appetite.

Returning upstairs, I tried to while away the time with the novel Rebecca had stacked on her nightstand, Ann Radcliffe's *The Mysteries of Udolpho.* At first I had to smile, thinking back to the day I told Robin I did not stoop to reading romances, but then I became so engrossed in the tale that the hours did at last pass quickly. Somehow, the increasingly frightening situations Emily faced, as outlandish as they were, made my own situation more tolerable.

The sun was setting late that evening when I looked up from the second volume, distracted by the sound of marching boots in the inn yard. Going to the room's south window, I saw a group of five redcoats approaching the building. Then voices rose from the bar-room below, but I could not make out what they said. Would the innkeeper give me up? For a moment I thought of climbing out the room's west window and making my escape, going so far as to search for a drainpipe down which I could climb. I found none. Besides, I was not Rebecca and had neither the strength nor the skill for such a feat. If the redcoats decided to search the inn, then I must rely on my wits.

The inn's front door banged closed and the soldiers marched off toward the west. I was just breathing a sigh of relief when a dun-colored shape darted out from the side of the building and took after them. It was the same strange figure in sack-cloth I had seen upon my arrival. It caught up to the soldiers, engaging them in a conversation with much pointing back toward the inn. Again I thought of attempting escape, but decided this would only make me appear more guilty were I to be caught. Back the soldiers marched, and I waited with racing heart, pacing up and down the room, as several pairs of booted feet ascended the stairs. The door burst open and two soldiers stepped in.

"Oh, thank God you've found me!" I exclaimed, having decided to play the relieved kidnap victim. "I was expecting those rogues to return at any moment and be off with me."

Neither of the soldiers wore the brighter coat or gold lace of an officer. The one who seemed in charge looked around the room for a moment before asking, "Are you Miss Collington?" I saw no reason to deny this. "We were told you were kidnapped, but now here you are, at your liberty." He was a large man with an open, round face, his mouth making a round shape of perplexity.

"Of course I was kidnapped!"

"Why aren't you tied up then? A young lady such as yourself, you're worth a lot to a lout like the highwayman, one way or the other. He's not going to risk you wandering off."

"The innkeeper has kept an eye on me, and the highwayman threatened my family if I tried to escape. I might have attempted it, but I couldn't put my father in jeopardy."

"Is that so?" the soldier said with mock credulity. He surveyed the room with the air of a man who was going to earn a promotion this day, poking into drawers and the chest at the foot of the bed before going to the wardrobe and pulling out one of the gowns hanging there. "Well, look here, it seems you've moved in quite comfortably." He gave a satisfied grin.

I held out my arm to show the sleeve extending far beyond my hand. "Does this gown look as if it fits me?" My tone made it unnecessary to tell him what a fool he was. "I wore only a nightdress when I was taken, and the rogue was gentleman enough to loan me this gown. As to what he is doing with such a collection of women's clothing, I cannot tell you."

The soldier seemed unimpressed with this argument, and as uninterested as most men are in the intricacies of female dress. He continued with his search, growing jolly as he picked up the volume of *Udolpho* and read the title printed on its spine. "Did the highwayman allow you to bring your own books? Quite considerate, that." Here he gave me another smirk.

"Of course he didn't. That book belongs to the rogue as well."

"A highwayman who reads romances? What do you take me for, Miss Collington?" He seemed so pleased with this discovery that he continued searching the room with even greater enthusiasm. He came to Rebecca's work bag, holding it aloft with evident glee. "Come now, you cannot tell me the highwayman knits – wait, what is this?" He reached into the bag and pulled out a small, curved bit of cloth attached to the needles. "A highwayman who knits booties for newborn babes?"

I couldn't prevent a low sob from escaping my lips. I hadn't noticed what she had been working on, but it was so like her, that even as she sat here plotting to steal thousands of pounds for the poor and the wretched and the charities that served them, she also took the time to perform such a small act of kindness. And that thought led to wondering what had become of her, whether she was lying dead on the road, or worse –

"No, Miss Collington," the soldier was saying, "it must have taken a good-size cart to bring you here with all your belongings. It's clear you've eloped with the highwayman."

"How dare you!" I tried to look down my nose at him. "When my father hears of this – "

"Now, there's no call to take that superior tone with me – you're only a vicar's daughter after all. And you wouldn't be the first young lady of decent birth to lose her head over an outlaw. Well-dressed fellow no doubt, cuts a fine figure, a bit dangerous, rides a spirited horse – a little flattery from that sort will turn many a young lady's head, make her forget propriety in a moment of passion – "

"You will pay for casting such aspersions on my character!"

He only laughed at this, then said, "Matthews, gag her. I've grown tired of her lofty attitude. Since the highwayman failed to bind her, we'll do the job for him." He turned to the other soldier. "Jones, see if there's a horse to be had and make straight away to report our discovery to Captain Harris." These orders given, he surveyed the room, measuring the distance between the bed and the south-facing window – a few feet at most. "Yes, we'll tie her to the bed post. That way, when the highwayman returns, he'll see her from the yard. We'll use her to lure him in and then we'll have him!"

I tried to struggle but there was no question of my resisting. First they stuffed a kerchief in my mouth and tied the ends behind my head, then they bound my arms behind my back and around the bedpost. They lit all the candles they could find so my upright figure would be easily seen by anyone approaching the inn from the road that passed by on the south – the road down which Rebecca could ride at any moment.

Then they did the strangest thing of all. "Bring me your musket, Matthews," the leader ordered. When this was done, he took the weapon and placed it against me, with its muzzle beneath my breast, lashing it in that position with more of the cord they had used to bind me. With a dreadful click, he cocked the hammer. What this was meant to accomplish, I do not know, though it certainly frightened me more than anything they had done so far. Perhaps they hoped the highwayman would rush in, see me bound, and set the gun off while hastily untying me, one shot killing us both. It seemed an absurd idea, but I could not question them, gagged as I was. I tried to stand as still as possible, finding this easy to do, lashed as I was to the bedpost.

With these preparations made, the leader left two of his men to spy out the window, while he went downstairs to await the highwayman.

The hours stretched on, the moon, visible through the open window, offering the only measure of time's passage as it inched upward. Soon the whole yard before the inn, and a good length of the road beyond, was bathed in a light nearly as bright as day, despite the glare created by the candles burning in the room. To the east, the road stretched across the purple moor, but to the west my view was cut off by an outbuilding of the inn.

The soldiers were not the most attentive, soon nodding off at their posts at the window. I thought of how I might escape, quietly struggling against my bonds. I moved my hands up and down along the post around which they were bound, then tried twisting them this way and that in an attempt to free them. It seemed there was a little slack in the cord, and if I could just work at it a bit more, trying to make my hand as slender as possible, I might be able to get free.

Time passed – it must have been hours, judging by the height of the moon – and I had made progress. I could move my hand back and forth for a considerable distance in its corded cuff, and move it farther down the bedpost, but still not enough to get it free. My hand had become slick – with blood, I knew by the stinging at my wrist – and I hoped this slickness would allow me to make better progress.

I was just renewing my efforts when boot steps sounded from the stairwell. The soldiers at the window jerked awake, sitting more upright just as the door to the bedchamber burst open.

"You two!" their leader shouted. "No falling asleep now – I can tell by those dazed looks that you've been nodding off." He looked me over, but noticed nothing amiss. "Stay awake boys. The rogue has to return sometime." With that, he left the room, shutting the door behind him.

With the soldiers more alert, I dared not continue my struggle to free myself. When their attention was once more fixed on the inn-yard, I quietly tested the reach of my hands. Perhaps they had left a knife on the bed where I could reach it. But my hands met only the bedpost and the musket lashed beside it. Leaning sideways, I slid my hand along the stock, finding first the trigger guard, and at last the trigger itself.

I gave a little gasp as I realized what this meant. I may not have achieved my own escape, but I had found a means of achieving Rebecca's.

Only one question remained: would I have the courage to go through with such a plan? I thought back over everything I had experienced with Rebecca. For two days, I had felt the greatest love a person can know. I had felt more alive than I could remember. I had felt myself to be the happiest of all women, wed to Rebecca as truly as had we married in church, before God and family. I would not have traded those two days for anything. It did seem a bitter loss for it all to end so soon. Yet when I had joined myself to her, I had promised to keep her, in sickness and in health, and surely there was only one way I could keep that promise now. If I could save the life of the one I held most dear, I would do it gladly. I knew Rebecca would have done the same for me.

I had not long to ponder my resolve, for in a few moments more, the sound of hoofbeats came through the open casement. The redcoats looked to their priming and peered cautiously out the windows. I leaned over, the muzzle digging into my ribcage, my finger finding the trigger once more. It was slippery with my own blood, and I hoped my finger would not slip. I took a deep breath as I waited, trying to calm my galloping heart.

The sound of hoofbeats grew louder. When would the rider appear? Would my warning shot come in time to warn Rebecca away? And in these last seconds, I thought of Father, and all the devastation he would face when this news reached him. But I could wait no longer. The rider would soon be within the redcoats' sights. I began to press the fatal lever.

Tlot-tlot; tlot-tlot! Had they heard it? The horsehoofs ringing clear;
Tlot-tlot; tlot-tlot, in the distance? Were they deaf that they did not hear?
Down the ribbon of moonlight, over the brow of the hill,
The highwayman came riding –
Riding – riding –
The red coats looked to their priming! She stood up, straight and still.
- Alfred Noyes, "The Highwayman"

CHAPTER TWENTY-SIX

A RIDER appeared, not from the east, but from the west. In the bright moonlight I readily saw it was not Robin. My finger eased off the trigger and I gasped, out loud this time, my whole body trembling.

Two more riders appeared behind the first, these dressed in military uniform. The soldiers at the window relaxed and uncocked their muskets. The riders dismounted, the one who had been in the lead looking awkward as he did so. Then words were spoken as the men disappeared into the inn, growing to shouts as they ascended the stairs. The door to the bedchamber flew open and in strode an officer. Behind him came Anthony, his right arm in a sling, a cloak thrown over his state of undress.

"Untie this young lady immediately," the officer ordered the men, but Anthony got to me first.

"Careful of the musket, sir," one of the men said.

Anthony paused, staring with horror at the strange snare the soldiers had caught me in. "Lizzie, are you well?"

I nodded, though my whole body still shook.

The officer came over to see what his men had done to me. "What in blazes?" he demanded.

The two soldiers who had been at the window stared blankly at him, but then the leader of the original five entered the room. "Begging your pardon, sir, but it was plain she had been consorting with criminals. We only meant to use her as bait, and maybe give her a little scare at the same time."

"Have you lost your mind? Clearly, you have the judgment of a flea, whether it's this business with the musket, or deciding whether Miss Collington is a victim or an accomplice. Now get downstairs and wait for me there."

Meanwhile, Anthony had knelt beside me, tugging ineffectually at the knots around my wrist with his one good hand. "Lizzie, you're bleeding!"

His gaze travelled from my wrists to the trigger of the musket and then back up to look me in the eye. I turned away, knowing he had just seen the blood that told him what I had been about to do.

Seeing how much difficulty Anthony was having, one of the soldiers offered to help him. In a moment I was free; without the cords and the bedpost to support me, I sank down to sit on the bed.

The officer considered me for a moment. I was still trembling, and I knew I must be pale, very like a frightened kidnapping victim. "Miss Collington, I'm afraid I must ask how you came here."

"It's as I told the other soldier." My voice was faint and quavering. "I was kidnapped the night before last. They brought me here, bound and gagged. The highwayman set the innkeeper to guard me, and he – he threatened to harm my father if I attempted to run away."

"It's just as I told you, Captain Harris," Anthony said. "I knew there would be some such explanation."

"Yes, it does seem most likely. See to her, will you, Burnside?"

The soldiers left the room. Anthony looked after them for a moment before turning to me. "Here, use this to stanch that bleeding." He handed me his handkerchief, suddenly seeming more distant, and less solicitous, than he had in the moments after entering the room. He turned away and stared out the window, while I daubed at my wrists. The blood was beginning to dry where it had run down my hand to the tips of my fingers.

At last he said, "This is quite a predicament you've gotten yourself into, Lizzie. My only question is why? Why would you do such a thing?"

"Because I love her."

"You believe you do, I am sure. Yet you must know your father is half mad with fear and grief for you."

"Then he will be glad for my safe return, thanks to you. Do you – do you plan to let us go?"

"'*Us*'? No, not *us*, if by that you mean you and this outlaw. Since I awoke from the laudanum and heard that you had been kidnapped, my one thought has been to preserve your reputation. I knew the kidnapping was a lie, of course, but so far I have managed to keep Captain Harris convinced of its truth, despite the report to the contrary and what he just saw. As for this Mrs. Burgess – "

"You haven't given her away have you?"

"Not as of yet, but her fate depends much on you."

"How? What do you mean?"

"You have a choice, and you must make it quickly. A larger contingent of soldiers will arrive soon and set a trap for the outlaws. Mrs. Burgess – Robin – could easily be captured or killed. But you can prevent both." He paused and turned to me. "Say you will marry me, and I will ride out and warn her not to return here. You will buy her life."

"And be parted from her."

"Of course. She must leave Leighton immediately."

I stared at him for a long moment, trying to gain control of my runaway thoughts and emotions. I was still distraught and trembling from what I had nearly done. Yet, as strange as it may seem, this decision was the harder to make. How had I misjudged Anthony so completely? This was not the honorable behavior of a friend. "You would force such a choice on me? You would have me wed you against my will?"

He turned back to the window, as if he could not look at me while speaking in such imperious tones as he had adopted. "Anything to keep you out of the hands of that – woman. I read your letter, and it did convince me you feel a great attachment to her. As time goes on, however, and her hold over you lessens, you will come to your senses. I know you feel some measure of attachment for me."

"You speak as if I were bewitched, as if I do not know my own heart and mind."

"You are young, it is likely just a passing passion. In a year or two you will be glad you have joined respectable society rather than throwing everything away on a woman and an outlaw, and you will thank me for saving you from yourself. Now come, time is short. Will you see your beloved shot down in the inn-yard, or will you save her life?"

"You know there is only one choice I can make; it is no choice at all."

He turned back to me, and his eyes bored into mine. "Then I have the promise of your hand in marriage?"

"You do."

He did not seem glad of this, but remained as serious as before. "I will not insult you with going to my knee or professing my love, though you know I do love you. We must save all that for later. Now, prepare to ride out with me. I will tell Captain Harris that I am taking you to safety." He turned back to me before leaving. "Oh, and before coming down, make sure there is nothing here that could tie Mrs. Burgess to the highwayman."

He left the room and I sat there for a moment more, pondering what I had just done. Then I realized there was no time to waste, as Rebecca could return at any moment. I followed Anthony's advice, searching the room for anything with Rebecca's name on it, a direction on an envelope, or anything else that might connect her name with this room. The gowns and the other feminine accoutrements could not be helped. I thought all was safe, but then I thought to look in the volumes of *Udolpho.* I smiled when I saw a bookplate in the first one; but it would not give Rebecca away, for it bore the name Robin Cantwell. I should have known she was crafty enough to keep her two lives separate, even down to her reading. A taste for gothic romances seemed to suit Robin, her life was so like to them. Just to be safe, I tore the bookplates out of each volume and thrust them into the pocket of the borrowed gown. Then I wrapped a cloak over all and went downstairs.

THE MOON rode toward the west as we rode east, Caius cantering easily beneath us across the purple moor. I sat aside behind Anthony, my arms encircling his waist, every moment regretting this necessity to keep from falling. I couldn't help remembering the first time I had ridden behind the highwayman. In that moment, I could never have imagined a person with whom I would less willingly share a seat, but now I had found him. I tried not to lean too close against him, but it was difficult, smooth though Caius's gait was. Yet somehow I trusted that Anthony would soon return to his senses, just as surely as he trusted I would return to mine.

"Are you certain she will come this way?" Anthony asked, his voice raised over the clattering of Caius's hooves.

"I am not certain at all. I know only that they took this road when they rode out yester-evening. By now they could be anywhere."

"If they approach the inn by another road, then there is nothing I can do for them. You must admit, I've done everything I could."

He spoke true; I had heard him give nothing away since leaving the inn to find him standing with the soldiers in the yard. They were questioning the strange fellow in sack cloth who had alerted them to my presence. He now seemed of middle age and not in his right mind. He had seen and heard but little – only our parting when I had leant out the window. I was thankful to my father for training me to such reserve as I had shown then, for our conversation had given nothing away.

"You see, Captain," Anthony said when the informant finished, "Miss Collington was a captive, obeying the highwayman's orders to lean down and let him touch her – the very thought of which makes my blood boil – and making her swear she would be here when he returned."

"I quite agree, Lord Burnside. Miss Collington, you are free to go."

"By your leave, Captain," Anthony said, "I will escort her to safety and warn her father of his danger."

"Of course. And I will send word to my men to post a guard on the Parsonage."

With that we had mounted Caius, somewhat awkwardly with Anthony's bad arm, and ridden west, toward Holbourne and Leighton. We had not gone far when we passed a troop of soldiers marching in the opposite direction, toward the inn. Then Anthony had steered his horse onto a little track heading north, and we had travelled in an arc, north, east, and south, until we once again struck the road on the moor east of the inn.

Now, as we continued east across the moor, the moonlight creating eerie shapes out of every rock and tree, casting long shadows, and etching every edge with silver, I had to agree that Anthony had done everything in his power to preserve my reputation. As for Rebecca's whereabouts, the road east seemed, by the slimmest of margins, the likeliest place to find her. She and her accomplices could have split up, or they could have gone far out of their way in eluding their pursuers, and even now be approaching the inn by another route. And this was not the worst of all the possibilities running through my mind. No, I could only trust to hope that she would return on the same road by which she had departed.

I tried to banish any other thought as we approached a dark wood. Anthony slowed our pace to a walk as we moved under the trees, for the oak canopy was so dense here that only shafts of moonlight penetrated it, leaving much of the road in dark shadow.

"Caius can use the rest," Anthony said. "This is but a narrow band of forest, and we should soon proceed more quickly."

We kept to this sedate pace for several minutes, Caius's hooves clip-clopping on the road's hard surface, then entered a more open stretch bathed in moonlight. As if announcing our presence, a whistle sounded from the dark shadows on our right and a little farther ahead. Anthony brought the horse to a halt and peered uncertainly ahead, but it was difficult to distinguish anything in the gloom. Something moved through the trees to our right, and in the next moment a rider emerged onto the road ahead of us, silhouetted against the black of the forest beyond.

Anthony turned Caius as quick as he could, but it was too late. A rider entered the road in the direction from which we had come and levelled a pistol at us. Anthony dropped the reins and reached to his waist for his own pistol, but before he drew it a voice came out of the forest, now on our left.

"Are you a better shot with your left hand than with your right, my lord?" I took what seemed my first full breath in many hours as I recognized Robin's voice.

Then she was beside us, sitting tall on Juno, the black horse looming like an apparition out of the blackness under the trees. Robin's eyes glinted in the moonlight as they peered at us from above her black mask, her pistol aimed at Anthony's chest.

"I came here to find you, not to let you rob me," Anthony said.

"Yet you have something I want." She tugged her mask down to reveal her face. "Good evening, Lizzie. I didn't expect to find you here. We were just taking our rest off the road, making sure no one was following us. I must say, I was surprised when you appeared." She smiled, but her face was drawn with fatigue. She took in my grim expression and returned her attention to Anthony. "But before we talk, you'll hand over those pistols, my lord. Two fingers only, please, as we don't need any of the foolishness of our last encounter." She took one pistol from him and hooked it in her waistband. "How is your shoulder, by the way?"

"To blazes with my shoulder!" Despite this outburst, he handed over the second pistol. "I am here to deliver a warning."

"That's bold, for a man in your position," said Jack, the one who had cut off our retreat. He glanced down at his pistol, still levelled at Anthony's chest, then gave him a wicked grin.

"Or a mite foolish," said Tom from behind.

"Listen to him, please!" I cried. When would they realize that this game was not to be won by pistols?

"What is this warning?" Robin asked.

"The militia found Lizzie at the Old Inn – through no fault of mine, I assure you. I did my best to persuade them that she has nothing to do with you, but was an innocent victim."

"Excellently done, my lord." She tipped her head to him, but there was still something of mockery in her gesture.

"And now I must warn you, they have laid a trap at the inn; they will surely kill you or take you to the gallows if you return there."

"Why would you give me such a warning?" She looked from Anthony to me and back again, a growing panic in her voice. "I thought you had no dearer wish than to see me hang."

"Oh, that is still true, but I have made a bargain, one much to your benefit, and my own. Will you tell her, Lizzie, or shall I?" I could only shake my head, and he went on. "In exchange for my saving your wretched life, Miss Collington has agreed to make me the happiest of all men."

Robin's eyes snapped back to mine. "Say this isn't true."

I could only nod, trying to put as much of apology into my expression as I could. She seemed to shrink in the saddle then, giving out a low moan. When she spoke, her voice was Rebecca's. "Why did you ever make such a promise? Are we not joined together? I would have died in the inn-yard for you, rather than submit to this!"

"And I would have done the same for you, but I never had the chance. This is the only way I could save you, though it meant breaking our vows. Don't dare tell me I had the easier choice." The words hung there between us, but I did not care to take them back. If we were truly bound together, surely the saving and the being saved could not go only one way. She bowed her head and said nothing.

Jack rode up beside us, opposite Rebecca, and aimed his pistol at Anthony's head. "Should I blow his brains out, Robin?" Admirably, Anthony did not flinch.

"No!" she exclaimed, sitting upright, assuming something of Robin's authority once more. "We've shed no blood in this operation so far, and we won't start now." Jack lowered his weapon and rode off a distance. Robin put Juno nearer to me, holding out her hand. "Come, Lizzie. You have only to take my hand, jump onto Juno's back, and we'll be off. We'll start a new life together, somewhere where no one knows us."

I looked at her gloved hand, just inches from me. How I wanted to take hold of it and have her carry me far away! A different life was before me, and I had only to reach out and take it. But I could not. I shook my head, still staring down at her outstretched hand. "I gave my word. I cannot break it."

She snatched her hand away. "Honor and gentility be damned!" She reined Juno around Caius and came up on his right side, where she could come close enough to grasp me by the arm. "By God, I ought to kidnap you in truth, and hide you away until you come to your senses."

Caius gave a stamp and tried to turn toward the other horse, pulling me from Rebecca's grasp as Anthony struggled to control him.

I shook my head again. "But there is my father to think of. I thought I could bear the thought of his distress over my kidnapping, but as it turns out, I cannot. I am sorry if I misled you, as I seem to have misled myself."

"And if Miss Collington refuses to honor her promise to me," Anthony said, "I will track you down. You've escaped capture so far only because no one has raised a concerted effort. But you won't get away so easily this time. I'll send to Bow street, I'll hire every thief-taker in the country if need be."

She gave a groan of frustration and rode a few paces off.

From behind us, Tom spoke. "I told you all this romantic nonsense would come to no good."

Anthony nudged Caius a pace or two forward. "I have given you your warning, and now I would take my leave."

"You'll leave when I give you leave, for you are still under my power!" For all the boldness of her words, her voice was that of a woman who knew the game was over, and she was not the winner.

Anthony went on as if she hadn't spoken. "Mrs. Burgess must disappear from Leighton immediately, and if so much as a letter goes missing in the neighborhood, I will reveal your identity, and have your likeness published across the land. I'm sure Lizzie can produce a truthful rendering from memory."

Rebecca sat her horse a few paces off from us, staring up into the trees for several moments, lost in thought. At last she rode back to face Anthony, more subdued than I had ever seen her. "If Mrs. Burgess disappears now, at the same time the highwayman abducted Lizzie, people will easily connect the two. From there, it will be a short leap to suspect Lizzie herself, since we have been so close. I'm sure neither of us wants that."

Anthony shook his head.

"If you will allow me to stay through this Sunday's auction, I will create a pretext that calls me away to London the next day. I promise, you will never hear of Mrs. Burgess or the highwayman again."

"I don't know why I should trust you when just now you encouraged Lizzie to break her vow to me. Why should you care to see the auction through?"

"It may surprise you, but I have a great interest in its success. Last night's escapade wasn't so lucrative as we had hoped, meaning the poor and the orphans in Exeter will continue as wretched as before. They will need every shilling we can earn at the auction. Also, I can only hope that you will change your mind in the meantime."

Anthony actually laughed at this. "That is hardly likely! But very well. I will consent to your plan, on the condition that you have no contact with Lizzie until the auction. No one will be surprised if she remains in seclusion after this ordeal. A guard will be set on the Parsonage, in case you have any further ideas of kidnapping her. She will be expected at the auction, of course, but I will have my eye on both of you."

I was growing impatient with this bargaining over my fate. "Do I have no say in where I go or what I do?"

"No, Lizzie, you don't. Remember, though I have preserved your reputation as far as possible, you will now be viewed as a ruined woman, whether you were taken against your will or not. You should consider yourself lucky that I will still have you, at considerable loss to my own standing. Do you truly wish to jeopardize that?"

"Here now, Robin, are you sure you don't want me to splatter his brains on the road?" Jack asked.

"No," she said, looking sadly at Anthony. "He only speaks the truth."

"Then we are agreed?"

Rebecca nodded.

"Now, if you will return my pistols, we will be on our way."

Rebecca rode up to him, keeping her eyes on me as if taking one last look, then handed the pistols over one at a time, her accomplices keeping their own weapons trained on Anthony. As he was preoccupied with hooking the last one into his waist band, she continued along to me and took my hand, giving me a look of the deepest regret.

"Do not give up hope, my love," I said. "Lord Burnside must know in his heart that this conduct does no honor to him."

Then Anthony put Caius in motion and we were forced to let go, our fingertips brushing as our hands parted.

"That went well, all things considered," Anthony said when we were out of earshot. I said nothing, wondering if it were possible to hate any person more than I hated him at that moment.

Anthony attempted a canter, but found he was too fatigued to maintain his seat at such a pace. After a time the effects of his recent wound became too much for him, and he could hardly stay on at all. "Lizzie, I'm afraid you'll have to take the reins, I'm so light-headed."

I did as he asked, guiding Caius and holding Anthony in the saddle at the same time. It was awkward, as I was sitting aside, and if he had been a larger man, I doubt I'd have been able to keep either of us ahorse. But somehow I managed it and, slow as our progress was, we arrived at the Parsonage just before dawn, both of us barely able to stay upright. Father and Mrs. Simmons burst out of the house at the sound of our approach. Both were still fully dressed, their looks of worry turning to relief as they realized I had returned home safe. Father helped me down, and I could only look on as they got Anthony into the house.

I followed, unsure of who had kidnapped or rescued whom.

CHAPTER TWENTY-SEVEN

WHEN I awoke late that afternoon, having slept soundly for the first time in days, my future became painfully clear: a life without Rebecca, and wed to a man I detested. The days following were torture. With four redcoats on watch outside, I could not leave the house and relieve my pent-up emotions with a long walk. Father and Mrs. Simmons treated me with gentle kindness, speaking in hushed tones and treading softly around me, as if I were a fragile teacup, which even the slightest noise or touch would shatter. They could do little to comfort me, for I could not confide my real troubles to them; left to their own devices, I was sure they would imagine that the worst had befallen me, yet I could not affect a happy mood to relieve their worries, my gloom was so great. The best I could manage was an air of blank imperturbability, wandering about the house as a sleepwalker might, unable to turn my attention to any of my usual pursuits.

The next day, Father visited Holbourne and learned that Anthony was still abed and feverish, his wound having reopened during his night-long ride. Rebecca's absence was more difficult to explain. "Mrs. Burgess returned yesterday from her business to do with the auction in Exeter," Father said. "I wonder why she does not visit?"

The answer came in a note to Father, carried to us by a village boy the following day. Rebecca explained to him that preparations for the auction had kept her too busy to spare even a moment for a visit, and asked him to pass an enclosed note along to me. "I wonder why she did not write you directly?" Father asked as he handed me the sealed note. I retreated to the drawing room to read it. Breaking the seal, I found the following:

My love, You cannot imagine what a torment these last days have been; or perhaps you can, as I have to think you must feel the same. It seems unkind to hope that you do, but I cannot help it. To be kept apart from you, never to see you again, never to hold you, never to coax another smile from your lovely lips – sometimes I think I will die from the pain of it – or wish that I could, that this pain might end. I cling to thoughts of our one day together, and only those sweet memories carry me through the mundane tasks of the auction. I am so out of my mind with missing you that I can hardly attend to my duties there, or remember the good that it will do. If there were any part of my heart left to break, it would break for the impoverished of Exeter, for the vaunted thousands we expected in the mail coach were a fiction, a ruse to lure us into a trap. We just barely escaped with our lives, and so were much delayed in returning to the inn.

I told you once that I had vowed never again to put myself in the power of any man. And now here we both are, in the power of one I consider far less than a man. And to think, for a moment I considered him truly honorable! [Here, she went on to abuse Anthony in terms I will not repeat.] *Oh, the thought of it galls me! My insides burn with indignation. How you can have any faith that he will change his course is beyond me. Why did I not release you from him when I had the chance? You must admit by now that it would have been better. I have half a mind to mount an assault on the Parsonage, redcoats be damned – four of those fellows are no match for the three of us. But no, Tom and Jack would never support me in it, and I could not do it alone.*

Please say you will come to the auction. Seeing you there, even if for the last time, even if I cannot say what I want to say, is the only thing that keeps me moving forward. After that, beyond leaving Leighton, I know not what I'll do. For the first time since those bleak nights in my husband's manor, I can see no future. But for now I cling to thoughts of my one last chance to see you again.

You know you have all my love,
Your darling,
Rebecca

I began folding the letter, but before I could compose myself, Father entered the drawing room. I must have appeared distraught, for he immediately came to sit beside me and took my hand, showing an uncharacteristic lack of reserve.

"Lizzie, have you received any troubling news? I fear – I fear that Mrs. Burgess has cut off her acquaintance with you after – recent events."

"What?" I asked, then realized what he meant. "No, nothing of that sort. She merely wanted to wish me a speedy recovery, and to apologize for not being able to visit."

He looked about the room uncertainly for a long moment. "Lizzie, I know I have always taught you to regulate your emotions, neither soaring too high nor sinking too low, but always showing a composed face to the world. I truly believed it the best way to protect you from all the hurts life would inevitably throw your way, and from any unscrupulous sorts who would play on emotions openly displayed. But, in recent days, I have realized this may not have been the best program. I know you have been much tormented in spirit by your recent experience, yet you seem unable to speak of it; I know you are troubled, yet you cannot show it. And so I must ask you – when you were held captive by the highwayman, did he – did he – lay a hand on you?"

"No! I told you when I returned, although perhaps I was so delirious with fatigue I could not make myself understood – I am well. Nothing happened, other than my having a great fright, contemplating what the highwayman and his henchmen *might* do."

"Oh, my dear, I am so glad. But the fright of not knowing what to expect – it must have been terrible."

"Yes, and I am still recovering from it, which explains my lack of spirits. But in fact, he was quite the gentleman to me, and insisted on the same polite behavior from his men. I believe he meant to hold me captive until I came to love him, like something out of a gothic novel."

"What would you know about those?"

I smiled for the first time that day. "I have my ways. Father, I am no longer an impressionable girl. Do not you think it's time I chose my own reading?"

"I daresay you are right, my dear. But tell me, you seemed perturbed when I entered. Are you sure there was no bad news in that note from Mrs. Burgess?"

"There was one bit. I don't know why it affected me so; perhaps my nerves are still on edge. But she must go away, right after the auction, and doesn't know when she might return. It was a silly thing to become so distraught over."

"Oh, my dear! Not to be able to show a tear when your best friend goes away, and just when you need a friend the most? I was a fool ever to train you to such reserve. Say you will forgive me!"

"Oh, Father!" Then I did fall into his arms and had a good cry, one long in coming, all under the pretext of the emotional strain brought on by my presumed kidnapping. I loved my father more at that moment than ever before. How could I have thought of deserting him? The fact that I had been prevented from doing him that great injury was the one bright point in the whole affair.

When he left me, I wrote a note to Rebecca asking her to do nothing rash, telling her that I still held out hope that Anthony would reverse his course, and if not, then the last happy moment of my life would be when I saw her at the auction on Sunday.

More news that should have lifted my spirits came in the next day's regular post, in a letter from Catherine Cowley. I was stunned to unfold the sheet of paper and discover within it a five-pound note. Her family had received my more detailed sketches, and her parents had viewed them with the greatest appreciation; the enclosed payment was to serve as a commission, with a promise of five more upon completion and delivery. Ten pounds for one watercolor! For a moment I was carried away by dreams of what independence my art could buy me.

But then I remembered what my life was to be, and that Anthony would in no way allow me to earn my living as an artist and a writer. True, I could pursue my art merely for the pleasure of it. I could complete this watercolor only for the enjoyment it would bring my new friend and her family. Yet I could muster little enthusiasm at the moment even for this favorite activity, or anything else. My food tasted like ash, my favorite books made no sense, Bach's most elegant minuet was crashing cacophony, and I would sooner plunge a pencil into my eye than put it to paper. I put the note back in the envelope and put off sending a reply until I was in better spirits, though I could not imagine when that would be.

As if to underscore my bleak future, Anthony visited that afternoon, his face wan and gaunt, his hair disheveled, his cravat sloppily tied. Mrs. Simmons smiled knowingly as she made an excuse to leave us alone in the drawing room.

"How is your shoulder, my lord?" I asked.

"My lord, is it? Is that the way it's to be?"

"I pledged to marry you, and I plan to fulfil that vow. You cannot also demand that I be happy about it."

I could tell that this wounded him. "Lizzie, what must I do to regain your affection, short of doing that which I will not do?"

"I can say nothing of affection, but you can earn my approbation by waiting until Rebecca is gone before you approach my father. I would not have him and Mrs. Simmons parade their happiness before her."

"I will do as you wish. Lizzie, I know you cannot understand this at the moment, but I want only to safeguard you from doing further harm to yourself. If only you could know how I felt when I saw you in the Old Inn, bound, gagged, and bleeding – then you would never doubt what my feelings are."

"I never doubted your affection for me, only the lengths you would go to have me; I certainly never thought you capable of the callous measures you have recently undertaken."

"In the end you will see that I am right and thank me for the good I have done you."

I thought of responding with a melodramatic outburst, perhaps slapping him and shouting, "Never!" But I knew I could push the boundaries of my promise only so far. "You seem not quite convinced of that," I said.

Indeed, he could not hold my gaze, but looked unsteadily about the room, his free hand fiddling with the loose end of his cravat.

"Anthony, you know this behavior becomes neither you nor your ideas of chivalry. You may believe you have come to my rescue, but I need none. Instead, you are behaving as a brute, with no regard for my wishes. A true friend would want to see me happy."

"But she is an outlaw, not to mention a woman."

"That she is a woman cannot be mended, nor can my attachment to her. As for her being an outlaw, I believe I can dissuade her from that course of life."

He looked at me then, as if measuring my resolve. After a few more moments of strained silence, he rose, bid me a stiff good-day, and left.

If Father and Mrs. Simmons had hoped to see me cheered by Anthony's visit, they were disappointed.

SUNDAY ARRIVED, and the parish church was more crowded than usual, the congregants planning to go to the auction immediately afterward. Many wanted only to gawk at the items they could never afford, a form of covetousness not entirely appropriate for Our Lord's Day, but an acceptable one, since the entire endeavor was meant to accomplish His work. The pews were so full that I caught only one glimpse of Rebecca across the nave; she must have left immediately after to attend to last-minute details, because we did not see her in the receiving line. I did, however, receive much sympathy for my recent ordeal, along with many looks of regret for what this damage to my reputation would mean, and much gesturing toward me from those in the crowd who had yet to move toward the village hall. It was a struggle to ignore all this attention and return my neighbors' sincere best wishes with a polite smile.

The challenges to my composure continued as Father, Mrs. Simmons, and I walked to the auction, Anthony falling in beside us. With an effort, I managed to behave toward him almost as I would have a month previous. He was still wan and lacking energy, appearing to have slept little, but at least he was suitably dressed. If my words on our previous meeting had had any effect, he did not show it.

Yet worse than this meeting with my tormentor was the prospect of my first encounter with Rebecca. It would take all my self-command not to throw myself into her arms the instant I saw her. Then wouldn't our neighbors have something at which to point and shake their heads!

Entering the hall, we joined the crowd viewing the auction items arrayed on tables and hung on the walls. I was familiar with much that was on offer, having helped gather and catalog it: vases of uncertain antiquity, paintings by artists no one would recognize, sets of china and silver in dated patterns, fireplace screens, jewelry of little value, and, surprisingly, several valuable items of *Orientalia,* carved ivory, jade, and even a beautiful three-paneled folding screen.

I pretended to look for any items not familiar to me while I scanned the room in search of Rebecca. Finally I saw her at the other end of the hall, surrounded by volunteers and potential bidders asking her question after question. Between answers, she let her eye rove over the hall until she found me and gave a little nod. With admirable composure she turned to her next questioner. I could feel Anthony next to me, measuring my reaction, but so far my mask of indifference was in place.

We started to examine the items on offer, an activity in which Father and Mrs. Simmons took great interest, while Anthony and I pretended to do the same. I was content so long as we kept moving toward the spot where Rebecca stood; I tried not to glance too often in her direction.

Anthony brought up short. "Look, there is your contribution." He pointed at the small watercolor Rebecca had insisted I contribute, hanging on a wall surrounded by other nature scenes. Mine showed a bit of meadow next to a pond, a purple orchid drawing the eye to the lower left. I caught my breath as I remembered the day I had taken that sketch; Rebecca had been with me, and she had expressed such an excessive delight over the flower's beauty and its sensuous qualities that I blushed to remember it.

But I could not let my mind follow where that thought naturally led, and so I turned away as Anthony said, "It's quite the best of the lot, and underpriced with a starting bid of only ten shillings."

"Do you really think so?" I asked idly, pretending great interest in a blue-patterned tea set.

"Absolutely. I believe I will bid on it myself." He lowered his voice. "You have an outstanding talent, Lizzie."

I found this hardly comforting, considering the fact that he was buying me as easily as he would buy this picture. Father came to my rescue, pointing out that Rebecca seemed to have a free moment, and suggesting that we make our way to her. I took a deep breath and arranged my expression for what was to come.

Rebecca saw us approaching and came to meet us with a most natural, easy manner. "Lizzie!" she exclaimed with all her usual open affection, shaking my hand and kissing my cheek. "It is so good to see you! Have you recovered from your awful ordeal? I am so sorry I haven't been able to visit you, but I thought you would need your rest."

I admired her self-mastery, for she had behaved just as anyone who knew her would have expected. I endeavored to do the same, giving her my usual restrained smile. "I am fine, thank you, but I am looking forward to getting back out into the world."

"And Lord Burnside," she said, curtsying to Anthony. "Our hero! Doing battle with the highwayman, even taking a wound from him, yet venturing into his den to save Miss Collington. I'm sure Mr. Collington is forever in your debt. Is your shoulder mending well?" Perhaps only Anthony and I noticed the touch of coldness in her voice and the flatness of her gaze as she said this last.

"Excellently, thank you," he said with a stiff bow. "And Mrs. Burgess, may I congratulate you on a splendid event. I'm sure the poor of Leighton and Exeter will be grateful."

"I daresay they will, though it hardly seems enough, does it?" Her tone remained cordial, but her eyes still had that same flat, judging expression.

Anthony could do no more than resort to platitudes. "'For ye have the poor always with you,' as our Savior said. But we should detain you no longer from your duties." He bowed and took my elbow, steering me toward the side of the hall we had yet to inspect. Father followed behind, while Mrs. Simmons went off to greet her acquaintances from the village. Rebecca allowed herself one mild look of regret before turning back to the volunteers who required her attention.

The rest of the day was a trial, with no further chances to talk with Rebecca, either in a crowd or alone – she was too put-upon by volunteers to allow for the former, and Anthony would not allow the latter. The bidding began and I insisted on staying when Father suggested I must be tired. Anthony had committed to staying until my watercolor came up, which unfortunately happened early on, an interested murmur going through the crowd when he bid the price up to an unheard-of four pounds three. He gave me a smug glance as the auctioneer gaveled him the winner, but I stared stubbornly at my lap, saying, "I am glad you think so highly of my work."

"And now we can be going, I should think?" He tipped his head toward me, trying to catch my eye, but I remained resolute. He would not so easily cheat me of my last farewell with Rebecca.

"Think of your duty to the parish, Anthony!" I said. "You must set a good example. I am sure there is room in Holbourne for many of these items."

At that, he subsided, making desultory bids on the occasional art object. Meanwhile, the auction dragged on, and I caught fleeting glimpses of Rebecca moving about behind the auctioneer's podium, ensuring that everything ran smoothly. No one observing her dedication to the work would suspect that she had volunteered mainly as a ruse to investigate the contents of wealthy estates and to become privy to their owners' movements.

At last the affair was over, the last item bid upon, the last successful bidders queuing to claim their purchases. Anthony had to leave us to claim his watercolor. I hoped during this lapse in his attention to have a moment alone with Rebecca, but she remained too busy, giving me one or two regretful glances.

Anthony returned, having given the wrapped picture to his man. Mrs. Simmons rejoined us from visiting with her friends, and Father again suggested it was time to leave.

"I would like to stay long enough to get some idea of how we fared," I said, "considering I put such effort into the event."

"I would be glad to escort Lizzie home, since she insists on staying," Anthony offered.

"Thank you, my lord," Mrs. Simmons said. "Always so considerate!" She beamed as she and Father turned away, always glad to have an excuse to leave us to ourselves.

We stood there in the middle of the hall, sharing a constrained silence, people streaming about us with their new possessions. Occasionally Anthony would make an attempt at conversation, but I stared resolutely at the floor, offering replies of one or two words.

Finally, I could stand it no longer. "I believe I will offer my assistance." I strode purposefully over to the cashier's table. Rebecca was busy elsewhere, and my offer was at first refused – "you need your rest, dear" – but at last they saw that I would not be turned away, allowing me to help with packaging the more delicate items. As I found a chair and set to work with paper and string, Anthony hovered nearby, looking out of place in the group of women, but unwilling to allow me even an instant with Rebecca out of his earshot. I had the satisfaction of a smile from her when she returned to the room and saw me working there. She flashed Anthony quite a different look, but no one noticed it.

At last, the final payments were made and only the volunteers remained. Rebecca called for their attention, thanking us for our great efforts and the opportunity to lead us, and announcing that the auction would easily clear three hundred pounds, to great applause. "And now I have an announcement. Tomorrow I must travel to London on a matter concerning my brother. I regret to say I do not know when I will return."

Only Anthony and I managed to remain silent at this news, the rest of the ladies murmuring and even gasping, for Rebecca had become an object of both affection and concern amongst our neighbors. "Nothing serious, I hope, my dear?" one matron asked over the rest.

"I can give no details, but I hope all will come right in the end. Still, it pains me to leave you all, when my return is so indefinite." Here she hazarded one glance my way.

Her speech over, the ladies gathered around her to give her their best wishes before turning to the cleaning and a final count of the proceeds. Wanting to avoid such a public farewell, I retreated to the center of the hall, Anthony following.

"Now we *must* leave." He put a hand on my elbow and tried to turn me toward the door.

I glared up at him, resisting. "Only if you dare to drag me away, my lord," I said in a low voice, and he relented. I turned to look back at the thinning crowd around Rebecca. She caught my eye, then quickly excused herself and came toward us.

She approached us with a deliberate pace, as if she could make these final moments last forever. Again I marveled at her composure, for she wore a smile, where I could hardly keep my lower lip from trembling; I felt as if my mask of composure were ready to split in two.

Finally she reached us, stopping a pace away; Anthony might not have existed for all the attention she paid him. "I wish my news could have come as a surprise to you, as it was for the other ladies. I know what these days must have been for you."

I could say nothing, having nothing to say that I would have Anthony hear. God forgive me, but in that moment I wished that Robin had run him through, no matter the consequences.

We were silent for a long moment, simply looking at each other, Anthony standing impatiently beside us. Another moment and her reserve would crack. Mine already had, as I felt a tear running down my cheek.

"Come," she said at last. "Will you shake my hand?"

I could not bear to do so little, even with Anthony standing there. I stepped up to her, placed my hands on her shoulders, and leant up to kiss her on the cheek. Two seconds, three seconds, five – I know not how long, longer than was proper – I let my lips tremble against her soft skin, and I could feel her whole body begin to tremble as well. I know she wanted to throw her arms around me and bury her face in my shoulder, but she did not, simply letting her hands rest on either side of my waist.

At last I whispered in her ear: "You have all my love, forever."

I felt her give a shudder. "Just say the word," she whispered back, "and we will escape together – somehow."

I pulled away to look at her and my resolve nearly broke. But it could not be. Were we to flee together, what could our lives be? Living as fugitives, constantly on the run – our love would founder under the weight of constant fear and recrimination. I had clung to the hope that my patient arguments would sway Anthony from his course of blackmail, showing him that his actions were the opposite of those ideals he held so dear. As this had not come to pass, I could see no other way out. I shook my head.

At this denial, her expression grew yet more forlorn, her eyes showing a hopelessness beyond all hope; then they turned harder as she steeled herself against a grief that would drown us both.

She reached up and took my left hand from her shoulder, the one with her ring on it; I had moved it to my middle finger to avoid uncomfortable questions. She bent over it, twisting the gold band for a moment before kissing it, gallantly, as the highwayman might have done. Then she straightened. With a last brief glance, she turned back to the other ladies, who were busy with their work and oblivious to our little scene.

I turned away as well, unwilling to watch her walk away from me, making for the exit as quick as decorum would allow. "There, there," one of the women said to Rebecca just before I reached the door, "it's not as if you're sailing to the colonies!"

I burst through the door Anthony rushed to open for me, finding the sun shining brightly and the people of Leighton enjoying a pleasantly warm day. But I was a creature made of ice, and the sunshine and the warmth were no friends to me. I began the long walk home, oblivious to Anthony trailing beside me, toward a future that could hold neither hope nor happiness. I felt brittle, as if one touch would shatter me into a thousand jagged shards.

CHAPTER TWENTY-EIGHT

A BANGING came at our front door early the next morning. Instantly there were stirrings from Father's room and from downstairs, Banks exclaiming about the early hour as she went to the door. I remained in bed, taking no more interest in this ill-timed visitor than to wonder if it were a tradesman who had arrived at the wrong house. Judging by the angle of the mid-summer's morning sun streaming through the window, it could not have been much past six o'clock.

Then the housekeeper exclaimed again, "My lord!" and I gave a groan as I dragged myself from bed. Could the man not give me one day of peace after yesterday's torment? But I had a role to play, and I must play it to keep Rebecca safe.

Shockingly, the sound of boots crossing the hall rose from the floor below, and then they were on the stairs. I threw a wrap over my nightdress as I heard my father greet Anthony, a question in his voice: "My lord?"

"I must speak with Lizzie immediately," Anthony was saying as I opened my door.

He spun around on the landing, with Father standing behind him and Mrs. Simmons beaming on the steps below with all the confidence of one whose prediction had come true. Anthony's dress was once more in disarray, his coat unbuttoned, his waistcoat askew, the legs of his breeches haphazardly tucked into his knee-high boots, and his jaw unshaven; most shocking of all, he wore no cravat, his collar remaining open at the throat.

In short, he appeared to have spent the night wrestling with whether to make his proposal; having decided, he could wait for neither a decent hour nor a proper toilette before making his feelings known.

"Lizzie, I must speak with you," he stammered, hardly able to look at me. "I thought, perhaps, a walk."

"Of course, my lord." I curtsied before turning back to my room.

"And – perhaps your riding habit would be best."

Was he planning an elopement? I did not pause to wonder, but closed the door on him and began to change, feeling that it was pointless to postpone inevitable pain. A quarter of an hour later, with Mrs. Simmons' help, I was ready to leave the house, dressed in riding habit and boots, my hair pinned up with all the neatness haste would allow, and my bonnet in my hand. I had Rebecca's letter in my pocket, for I had kept it with me since receiving it.

"We're so happy for you, dear," Mrs. Simmons said, my father standing beside her, nodding his approval, before closing the front door behind me. I found Anthony pacing up and down in the lane, squinting into the sun cresting the forest to the east.

"Is it really necessary to go through these steps of a proposal?" I asked him as I tied my bonnet. "You could simply tell Father you have already won my affection."

"No, I must have my say before I would speak with him."

"What more could there be for you to tell?" Despite this mild resistance, I lowered my gaze and stepped through the gate, thinking again that the sooner I grew used to living under his rule, the better. Caius was tethered to our picket fence, and Anthony took up his reins, leading him behind us.

"You've only brought one horse. I thought we were to ride."

"We will walk back to Holbourne's stables; that will give me time to say what I must."

For a man with so much to say, he was remarkably silent, remaining lost in thought as we walked down the lane in the direction of Leighton and the turning to Holbourne. It was a beautiful morning, with the fog just rising out of the hollows and catching the light of the sun in wisps and shoals – the kind of sight seen mainly by servants, workers, and artists, and seldom by the slumbering gentry.

"We are making good progress toward your stables," I said as we arrived at our turning, "but less so in what you have to tell, I'm afraid."

"Yes, well – " He stirred from his reverie. "You see, Lizzie – Your words of the other day stung me more than I could readily admit. Since my return from London, after a despicable lapse, I have once more attempted to live up to those ideals of nobility, chivalry, and gentility which bind those of noble birth to their people. But recent events have forced me to acknowledge the ways in which I still fail to uphold them, and have even failed in my duty to my people."

"Go on," I said, thinking that his recent behavior toward me was an excellent example of his failure.

"Over these last days, I have found myself preoccupied with the highwayman's boasts of helping the poor, wondering whether they could possibly be true. Such selflessness in a rogue seemed highly improbable, and if I could prove that she lied in this, it would change your opinion toward her. Two days ago, I went to the orphanage in Exeter and asked if they had received any large, anonymous gifts. You can't doubt my surprise when I learned they had, in fact, beginning this spring, and in quite large amounts, too. The money would appear in the hands of a humble messenger, who would say nothing of the person who gave it to him. The head of the orphanage told me, too, that the poor spoke of a mysterious gentleman who came among them, handing out food, medicine, and silver, even going so far as to offer to pay their debts. Lord Rob, the people called him."

"I knew she could not have lied! And will you do the same once she is gone?" *Now that she has gone,* I corrected myself, my heart giving a catch, for she must have been riding out in the post chaise for Exeter even then.

"It did make me think, how could I let her outshine my father and me in performing duties that should rightly fall to us?"

"And so you have another reason to send her away."

He only shook his head and looked at the lane in front of him. "You still don't understand, but maybe this will make you see. Another image has been in my mind these last days, one that, when I came to understand its meaning, put all my pretense at nobility to shame: a musket trigger wet with blood – your blood, Lizzie! At first I could not believe it. I told myself it must have run down the stock as you struggled to free yourself. But over and over the image would return, in my waking hours and in my dreams, during those few moments when I have been able to sleep. Then, last night, I came awake with the image so clear in my mind, I could tell that your blood would never have reached the trigger, unless you had placed your finger there."

I knew he expected me to confess something here, but I stared resolutely at the ground.

"And then I knew – had Rebecca arrived in the inn-yard before me, you would now be dead, your breast shattered in an attempt to warn her, and my own heart shattered by grief. And then I had to wonder, what could possess you to do such a thing?"

"Yes, what could possess me? For certainly I must have been possessed, or seduced, or out of my mind."

"Yes, and so I have told myself, many times over the past week, since I first suspected your attachment to Mrs. Burgess, for women are weak creatures – only, you have never seemed so. Yet what other explanation was there? As much praise as some would give to sentimental attachments between women, I believed that these could never supplant that more natural and sanctified bond between woman and man. Those women who would go beyond pure romantic friendship and indulge in Sapphism must do so only out of twisted lust and depravity – "

He fell quiet as I stopped in the lane and stared at him. "And you would still have me, though you think me depraved?"

"No – yes – I mean, you must let me finish."

"I have no choice but to let you finish, for you now rule me in all things. Yet I can see no point to this, other than to make my acquiescence that much harder to bear."

"That is not my intention, Lizzie." A note of pleading had crept into his voice. "I meant only to describe what my *former* thoughts had been. But come, let us continue our walk, for it is difficult to tell you what I must while you stare at me with such scorn."

I relented, and we began walking once more. The stables were just visible a quarter-mile up the tree-lined gravel drive, and partially hidden behind the great manor house.

"Last night my thoughts on the matter changed," Anthony went on. "Strange to say, the change was prompted by thinking back to that club where my companions brought me on my last night in London."

"I had hoped you would never again speak to me of the place."

"Yet I must, for there is something I didn't tell you. When the two women entered the room, they were disguised, as to a masked ball. But once the door was closed, they seemed to recognize each other, and they said each other's names, and each took the other's mask away. They fell into each other's arms with cries of delight. One said something like, 'Oh, how I have waited for this day, wondering if you felt the same as I do!' Then they were kissing, and it was the most passionate kiss I have ever beheld."

"And were you aroused?" I gritted my teeth, my fists clenched.

"I am ashamed to say that I was, though I left the place before they could do anything more, and I even tried to alert them to the other lurking men by shouting and banging on the wall – but none of that matters. The point is this: what I saw there was not depravity; no, all the depravity was on our side of that wall. What I saw in that room was love, and it was – beautiful. That is the only way I can describe it." He was silent for a moment as we continued slowly up the lane. "And now I have to ask you, is it the same between you and Rebecca?"

I stopped again, turning on him. What happened between Rebecca and me was none of his business. "Why must you torment me so?" I demanded. I lost any control I had left, flying at him and hitting his chest with the fleshy part of my fists.

He did his best with his injured arm to grasp at my wrists until he finally caught them. "I don't mean to torment you, but I must know – do you truly love her?"

I stopped struggling. "How could you not know? I told you everything in my letter."

"I must hear it from your lips."

"If that is your question, then yes, I love Rebecca with all my heart and soul." I held out my left hand to him. "I wear her ring, and she wears mine. She is all to me and I am all to her. We are bound together. Though you may call it blasphemy, if I wed any other, it will be bigamy in God's eyes. Do you truly believe I would throw everything away for mere lust and pleasure?"

Anthony regarded me for a long moment, then shook his head. "Only the greatest love could prompt such an act of nobility and self-sacrifice as you were about to make that night in the inn. I saw it again yesterday when you parted. I know that you could never look on me the way you looked on Rebecca then. And in contrast, how have I behaved when prompted by love? As a tyrant and worse. I told myself I was trying to protect you, but I was merely pursuing my selfish ends. And all this time you have been patiently persuading me, presenting me with an example of love and duty that put me to shame."

My heart rose at this declaration, yet he turned his back on me and his voice became harder. "But I will not be outdone in noble deeds, not by you and certainly not by the highwayman. At the same time, there are other considerations. Preventing crime in our neighborhood and protecting its people are still duties I hold sacred."

He stopped there, and I waited for him to go on, wondering what new means he had concocted to keep me from Rebecca, and how any noble deed could play into it.

"And so I must ask you one more question."

"Yes?" One syllable was all I could risk, or my voice would break.

"Do you really believe she would abandon her life of robbery to have you?"

"I do." My voice trembled with unexpected hope.

Anthony turned back to me, taking my hand and going to one knee. "Then, Elizabeth Collington, I release you from your vow to me. You are free. I only hope you can forgive me for behaving so ignobly toward you, and for taking so long to come to my senses." He raised my hand to his lips, looking first at the ring I wore there, while I stood trembling with joy and relief.

He stood and I threw myself into his arms. "Oh, Anthony! I will love you forever for this! I don't know how to thank you."

"No, do not thank me," he said, pushing me gently away. "I deserve no thanks for doing what I might have done from the beginning. It is no kind of love that would see you unhappy before seeing you in love with another. And remember, I am not totally disinterested, for the highwayman's career will come to an end, and I'll have the lout right under my nose." He actually managed a grin then. "But why are you still standing here? Your horse is saddled and waiting, and Rebecca must be halfway to Exeter by now."

I looked toward the stables, still a good distance off. "You are right, I must hurry. Might I take Caius?"

"What? Your horse is right there, it won't take long."

"Caius is faster, and I can go faster still while riding astride."

"You would ride astride? But Caius is too large for you, and too spirited."

"I managed him quite well the other night, though I had to sit aside and hold onto you at the same time."

He still seemed uncertain. "Well, I've heard of other women doing it. But I thought to accompany you. Going so far alone – think of your reputation!"

He had only to glance once at me to see how little this meant to me now.

"At least allow me to adjust the stirrups, won't you?"

The stirrup was already so high that Anthony had to boost me into the saddle. It was awkward getting my skirts arranged, and they still rode up, revealing my stockinged calves. Anthony adjusted the stirrups to the correct height, then I turned Caius around in the lane with a nudge of the crop.

"You'll use your crop less when riding astride," he said. "Use your knees instead."

"Yes, I have heard that," I said, smiling. "And thank you again, whether you will accept my thanks or no." I reached down and shook his hand, giving him a look of the truest friendship I could muster. Then I nudged Caius forward and soon we were cantering down the lane.

Riding astride was jarring at first, but at length I found the horse's rhythm, letting my hips rock with the motion of his stride. Then I dared urge him to a full gallop, the horse flowing over the ground like water while I marveled at our speed, feeling no danger of falling off. My bonnet, which I had tied poorly, blew back so that it dangled by its ribbons, flapping in the wind for a moment before coming free. Soon my hair was flying loose from its pins.

How must I have looked, racing down the lanes on a horse that was far too large for me, riding astride, showing my legs, my head uncovered, my hair streaming behind me like a black flag? I certainly did not avoid calling attention to myself, giving wild whoops of abandon from the thrill of our pace and the strength of the horse beneath me. For a moment I consoled myself with the thought that few people of good breeding and gentle birth were awake at such an hour.

And then I gave a laugh, for truly, I cared not.

I decided I would make better time by avoiding Leighton, taking a shortcut across fields directly to the Exeter road. Caius slowed to a canter across the rougher meadow, but still his stride was smooth and I held my seat easily. Ahead, a stone wall, some four feet high, stretched across our path, separating the sloping meadow from an enclosed paddock and the Exeter road beyond. Caius did not hesitate or slow his pace, and I urged him forward, rising up from the saddle with his leap. For a long moment we soared through the air, my heart leaping with the horse, the world suspended with our flight. My breath caught as I saw how far we had risen above the downward-sloping side of the wall; my belly gave a little flip as we hung there. Then Caius landed in stride. With my feet anchored in the stirrups, my legs absorbed the shock of the impact, and I kept my balance.

I gave another shout of exhilaration as we continued down across the paddock. There was one more wall to jump and then we were on the Exeter road. It was smooth and straight here, and I let Caius run, his stride stretching full length as I leaned low over his neck, the wind of our speed bringing tears to my eyes.

We were nearly to Exeter, its western wall just coming into view, when I caught sight of the chaise with its postilion driver riding the horse on the left. I slowed Caius to a trot as we came up on the right, giving a shout to the postilion, who turned to look back at us, his mouth dropping open when he saw me. I knew I must have some excuse for waylaying him. I reached into my pocket for Rebecca's letter and waved it at him. "Message for Mrs. Burgess," I called to him. Finally he brought the chaise to a halt, and I stopped Caius alongside.

Rebecca opened the door. "Lizzie?" she asked, getting down from the carriage.

My heart was racing and I had to take a moment to catch my breath. Caius blew and shook his head, his coat glistening with sweat. Rebecca came over to pat his neck, then smiled as she realized I was riding astride. "What is it?" she repeated.

I held the note down to her. "This letter came after you left," I said for the postilion's benefit, leaving him to wonder how a letter could have arrived at that hour, or why I would have it. "I hope you don't mind that I opened it. Your brother no longer needs you in London. I wanted to save you the trip."

She looked down at the letter she herself had written, then back up at me with a question in her eyes. "Well, this is excellent news! Will you get down?"

She held her hand out to me and I took it, but found that it was little help in dismounting when riding astride. I threw one leg backward off the horse, as I had seen men do, then lowered myself toward the ground, finding it farther than I had realized. Too, riding astride taxed different muscles than I had been wont to use, and my leg would hardly support me when my foot finally touched the ground.

Rebecca was there to catch me as I fell backwards, my left foot finally coming free of the stirrup. "You've both had a tiring ride," she said. "Will you ride back in the chaise with me?"

Feeling her arms around me, I could not help turning toward her, though I could hardly manage it with the weakness in my legs. I clung to her and buried my face in her neck, giving a low sob. At last I whispered in her ear, "Anthony has freed me from my vow. You are free to return to Leighton. We can be together!" I felt her tremble as she received this news.

"Oh, I am so glad to hear my brother is well," she said, loud enough for the postilion to hear. "And your concern for him is so touching!" She held me away from her and looked at me, her eyes beaming, then dug in her reticule for a kerchief. "Why, Miss Collington," she asked with a restrained smile, "what has become of all your reserve and composure?"

"I believe I lost them both, along with my bonnet. I don't know if I will ever find them again."

Rebecca's smile grew wider, then she helped me into the carriage as the postilion tethered Caius to the back. One may imagine with what smiles, tears, and tender caresses we comforted each other during the journey home.

EPILOGUE

"IT'S MARVELOUS, Lizzie!" Rebecca stood behind me, looking at the watercolor on which I had been working for the past week. We were in the room Father had given me to use as a studio, a front bedchamber upstairs, with a wonderful view across our yard to Holbourne and the moors beyond. "But isn't it finished? I can't see what you have left to do. That is certainly the Pump Room, and you've caught not only the Cowleys' likenesses, but something of their spirits as well."

"I'm not sure." I tapped the handle of my brush against my teeth – a bad habit. "It just seems that *something* is missing." I regarded the picture for a moment more before setting down my brush. I had used a combination of pencil, pen and brown ink, and watercolor; I was satisfied with it, in truth, but *satisfied* seemed not quite enough. For ten guineas, it must be stunning. "Sometimes it helps if I wait for a day before deciding whether I am finished. But not to worry – it will be ready in time for our trip to deliver it next week."

"Oh, I'm not worried," she said, rubbing my shoulders and neck, for she knew that these areas became stiff when I had been long at work. "I have the utmost confidence in you. So much so that your journal entries are nearly ready for publication. I have selected and collated them in such a way as to make a wonderful book. You'll need to do some fleshing out of the text when we return from our trip, but then I believe it will be done. And I have a title for you: how does *A Year in Devonshire, as told by a Young Lady familiar with that County's Flora, Fauna, and Environs* sound?"

"Wonderful! Though I am not sure that 'lady' remains an accurate title." I took her hand from my shoulder and kissed it, turning to give her a wink.

"Now don't be silly. Many are the noble ladies of the *ton* whose virtue and gentility fall well short of your own." She grinned at me and bent down to give me a kiss.

A fortnight had passed since I had waylaid Rebecca on her trip to London. Since then we had settled into something like our former routine of walks, horseback rides, visits, and musical evenings, the differences being that instead of our work on the auction, we now labored over my art and writing; and, on those evenings when one of us had stayed late at the other's house, we would spend the night together. This was hardly remarkable, since neither my father nor Rebecca owned a carriage. When she stayed with us she used the guest bedroom, but we weren't above a certain amount of sneaking back and forth in the middle of the night; Father was known to sleep soundly, and everyone else was on the floor below.

No, if anyone in Leighton looked at me strangely, it was not because I could sometimes be seen walking home of a morning from her house, but because I was now the ruined woman of the village, an object of pity, or worse, since the highwayman had destroyed all my prospects. For the first week, I had been unable to walk twenty paces without someone, a girl I considered a friend or a matron of my acquaintance through my charity work, approaching me to express her sorrow and concern. I did my best to show stoic resignation to my straitened circumstances, rather than bursting out with the happiness I truly felt.

By the second week, most of my acquaintances were crossing the road to avoid me, or pretending to be deep in conversation as I passed by, while giving me covert looks. I had brought this on myself, I reasoned, by concocting the kidnapping story; my only consolation lay in considering how much worse the villagers' opinion of me would have been had they known the truth. Still, the prospect of our upcoming week in Gloucestershire, followed by another week in London, was all the more enticing for this.

The addition of London to our itinerary would allow Rebecca to check on her brother's recovery and to take me to the theatres and galleries of that great city – or so we had told Father. The real purpose was for her to purchase five-percent bonds with her ill-gotten gains, as I liked to call them. Her one source of worry was the number of these bonds she could afford, since her last outing as the highwayman had fallen far short of expectations, and she had given her entire share to the orphanage in Exeter. Her resulting income would be considerably short of the five hundred pounds a year she had set as her goal.

"I will do well enough for now," she had said, "but what of that inevitable day when I must also support you?"

"Oh, that is no worry, for you know that I am to be a famous and wealthy *artiste*," I teased her.

"Lizzie, you know I do not doubt your abilities as an artist or writer, or your ability to earn money from them; but it does trouble me to think that there might come a day when you *must* rely on your art in order to get by. I would rather see you pursue your passions purely for the love of them."

"My, how like my father you sound today! Are you the only one who will be allowed to support us? What happened to Mrs. Wollstonecraft and independence?" At that, Rebecca laughed with me at her own folly.

Our mirth was interrupted by the sound of horses slowing in the lane outside the Parsonage. Rebecca went to the window and looked down. "It's Lord Burnside, and he has his footman with him. So he really means to leave!"

"I knew he was serious about it," I said, rising and taking off my paint-spattered smock.

By the time we got downstairs, Father and Mrs. Simmons were greeting Anthony, rather frostily, in the drawing room. They had yet to forgive him for failing to propose when he had seemed so close to doing so. It had been difficult to explain his early arrival on that morning a fortnight previous, and precisely what he had wanted so urgently to discuss, if not to ask for my hand in marriage. Another difficulty was explaining why I, and not Anthony, had been the one to chase after Rebecca's chaise, but they had at last put this rash behavior down to my relief that my dearest friend was not to leave us. This, combined with my recovery from my frightful ordeal, was enough to explain my dramatic change in mood upon my return – for, despite all my efforts at reserve, tell-tale signs that I was the happiest of all women had been too numerous to keep hidden for long.

"We will regret not having you in the neighborhood for the summer, Lord Burnside," Mrs. Simmons was saying as we entered the drawing room, though her tone implied that Anthony's whereabouts were now of no concern to her. "And I am sure your parents will miss you when they return from London." Anthony accepted these compliments with good grace, considering that avoiding his parents was a principal reason for his rapid removal.

"Well, if Mrs. Burgess is staying," Father said (for they had become careful to ensure that Anthony and I had no more tête-à-têtes), "we will leave you young people to yourselves. I am sure you have much to talk about."

Mrs. Simmons and Father left the room, shutting the door behind them as I turned to Anthony. "You really are leaving?" We were still standing, as Anthony had risen when we entered.

"Yes, Lizzie. I was thinking of crossing to the continent. Or perhaps some time in the West Indies would do me good. Father has properties there, which need looking after with this war on."

"So far away, and to such a dangerous place?" I found it an effort to keep fear out of my voice; Father and I had dreaded Jamie's ship being sent to the Caribbean, the yellow fever was so rampant there.

"I'm afraid so. Much as I tell myself that I am happy for both of you, there is a certain lowness of spirits, and even a bitterness to see so much happiness from which I am shut out, that only time away in vastly different scenes can cure. As to the danger, I care not."

"Oh, Anthony!" was all I could say.

"My lord," Rebecca said, "you are the most truly noble nobleman I have had the pleasure to meet. If every aristocrat only followed your example, our country would be much better off. Will you shake my hand?"

"I will, if you will reassure me that Lord Rob will make no further appearances while I am away, save to distribute money and goods to the poor of Exeter."

"I will gladly do that, for not only have I sworn it to you, but our mistress here will hold me to it." She smiled and shook his hand, then gave him half a bow.

Anthony returned the bow and handed her a card. "My agent in Exeter has instructions to present you with monthly payments in the amounts we agreed upon. Will that be enough to allow you to continue your work?"

"It will do much good, my lord."

"Oh, and by the by, my agent is expecting a gentleman named Robin. I trust you can do this without your mask?"

"As it should be," she said. "I have passed as a man in London without it."

Anthony turned to me. "Lizzie," was all he could say.

With my newfound sensibility, I couldn't avoid shedding a tear. "I am sorry I hurt you so much that it's driven you from the country."

"I told you, you've done nothing for which you need to apologize. You were ever scrupulous to avoid luring me into an attachment; I did it all on my own. I look forward to returning when my feelings have moderated and I can once again be your true friend."

With that, he kissed my hand and turned to go. Hearing him in the hall, Father emerged from the library to say his farewell, and Mrs. Simmons soon joined us.

When the door had closed behind him and the horses had trotted down the lane, Father turned to me. "I still cannot help but think he played you false, my dear. If only I had warned you against the wiles of these nobles."

"Father, that is silly! Cannot you see that I'm perfectly happy?"

"But he paid you such attentions," Mrs. Simmons said, "as could only lead everyone to expect a proposal. And then to cast you off! Oh, Lizzie, I don't know what chances you'll have now, not after the harm the highwayman did you."

I reassured her for the hundredth time that I was quite content to make do with friends, family, and my drawing and writing.

"But such a beautiful girl as you are, to be forced at such a young age to give up on any establishment! And to forego the possibility of children! I can't help but be sad for you, even if you are not."

"Jamie will be home in a few years, and soon after he will be married, for what girl can resist an officer's uniform? Then we will have enough children about to keep us all occupied."

"But think of your future security, my dear," Father said. "I worry for you. Once I am gone, how will you possibly live?"

"I hope to make something from my art and my writing. You have already seen how much I might earn."

"But a woman of genteel birth, having to make her own living – it is not proper."

"Proper or not, I find the prospect somehow exciting. Besides, if it came to it, Jamie would not leave me destitute."

Rebecca, who had been hanging back from this conversation, now stepped forward. "As well, Mr. Collington, it is not unheard of for two single women, having no other options, to pool their resources and share a household. I could certainly use the help in paying the rent on my current lodgings, and there is plenty of room for Lizzie – when the time comes, of course, which I'm sure will be far in the future."

"You would do that for my daughter?"

"I assure you," she said earnestly, though with just the faintest trace of a smile about her mouth and the corners of her eyes, "it would be a pleasure – more than a pleasure – and no burden at all."

"Oh, Mrs. Burgess!" Mrs. Simmons exclaimed. "Lizzie couldn't have found a truer friend than she has found in you!"

Father readily agreed with this sentiment, and the two returned to their former activities, Father to his library, Mrs. Simmons to her room at the back of the Parsonage.

Rebecca and I looked at each other and laughed, holding hands as we made our way back upstairs.

It does not embarrass me at all to say that I laughed the longer, for I had much catching up to do where laughing was concerned.

ACKNOWLEDGMENTS

My first debt goes to all the writers who inspired me, Ellen Kushner chief among them. *Privilege of the Sword* showed me what was possible in combining a comedy of manners with melodrama, all while imagining an alternative Europe where people were pretty much free to love whom they chose. Emma Donoghue's *Life Mask* introduced me both to late-eighteenth-century England and to ways of imagining how those of non-conforming sexualities might have fit into it. Nicola Griffith: both she and her vision of St. Hilda, as told in *Hild*, are my heroes. Though I came to it after I finished this book, Heather Rose Jones' *Daughter of Mystery* inspired me to keep seeking a home for my own novel. You should probably read these #ownvoices before reading my attempt at historical representation of women who love women, which must inevitably rely on imagination (and research).

Both Mari Christie's (Mariana Gabrielle's) *La Déesse Noire: The Black Goddess* and Katharine Grant's *Sedition* provided examples of how to gracefully include voices that are not our own in historical fiction.

Is it appropriate to thank a dead author? I wouldn't be anywhere without Jane Austen. And Alfred Noyes may be dead, but it was Loreena McKennitt's superb musical rendition of *The Highwayman* that first put the idea for this novel into my head.

Thanks to my beta readers, Jeannie Miernik, Judy Spanogle, J Marcus Newman, Anne Simon, and Christina Mitchell, all of whom gave me valuable encouragement and advice. Without them, this novel would still be just a file on my computer.

Thanks to historian Jacqueline Reiter (author of *The Late Lord*), who checked the manuscript for obvious historical gaffes and anachronisms; any that remain are my own. (And here I should point out that Dora Jordan didn't appear in *As You Like It* in Bath in the spring of 1796, although she did tour there in other years, and she was famous for her portrayal of Rosalind/Ganymede. This was one liberty I felt I had to take.)

Numerous books and sites helped in research for this novel, including Kirstin Olsen's *Daily Life in 18th-Century England*; David M. Shapard's annotated editions of Jane Austen's novels; Emma Donoghue's *Passions Between Women*; the Jane Austen's World blog and many other Regency-centric history sites, so numerous thanks to the popularity of the Regency Romance; Rictor Norton's website, which includes not only eighteenth-century British gay and lesbian history, but also a section on the Georgian Underworld; and Stephen Hart's *Cant: A Gentleman's Guide*, as well as his Pascal Bonenfant website.

Capital City Writers Association (my RL writing community) and Speakeasy Scribes (my online one) provided invaluable support and camaraderie during the long process of finding a home for *Daring and Decorum*.

And finally, thanks to Diane Willcox, my alpha reader, partner, and wife, who has shown superhuman patience with my transition from nonfiction to fiction. Without her, I would still be a typesetter, or more likely (given what has happened to that occupation) unemployed and homeless. All my love always.

ABOUT THE AUTHOR

Lawrence Hogue's writing is all over the place and all over time. He started out in nonfiction/nature writing with a personal narrative/environmental history of the Anza-Borrego Desert called *All the Wild and Lonely Places: Journeys in a Desert Landscape.* After moving to Michigan, he switched to writing fiction, including contemporary stories set in the desert and fan fiction based on the videogame *Skyrim.* He's a fan of folk music, and got the idea for *Daring and Decorum* while listening to Loreena McKennitt's outstanding adaptation of Alfred Noyes' poem, *The Highwayman.* When not speaking a word for nature or for forgotten LGBT people of history, he spends his white-knighting, gender-betraying energies on Twitter and Facebook, and sometimes on the streets of Lansing, MI, and Washington DC. He's sometimes been called a Social Justice Warrior, but he prefers Social Justice Wizard or perhaps Social Justice Lawful Neutral Rogue.

www.ingramcontent.com/pod-product-compliance
Lightning Source LLC
Chambersburg PA
CBHW060558310726
48982CB00008B/1158/J
* 9 7 8 1 9 4 4 5 9 1 4 2 7 *